THE DAMAGES

THE DAMAGES

A Marian Warner Mystery

SHELLEY COSTA

First published by Level Best Books 2024

Copyright © 2024 by Shelley Costa

All rights reserved. No part of this publication may be reproduced, stored or transmitted in any form or by any means, electronic, mechanical, photocopying, recording, scanning, or otherwise without written permission from the publisher. It is illegal to copy this book, post it to a website, or distribute it by any other means without permission.

This novel is entirely a work of fiction. The names, characters and incidents portrayed in it are the work of the author's imagination. Any resemblance to actual persons, living or dead, events or localities is entirely coincidental.

Shelley Costa asserts the moral right to be identified as the author of this work.

Author Photo Credit: Bloomfield Photography

First edition

ISBN: 978-1-68512-670-4

Cover art by Level Best Designs

This book was professionally typeset on Reedsy. Find out more at reedsy.com

For Michael.
Part of our story.
And a small one, at that.

Chapter One

Late May

He watched her pull into the deserted rest area. He had waited for her, smoking a rare cigar, but it was that kind of night. She hit a puddle, and in the headlights he hadn't shut off, the water from her tires sprayed like sudden white stars and disappeared. *You busted it all to flinders, boy,* Pop used to say when he'd drop something—just drop something like kids do—a cup, a fishbowl, a carton of eggs. Even as a boy, all he knew finally was he wanted to put himself out of the way of that old man's voice, and the only way he was going to damn well do that was by getting so much money he'd baffle the old man into silence. No matter how.

She stepped out of the Kia—slower than usual, he thought, but then, she had things on her mind. She was slender, tall, her short hair whipped over her face by the wind in the dark. She straightened up, and he felt an absurd love for the round shoulders he teased her about, gently pressing them back into some kind of posture. *You've got good hands,* she'd murmur, and they both liked the way his hands moved over her body, all those times, when he knew he had come a long way from busting things all to flinders. He had watched the wind race up through the trees, pushing the branches from side to side, flipping the leaves, and he thought for the two of them tonight, a storm would be welcome. *The leaves are turned wrong side up,* was how his grandmother predicted rain.

Closer now.

All of it.

Her, the rain, the air whipping up wet and fresh from the parking lot.

He opened the car door and tossed out what was left of the cigar. She stopped, then continued around the front to the passenger side, her heels sharp rasps on the pavement. In the shock of the headlights, she looked inexpressibly beautiful, and he thought how it might be nice to have her right there in the car, but he didn't want to stain the brown leather seats he had waited an extra six weeks for—either way, do it, not do it, he saw with the sudden clarity of all boys cleaning up broken glass and flopping fish and egg slop, if she liked his good hands then that was what he'd use to kill her, so his foot shoved the gun out of sight under his seat.

It only seemed right.

* * *

Early June

"Is this Marian Warner?"

She came clean. "Speaking."

"This here's Rodie Prescott," the caller went on. "From Carthage."

Rodie Prescott. Of course. Tall, lanky, early twenties. Drove a cement truck for Jack Girard, the unfinished business she had from a case in Carthage, Ohio, back in January. "Hi, Rodie," she said, wary. "What's up?"

"It's my sister Beth." His voice was spiraling up, like he was yelling to her across the gravel pit at Girard's construction company. "She's turned up missing."

As a way of cutting down expenses, Marian let go of a Manhattan sublet and moved into a winterized cabin on the Delaware River in Pennsylvania that she had inherited from Aunt Greta a year ago. She also left Marian the back taxes and a hot water heater that was more incontinent than Greta herself was. But Marian had already paid off the back taxes and bought a hot water heater that some nights was the closest thing she had to

CHAPTER ONE

companionship, so she wasn't keen to go looking for Beth Prescott. "Have you talked to the cops?"

"Yeah," he sounded aggrieved, "but they say for the first forty-eight hours she's a voluntary missing person, and they don't do anything until after that—"

"Her co-workers, her neighbors, her friends?"

"Yeah, all of those."

Marian rubbed her face, hard, and stretched out on the couch. The boy had been devilishly thorough, but she had saved her finest persuasion for last. "I charge..." she told him slowly, like they were bargaining for unnatural acts, "a lot."

"That's not a problem. I got the money."

The Teamsters must be one hell of a union.

Compared to locking up, getting in the Volvo, and driving eight hours to Carthage, Ohio, to spend a high-priced week turning over rocks, the unnatural acts were beginning to look pretty good.

"Marian? Are you there? Hello?"

She grabbed her date book off the table and eyed the spaces for the week ahead. Since the New York longshoremen had walked off the job less than a week ago, nothing was getting unloaded, and no potentially sketchy imported artifacts were keeping the Artifacts Authentication Agency busy. Her half-sister Joan Fleck, the director of the agency, put Marian, her one licensed investigator, on a desk job—meaning, working remotely from her kitchen table in pajamas—researching fake Chinese porcelains. Marian learned everything there was to learn in two half days and was wondering how best to wait out the longshoremen, when apparently Rodie Prescott's sister went missing.

Scanning the date book, she saw no time fillers like teeth cleaning, haircut, oil change, Italian lessons—what the hell kind of life *was* this? Marian sighed. At that moment, she heard a squeak in the rafters and looked up just in time to see a brown bat swoop into the room. Somewhere in the time it took her to cover her hair with her arms and roll off the couch, she told Rodie Prescott that she'd take his case.

THE DAMAGES

* * *

Carthage Business District, next right.

Marian swung the Volvo off the highway, a full eight hours' worth of elated that before setting out that morning, she had made a deal with her only neighbor, Ellen Harper, a retired school bus driver with a riding mower, to roar all over Marian's yard for eighty bucks a week. She liked wheels, mechanical things, money, and Marian. Only now, what with an actual employee, Marian would really have to do some serious looking for Rodie Prescott's sister.

The first clue that Marian was back in Carthage was the gauntlet of fast-food places along Cold Spring Boulevard, the four-laner on the outskirts of town, where opportunities to clog the arteries went three and four brick boxes deep. There was an Arby's in the parking lot of a Burger King in the parking lot of a KFC. Behind them all sprawled a Wal-Mart like a creature from the deep. Four-by-fours squealed in and out of what had become one long two-mile parking lot, blaring Alabama out of open windows. As she got closer to the center of Carthage, she drove by an abandoned gas station and a boarded-up motel. At some point in time, hard as it was to believe, even Wal-Mart would go.

Marian idled at the stoplight at the center of town, her eyes already stinging from the smell. When she was in Carthage last January, the cold kept the overhanging, eye-watering stink of the paper mill at bay. She flicked the blower to Off, pushed the vents shut, and checked that all four windows were closed tight.

A dented blue Dodge Dart sputtered to a stop next to Marian's old Volvo. Inside were a couple of boys with half-shaved heads and a tank-topped woman with a stringy perm behind the wheel. While Carrie Underwood begged Jesus to take the wheel, everyone in the car swayed in time to the music. Then the driver thrust an arm out the window, where it landed like a sandbag against the dented door. All of them were eating, passing bags of Ruffles and an open jar of Cheez Whiz, seeing themselves through that difficult time before dinner.

CHAPTER ONE

As the light changed and the Dart showed itself surprisingly fast off the mark, Marian felt a pinprick of doubt. How could she face her old friend Charlie Levitan, from high school days back in New Jersey, who was now the editor-in-chief of the Carthage daily newspaper? The one time his sexual availability hadn't been laid on Marian's doorstep for her perusal, he got a girlfriend who wound up murdered. And after ten years of foot-dragging toward a bedroom with Charlie, she had let Jack Girard cut into line after a five-day acquaintance.

But now there was the missing Beth Prescott. To get the job done, she'd have to chance running into Jack Girard, who might want her to explain why she left town without saying goodbye. There was the little matter of bloodying his front hall in a shootout with the killer, nearly catching Girard himself in the crossfire, then throwing up her lunch in his front yard. What worried Marian the most was that he would want her to explain their lovemaking, her suspicion of him, and the final number of pi.

* * *

Rodie Prescott pulled into the pitted gravel lot next to a little place called Ernie's in a new red Toyota pickup. Marian beat him there by five minutes, enough time to wonder why he chose this cinder block watering hole in a shabby east-end neighborhood where everyone's a bag lady, even the guys. Rodie and Marian shook hands solemnly and went inside, where it was cool and dark.

Ernie's wasn't a theme bar, or a sports bar, or a biker bar. The fanciest thing about it were the fake alligator seat coverings Marian ran a hand over as soon as her eyes got accustomed to the place—and the fact that Ernie Diodakis was a pretty brunette with hoop earrings who seemed to know Rodie better than anyone else over the age of forty had any hope of knowing him. She was adorable in a smirky sort of way, like the only thing owning a modest little bar in that sketchy Carthage neighborhood had taught her was that you didn't need conversation when what you've got were quips. Hanging just under a metal wall sconce was an 8x10 sign: *Ernie's Is Not*

Responsible For Anything You Yourself Fuck Up

Marian ordered a vodka martini, medium dry, Smirnoff for the vodka, one loose olive, no stick, two rocks but only if she had the olive, if not then straight up. Ernie nodded like it all made sense to her and came up with the goods in ten seconds. Suddenly the door was wrenched open, and a man built like a refrigerator stood uncertainly in the hazy rectangle of daylight.

"Chopper, you just go on and get out of here."

Chopper took a step inside and articulated something that sounded like peach pits in a garbage disposal. His backlit hair started at his ears and went down to his shoulders. Ernie leaned on the bar. "Chopper," she pointed a manicured finger at him, "I told you I'm not serving you until you settle up for your kids."

Rodie turned to Marian. "Deadbeat dad," he said just a little too loud, like he was trying to be heard over bar noise, but they were the only ones in the place. She nodded, whispering to him it was a bad time to be discussing Mr. Chopper's financial difficulties.

Fists the size of pumpkins pounded both sides of the doorway. Ernie was unmoved. "You can have any kind of hissy fit you damn well please," said Ernie, with a shake of her head, "but I'm not serving you, and you know why. Now go on home. Go *on*," she made a shooing gesture like he was a stray mutt. He reeled out, slamming the door with a boom. Ernie, on the other hand, uncapped Rodie's beer bottle with one hand, set out a cocktail napkin and winked at him.

Marian followed Rodie Prescott to one of the three booths. On the beige stucco wall were framed photos from a hundred years ago of a hard-luck town called something like Gormless, Tennessee—Great Fire, Great Drought, Great Train Wreck. Ernie breezed over with a bowl of what Rodie called the best guacamole east of the Mississippi, "God's honest truth, Ernie here's won awards," and a basket of Tostitos.

As she turned away with a quick stretch, Ernie's top rode up and revealed a couple of silver bellybutton rings that got in the way of her unicorn tattoo. Marian was about to give Rodie the single best piece of advice she could muster—namely, get Ernie to go after Beth. She'd cost less, put out more,

CHAPTER ONE

and yell at anyone who needed it. Suddenly, he slumped in the booth and told her how much it meant to him that she came to help. Jack told him she would.

Stuck. But good. "When did you last see Beth?"

Rodie held his beer with two hands like he was afraid it was going to go somewhere without him. "Ten days ago."

"Okay."

"Maybe twelve."

"Which is it?"

He bit his lip. "Twelve. Shit. Really, twelve." His face started to fall apart. "Okay, sometimes that happens, but I ran into someone who works with Beth who says she hasn't been there all week—" He gave up, chugged his beer, and waited for Marian to say something sensible.

She felt like telling him her drink had all that shimmering oiliness she loved in a martini, but she noticed he needed a shave, and one of his front teeth was crooked, and he held a cocktail napkin to his lips to catch some beer, only it looked like he was trying to stop the flow of blood. Great fire, great drought, great train wreck, all right there inside his poor rib cage. "So you called the cops."

He nodded, and when his anxious blue eyes settled on her, they were wet. "They told me they wait two days before putting out the word, in case she's a voluntary missing, they call it. I ask them what good's *that* when she's already been gone maybe over a week, like, and I only just found out. Two days from the first report, they tell me again, which means you, which means now—like I'm fucking four, Marian—and let us know if she comes home in the meantime."

He put his head down on the table and curled his forearms up over his dark hair, shutting out the racket of sisters who turn up missing and cops who quote rules when the world goes up in flames. Marian grabbed his wrists, just to take hold of him somehow, and he shuddered.

"Where did you see her?"

"I passed her on the road," he mumbled, his lips an inch from the tabletop.

"Which one?"

"Hopewell Avenue. She was heading east."

"What time?"

"Not even nine in the morning. She must have been on her way to work."

"Which is where?"

"Mercy Hospital." He came up for air, laying his cheek against his arm, his fingers tracing circles in some spilled beer. "Beth's a courier for the lab."

"What does that mean?"

"Oh, she picks up blood samples from doctors' offices and takes them back to the hospital lab. For tests."

"You sure it was Beth you saw?"

He sat up. "Yeah, it was Beth. She's got this yellow Kia Soul. And vanity plates."

"Where is it now?"

Marian watched him lick the guacamole off the business end of a chip. "The cops checked Beth's place, the hospital lot, all the stops on her route. Nothing. They'll put it in the computer to see if something turns up."

"Does she have any history of just taking off?"

"Not for any twelve damn days. No."

Not looking good. "Any history of instability?"

"Instability?"

"Apartment hopping, bed-hopping—"

He flattened his hands across his jacket. "I'm her *brother*."

"—job hopping—"

He made a blowing noise. "Well, office work, yeah, but—"

"Drug or alcohol problems?"

"No, no." He waved it away.

"Psychiatric problems?"

"Hell, no."

"Anything out of the ordinary in the way she seemed lately?"

He shrugged, staring at a point on Marian's nose. "Like?"

"Elated, worried, despondent."

Something clicked. "Jesus, Marian," his voice rose, "are you saying she *killed* herself?"

CHAPTER ONE

Marian held up her hands. "I'm just trying to get a fix on her state of mind, that's all." She knew he'd lose no time telling Jack Girard that the PI he recommended thought Beth offed herself. She looked quickly over toward the bar at Ernie, who gave her a look that said, *sounds reasonable to me,* then pensively scraped some caked lipstick from the corner of her mouth.

What Marian couldn't tell Rodie—not now, not yet—was whether his sister had dropped out, shacked up, or managed to wind up dead in a ditch somewhere.

Chapter Two

There was never a time she did something useless that she didn't feel better for it. Unless it was a date. She agreed to go with Rodie to his sister's apartment even though he'd already been there earlier in the day. They left Ernie's, and she followed the red Toyota west three miles out of town, past all the fast-food joints, toward those soft green hills of Carthage. At the sign for Coconut Palm Estates, where the only coconut palm within a thousand miles was painted on the sign, they pulled in. *Entering Coconut Palm Estates, 10 MPH Strictly Enforced, We Will Ticket!!, Park at Your Own Risk, Lock Your Vehicle, No Dumping, We Will Ticket!!, Proud to Be an American.*

Rodie Prescott headed around the corner of the building, and Marian followed. There, he whirled his pickup into a parking space as she watched the sunset start to lengthen into soft purples. She got out of the Volvo and looked around, then trotted through the walk-through passage just to see what was going on out front. Two young moms with banana-clipped curls were running after toddlers, ripping marigolds out of the strip of brown that passed for a garden. "Jaden, now what have I told you about doin' that? You gotta listen to Mama—" Then she grabbed an arm and hauled the kid to his little feet.

Four parallel rectangular buildings with exterior metal stairs, what appeared to be two units down, two up in each building. White stucco, casement windows—the complex reminded Marian of student housing. She jogged behind Rodie up the steps to his sister's apartment on the second floor. While he fumbled with the keys, Marian leaned against the railing at the back of the landing as a breeze whipped through, and her eyes swept across the back of the apartment complex. Behind them was what had to be the Wade County landfill. Terraced rises, stunted greens, the Chichén Itzá of garbage. Which, she considered, made Coconut Palms Estates oddly private.

Maybe even convenient for dumping a body.

With a shiver, she joined Rodie as he unlocked the front door to A4, Beth's apartment, on the right of the stairs. Inside, he flicked on a light they didn't quite need and looked around edgily, like the place was responsible for her disappearance somehow. Marian picked up a framed photo of Beth and Rodie from an open shelf in her entertainment unit. Beth, decked out in a shiny green rayon dress, was in her mid-twenties, short black hair, large sharp eyes, and a lopsided smile.

"You can take this, Marian," said Rodie, "if you want to show it places." He started to work it out of the frame while Marian took a quick look around.

In the refrigerator, there was a half-gallon of sour milk, a Pizza Shack box with what was left of a margherita pizza, and a flat little ribeye steak that smelled even worse than the milk. At the back of the counter was an old Walkman, and behind that were a couple of cassettes—Queen, Bon Jovi, the tape sticking out, slack, overplayed. The sink had a glass carafe with a varnish of dried coffee, and all that was left in a cereal bowl was a slick of dried milk that could be peeled off. Normal life, interrupted. Framed movie posters hang on the white wall of Beth's living room. Robert Pattinson as a vampire, Robert Pattinson as Batman. The couch was an acre of shapely leather on a wood frame, and two matching chairs were on either side of a glass coffee table—Thayer Coggin stuff she'd only ever seen in pricey furniture store catalogs.

Lab courier must be one lucrative gig.

Rodie watched himself slowly handing her the photo, and Marian could tell he was handing his sister off to some reality he didn't understand. "Did you bring a list?" She tucked the photo into her bag.

From his shirt pocket, he pulled a wad of paper the size of a chess square, unfolded it slowly, and handed it to her. What was he, twenty-two, tops? Angular shoulders, loose cotton shirt, nicely broken-in jeans. A boy who made things small to keep them close and take care of them. Only sisters didn't fold so easily. As Marian smoothed out Rodie's list of Beth Prescott's contacts, the only thing she knew for sure was that Ernie was a good thing. In a neat little hand, he had put down the names and numbers of Beth's family, co-workers, doctors on her route, friends. Then there was "other," the category that always interested Marian the most.

Buddy Bryson, old boyfriend, still here, camera shop.
Lila Ketchum, Ketchum Rays, Beth tans with her.
Eddie Estremera, Gringos???

Very thorough. She refolded the list, joking. "Anybody you leave off?"

"Well, there's her work."

"But you got them, all the Mercy Hospital folks, all the docs on her route." She didn't get it. "Isn't that her work?"

"Well, mostly."

"Mostly?"

"Nine to one."

"Lab courier's her part-time job?"

He considered. "That'd be about right."

Leaving half of Beth Prescott's work week unexplained. "What does Beth do in the afternoons?"

"Her other job."

"As?"

At that moment, three knocks hit Beth's door, and Rodie started over. "A home health aide."

Marian found herself sinking into a chair that cost more than her car. Home health aide meant maybe half a dozen patients and a county agency crawling with human resources. In the doorway stood a tall, stooped guy with startled eyes and a thatch of white-blond hair, dressed in a red Pizza Shack vest.

"Hey, Flyboy," said Rodie.

"I got Miz Elizabeth's pie." He was clutching a thermal zippered bag like he was a driver for Brink's.

For Rodie, it sounded like normal life. "She ordered a pizza?"

CHAPTER TWO

Flyboy drew himself up. "Standing order. Second and fourth Tuesdays. She here?" He took a step into the apartment and craned his thin neck.

"No, Flyboy, she—"

"Is Miz Elizabeth back from her trip?"

Suddenly, Marian felt alert. "What trip was that?"

"Wherever she went," he said reasonably.

She walked over to them. "What makes you think she went somewhere?"

The pizza delivery guy widened his pale eyes. "Because she wasn't here last time, was she, when I delivered her margherita pie. I knocked and knocked and had to take it back."

Rodie nodded.

Then, the pizza in the fridge was a month old.

Flyboy went on, "Is she like here?" He offered them the box.

Rodie clamped his arms over his chest. "No, Flyboy," he mumbled, "and we don't know where she is."

At that, Flyboy stared hard at Marian, like she knew more than she was damn well telling. When she handed him a twenty, Flyboy looked over their heads as though he was consulting the future, and it was writ large on Beth Prescott's living room ceiling. Finally: "Miz Elizabeth be turning up, see if she don't." He thrust Beth Prescott's forlorn pizza at Marian, sighed mightily, and backed out of the doorway. "I'm a lotta places," he said conspiratorially, then started down the hall.

"I know that, Flyboy," Rodie called after him. "You're a good man. Keep your ears open."

When he shut the door, Marian took him on. "Why didn't you put all those numbers on the list?" She set the box down on Beth's kitchen counter.

"All what numbers? She does it private." He ran his forearm over the top of his head. And she just goes the one place."

Clients. Marian reached in her bag for a pen. "What's the name?"

"Clayton Girard."

She sat back, sacked.

"Well, actually," Rodie went on, "Beth works for Jack because Jack pays her, but she really takes care of his father. Jack's got him at his place now, maybe you didn't know that—"

Marian shook her head.

"—and Beth's there three to seven, weekdays."

"That's nice."

"She went to school for it, even, for six whole months, after she saved up enough from her office job. Only she's never really worked in her field until now. She calls it a foot in the door."

When Marian asked him why he left the Girards off the list, Rodie looked away, shocked. For the first time since college, when she knocked back three tequilas at a Sigma Alpha Mu party and blazed out "Me and Bobby McGee" on their pool table, someone found her embarrassing. Not a good feeling for a client about to hand over a retainer. But he gave a small shrug and looked her in the eye. "It's *Jack*," he said, and Marian was left feeling like she'd asked the stable owner why he didn't charge Jesus for the use of the donkey.

"Okay, Rodie, I need some time alone here."

He nodded, then turned around quickly with his arms out, like Beth's apartment had outfoxed him somehow. "It's worse that it's no damn different, you know." At that, he dug into his jeans pocket and teased out an envelope with check-sized creases. "Here you go, Marian, here's the whatchamacallit." Her retainer. The truth was, as she took it from him, Beth Prescott's place— the poignant normalcy of it, the shrieking absence of just Beth herself—was beginning to give her a bad feeling.

A few flipped chairs, yanked and scrambled drawers, stains, would have gone far toward settling her down—there's nothing quite like chaos for finding the underlying mechanisms of things. But to look at the strange composure of Beth Prescott's apartment— while Rodie stared at his work boots and Marian held the envelope, even the tick, tick, tick of Beth's wall clock was sickening—you'd think she just went down to check her mail or take out her garbage. Nothing ham-fisted like Chopper was at work here.

"Can I get a set of keys?"

"Tomorrow, okay?"

She nodded. "If there's something I need to take with me—"

"Take it." He started to shake Marian's hand, then grabbed her in a

CHAPTER TWO

wrenching half-hug and hurtled out the door.

"Wait!" She called after him. "Where's the super's unit?" But as he clattered down the stairs, his voice was just a blare in the open stairwell. *Bottom of this* was the only part she caught. Then he was gone. Through the flapping vertical slats in the living room blinds she watched the Toyota roar out of the parking lot.

She ate half of the pizza at Beth's cheap dinette set, the kind someone buys who's hoping to eat most of her meals out. Then she washed up, pulled on a pair of thin latex gloves, and started in on Beth's small collection of CDs, which consisted mostly of pop. Billie Eilish, Coldplay, Taylor Swift. Marian pressed the eject button on the old Bose player, and out slid the last CD Beth Prescott had listened to here—*Aida*, for God's sake. It would be like discovering Nora Roberts on her mother the intellectual's bookshelf. Handling it by the edges, she dropped the opera CD into a Ziploc bag and slipped it into her bag.

In the medicine cabinet in the bathroom was the usual jumble of drugstore helpers—tweezers, clippers, razors, Q-Tips, extra-whitening toothpaste—but there were also three prescription meds. The Pill, prescribed by a David Barish, M.D., in a hot pink slip case with a graphic of a bee closing in on a flower. Beth had taken the first nine pills of the cycle, so wherever she was, she'd better not be having sex. The second prescription was for Bactrim—eight pills left. Someone named William D. Rinaldi was treating Beth Prescott for a urinary tract infection. The third prescription was Tylenol III dating back to the previous October, one every four hours as needed, prescribed by Jim Carney, the local surgeon who doubled as coroner.

Beth's taste in the bedroom ran along the lines of Adam Driver, looking wet and menacing in a framed movie poster from *Star Wars*. Marian rippled her way across the queen-sized waterbed and checked out the books stashed in the built-in headboard. A few bodice rippers, but mainly a bunch of curling paperbacks by Robert Ludlum and Danielle Steele. The only hardcover book was a pricey volume of Oriental erotic art, featuring page after page of open kimonos and fantasy samurais. On her long, low dresser were bills, bank and Mastercard statements, and a floral-covered date book. Marian picked up the date book, riffling quickly back to May 25th, the last day Rodie saw his sister. Nothing. Stashing the bills and statements in her bag, she headed for Beth's closet.

At the bottom was a clothes basket with dirty laundry, which she dragged into the light, along with a small, gray Rubbermaid bin. Tossed on top of the laundry pile was a two-piece white uniform, inside out, with tomato stains in three places. Beth had come home from the Girards' and changed in a hurry. The bin held a jumble of cocktail napkins from the weddings of her friends, some old report cards, a red ribbon for baton twirling, a souvenir coconut with a painted face from St. Thomas, and the front page from an issue of the *Toiler* dated ten years ago. A grainy photo showed the Tulip Time Queen and her court—third from the right, Beth Ann Prescott.

Second place for twirling.

Runner-up for queen.

A guest at other people's weddings.

An average student always making "satisfactory progress." Toward what, no one said.

Finally, there were blank forms, applications she had sent away for and never completed—Save the Children, Delta Airlines, Ohio University, birth certificate, all creased, all forgotten at the bottom of her closet. She looked around. There were no incriminating love letters, no tell-all diary, no hot snapshots. Beth Prescott worked her jobs, paid her bills, and had some dates.

Marian shoved the laundry and the Rubbermaid bin back inside the closet and went over to Beth's nightstand, where a red light was blinking on an old-school answering machine, next to a pink Trimline phone. For a Millennial, Beth Prescott had some pretty old-fashioned tastes. Jabbing the playback button, she listened to a string of calls, the first from Cooper Dental Associates, reminding you of your cleaning tomorrow at noon. Lila, laughing, asking when you're gonna get your sickly white buns on over there. Rodie saying hi, Boopster, call me back. A warm and easy Dr. Carney, calling to see how you're doing and to remind you of your appointment for 1:30 tomorrow. Jack Girard saying we're concerned about you, Beth, please call. Cooper Dental Associates again, this time asking did you forget your

CHAPTER TWO

cleaning yesterday? A hang-up. Someone starchy named Paulette Baron saying that one usually *requests* vacation time before one *takes* it. Another hang-up. And then the last—Rodie again—saying where the hell are you?

She played Jack Girard's message three times—it was an easy way to hear his voice without having to answer a damn thing—and she wondered what it would have felt like if she had heard that message on her own Voicemail. *We're concerned about you. Please call.* Instead, all she had was his infernal silence—and her own deep embarrassment. So she listened to what Beth herself had recorded for incoming calls. "Hi. It's Beth. Leave a message. Thanks." Every phrase, an invitation. She had one of those sexy voices, like a torch singer who smokes.

She'd take the answering machine with her.

Marian picked up her phone and hit Rodie's number.

"Hey!" came his voice, high and curious, backed by some soft jazz. Back at Ernie's was her guess.

"Rodie, Marian."

Again: "Hey!" Like he hadn't just left her an hour ago. "How's—"

"Beth's got some really retro stuff here. A Trimline phone. A phone answering machine. A Walkman. A George Forman grill."

"Oh, those. Sure. Those were mom's."

"Beth's sentimental?"

On the other end, Rodie hummed, thinking it over. "Well, my sister, she doesn't have a head for what you might call technology."

"A Forman grill?"

"More like Voicemail. Spotify. You know."

"Listen, Rodie, I need to take Beth's answering machine with me. Can you set up Voicemail for her number in case any more calls come in?"

"You bet. I'll use your phone number for the PIN."

"Good, thanks."

They disconnected.

Through the slats of the miniblinds, Marian looked out on a view of the parking spaces at the front of the small complex. Next stop, the Super's. She gathered her bag and keys, locked up, and hurried down the steps echoing in the late afternoon. A quick check of the complex's directory named Randy Gillison the manager, Unit B1 the office, in the building next door to Beth's. A1, V. Varnum. A2, D. Franklin, L. Bishop. A3, G. Cathcart. A4, B. Prescott. Somewhere farther down, a baby was crying. And farther even than that, Marian heard squeaky scales on a saxophone. Just as she was heading to B1, a silver van pulled crookedly into a parking space, the taillights went out, door opened, and out stepped a guy in a brakeman's cap. He carried a Lil Oscar and a Coleman thermos, so he was home for the night, here in Coconut Palm Estates. Marian wondered whether the weeding little Jaden was his kid.

Ten feet from Marian, he pulled up. "Help you?" he asked with a narrow look like he hadn't quite gotten to that chapter on customer service.

Marian pulled out the photo of Beth and Rodie and handed it to him. "Name's Marian Warner. Looking into the disappearance of Beth Prescott." What was happening to the beginnings of her sentences? "Neighbor?" She gave him a bring-it-on jerk of the chin.

"Manager." He worked his jaw.

Marian tried him out. "Randy Gillison?"

He grunted an affirmative. "Prescott girl gone?" Louder: "Moved?"

"No." Then: "Names in Building A?"

"The others?" He ticked off his fingers, shifting his weight. "A3 old shut-in hoarder lady never takes a bath should be in a nursing home. Excuse me," he flashed a sickly smile, "assisted living comfort spa. A2 husband and husband retired schoolteachers of all the damn things, tooling around the country in an old Airstream. A1—" Randy Gillison screwed up his mouth, "—quiet, hard-luck kinda guy, Vince Varnum, works night shift at the Amazon warehouse out Scioto Pike. Try him. He's got a kid two counties over the ex lets him see a lot, which means he's not around much."

"Try him now just the same."

Randy Gillison tugged at his cap, nearly slit-eyed with thought. "Prescott not coming back, you let me know?" He'd be finding out soon enough, what with Charlie's newspaper. "Got a waitlist as long as my—" here he stopped short, considered the chapter on inappropriate language in public, then

CHAPTER TWO

finished with wide eyes, "—truck."

"You work two jobs?"

"Three if you count my Etsy shop. I whittle." His chest puffed out, and he tightened his grip on his Lil Oscar and his thermos. Leaning half an inch closer to Marian, he wrinkled his nose. "Ain't nothing to managing Coconut Palms. Cooshy, even. Show the vacancies, collect the rents, report the deadbeats."

With that, the man tightened his grip on his Lil Oscar and shouldered his way into his apartment, where, through the open door, Marian heard the banana-clipped mother hush-hushing a screaming Jaden, and the returning Randy joined in with a round of hot accusations about how she don't give the kid enough to eat.

Marian knocked on the door to A1, the unit down one floor and across the hall from Beth's. The hard-luck dad who was working an Amazon warehouse job and trying to stay a dad for his kid two counties over. No answer. She pulled out a business card, the one that held just her name and, underneath, *Investigations*, and scribbled on the back. *Looking for Beth Prescott. Call me.* Wrote the number carefully, then tucked the card behind the brass knocker, with enough of a tip showing.

As she turned away from the quiet apartment, Marian looked hard at the photo of Beth and Rodie, studying the missing woman's face. The large, sharp eyes, the wry, appealing smile. What were the chances she threw over her jobs for a sudden trip to the Bahamas? Getting a tan without Lila's help would have to be pretty persuasive for Beth to close the door on her own foot at the Girards'—not to mention the hospital. Chances are—Marian flicked the photo with her fingernail—Beth Prescott just made the wrong damn date.

Chapter Three

It was dusk by the time she got back to The Briars, the inn where she'd stayed in January. It was a rambling, late Victorian house with a porch the size of the Boardwalk in Atlantic City. The owners, Cy and Barbara Hauser, were a lookalike couple in their forties who wore matching sweaters and khaki pants. Back in January, The Briars' pale green exterior stood out kind of sickly against the snow that never went away, although, in the daylight, the white smoke curling out of its three chimneys gave the place some life. Now, blue flowering vines had thickened around the stonework of the porch, and orange rockers were set out on either side of the oak front door. Marian pulled in behind a toffee-colored Saab with Ohio plates and turned off the car, right in the middle of Linda Ronstadt explaining why sometimes the heart is just like a wheel.

A couple of bony guys with very groomed goatees were rocking on the porch. They nodded at Marian and went right on discussing whether the worst hill in the race was Scioto Pike, which was steeper, or Great Seal County Highway, which was longer. In the parlor, Cy Hauser—Flyboy with better posture and a barber—was stumping a gray-haired grand dame and her middle-aged daughter with a baffling antique he was turning over in his hands. "Looks like a plane, wouldn't you say? Feel that smooth cutting edge?" The women had an unentertained look like they were wondering whether the Holiday Inn had any rooms. When he saw Marian, Cy waved, which looked a lot like he was trying to extinguish five flaming fingers.

Barbara Hauser and a woman with hair the soft orange color of an old sunset came together out of the kitchen. Marian got collared and turned

CHAPTER THREE

into the hall, where Barbara introduced her to Nan Kemp, Esquire. The lawyer had brown eyes and sandy eyelashes, a narrow nose, and a wide mouth. She was older than Marian, but not by much, and her sunset-colored hair was pulled into a French twist, with stunted little flyaway curls just at her hairline. She was wearing a Karl Lagerfeld houndstooth shirtdress and high boots.

"The trial —"

"Starts in the morning. It's a medical malpractice case against a local doctor."

Barbara leaned in. "She defends."

"My firm's on retainer with PQA—Physician's Quality Assurance. All we do is defend medical malpractice cases."

"Must be a living," said Marian.

The lawyer fluttered an eyebrow. "I think of it as piling up sandbags along the Mississippi."

"Ah."

"What about you?"

"Investigations."

Nan cocked her head. "I could use you."

"Sorry," I told her, "I'm tied up."

"Ah, well," said the lawyer as she started upstairs. "Stop by sometime."

"Your room?"

"The courtroom." She looked back with a grin. "More action."

Barbara grabbed Marian's sleeve and pointed fiercely into the parlor. "I'm going to need a lawyer. That Mrs. Garber was at me not two hours ago, howling theft. Her diamond, ruby and sapphire brooch in the shape of an American flag is missing. She had left it in her suitcase —" Barbara started waving her arms like she was doing the hokey-pokey "—and now it's gone, and she just knows it was the maid."

"What did you do?"

"Well, of course, what I *couldn't* say was that the best we can hope for is that ugly shit like that continues to disappear, so what I did was call the cops and report it. She says it's valued at thirty-two thousand dollars, and she doesn't want that sneaking little sticky-fingers maid to come near her room the rest of the time she and LaVerne are here. She insisted on showing the cop and me how she had wrapped the hideous thing in tissue paper and stuffed it way down inside a pocket of her suitcase. Then LaVerne pushed her on it a little, saying, are you sure you packed it? And the old lady said, 'Oh, *please*, LaVerne, I'm not *senile*.'"

The two of them peeked into the parlor, where Cy kept working cheerfully, with mysterious items he picked off the bookshelves. The Garbers tolerated him with expressions Marian had only ever seen in pictures from the Nuremberg trials. "Shit," Barbara leaned back against the wall, "we're going to get our asses sued off, and he's in there doing Antiques Road Show." Then she tugged at her spiky salt-and-pepper hair in a quick fit.

The screen door opened, and two goatees were the first things across the threshold. One of the knobby guys zeroed in on Barbara. "And breakfast would be—?"

"I could do eggs—"

"I meant time."

"Eight."

"But we leave at seven-thirty."

"Then, seven." They spread grim smiles and flowed into the parlor, where Cy was demonstrating how to churn butter, and an audience. As soon as the cyclists were out of the way, Barbara steered Marian toward the stairs, pulling a framed notice from a stack resting on an antique hall sideboard. "I'm sticking these in all the guest rooms." *The Briars Cannot Be Responsible For Lost or Stolen Items. Please Place Your Valuables in Our Safe.* Upstairs, they sailed down to the room at the end of the hall, which had an iron-frame double bed and wallpaper with a plague of violets.

With a quick look around, Marian unzipped her bag.

"Tour d'Ohio's going through, hence all the spandex," said Barbara as she shook out Marian's brown jersey dress and hung it up. "You met the lady lawyer from Columbus."

"The Saab out front?"

"That's hers." Barbara stuck a fist on her hip. "She's getting hit on by the

CHAPTER THREE

blacksmith—"

"What blacksmith?"

"—whose name, if you can believe it, is Jerry Vulcani, and he pretends to limp. Which brings me to Tulip Time, Carthage's annual salute to freaks and farm animals. I've got a blacksmith, a gunsmith, and a saddlemaker here all week." She spanked my black dress pants and hung them up. "The place is goddamned *Gunsmoke.*"

"And the lawyer?"

"Frosted the fake gimp."

"I see."

"What about you?"

Marian set her Dopp kit on the highboy dresser and dropped some underwear into the top drawer. It was a sad state of non-affairs when white Jockey for Her briefs were all she needed. "It's a missing person."

Barbara jiggled her blue-framed glasses. "You?"

"No one's paying me for that one."

"Someone should."

"What makes you think I'd take the job?"

"Oh, hell, Marian, don't get all dramatic. Just go call Jack and get it over with."

"No." The problem with Carthage, besides the paper mill, was that everybody was either related or in the same bowling league. Barbara Hauser and Jack Girard had done a fair amount of making out back in high school—Marian was reasonably sure they weren't related—and now they belonged to the Greater Carthage Growth Association, where they shared a pancake breakfast featuring bad local speakers once a month.

Barbara pitched a pair of pantyhose at Marian. "Then can you at least do something about these damn Garbers?"

"Like what?"

"Like find the hideous object."

"Look, I've got all I can handle—"

"We can't take another insurance hit—"

"—without looking for some overpriced—"

"I'll tell Jack you're here."

Marian sucked in air. "Low, Barbara, really low." She eyed the other woman with new respect.

"We can't take another insurance hit, Marian, not after the fall that rickety old ghoul the visiting professor took out front last March. We'll go under."

"All right, all right." Marian flicked at a speck on her blue acetate top. "Have you seen him?" They both knew she was talking about Girard.

"Yes," said the innkeeper, "I have," and she turned on her heel and left, maddeningly, in a rustle of khaki.

Different season, same damn skid.

* * *

"See Weezie," said the thin woman in a white lab coat, pointing elegantly to the back of the fluorescent-flooded room, when Marian asked about Beth Prescott. *Narkeytah Sayles* was embroidered in red on her pocket, which drooped from a clip-on photo ID worn by Mercy Hospital employees. Two other white-coated techs were spinning crits to the boom box strains of U2. Narkeytah returned to her microscope. "You want to steer clear of Paulette," she went on, without looking up, "who's looking to chew Beth's ass, and since that's not a happening thing, she might just take a shine to yours."

"Paulette—Baron?"

"Mnh hnh."

"She the boss?"

"She's the COO." Narkeytah's eyes slid her way. "Remember your Vice Principal?"

"We called him the nutcracker."

"That'd be Paulette."

"Thanks." From a back room huffed a short gal in civvies carrying an empty metal tray with slots for vials of blood. She was wearing beige palazzo pants and a red and blue plaid jacket with a nameplate: *Louise Tiller*. No embroidery for the blood schleppers, Marian guessed. "You Weezie?"

"That's me, all right."

CHAPTER THREE

"I'm Marian Warner. I'm here about Beth Prescott."

"Oh, *Beth*," she heaved, explaining how she'd had Beth's job shoved at her by Paulette Baron herself not even an hour after Beth didn't show up for work that first morning. Up to then, Weezie had done clerical. She shook her head, flinging around one of those perms that look like wet corkscrews, then lowered her voice. "Everyone is mucho pissed. Us," she said, "and a few of the docs on the route." Well, she went on, mostly the first day, really, cause bloods had to get drawn all over again, and it was a real pisser. "I mean," Weezie confided, "she's gonna hafta be like *dead* or something for Paulette to take her back."

When Marian handed her the list Rodie had drawn up, Weezie looked it over, like it was the glove in the O.J. case, and declared it to be Beth Prescott's route—now, she rolled her eyes, hers. Marian put it to her. "Tell me who's been cool about Beth's absence—and who hasn't."

Barish she didn't see.

Briggs was huffy.

Carney kinda frosty.

Rinaldi friendly.

Down the list she went.

"Did Beth ever talk about these doctors?"

"No."

"No," Narkeytah chipped in, still eyeballing slides.

"Well," Weezie shifted on her feet, "except to call Briggs a peckerhead." No, she added, her and Beth never socialized outside of Mercy, but she probably knew Beth better than anybody there. When Marian asked about Beth's afternoon job, her mouth went slack. Beth's job as a home health aide was news to her. She shrugged, tripling her chins. Beth came to the lab, punched in, drove her route, and punched out. "Now that you mention it," Weezie looked distant, "it makes sense." There were days Beth sprayed herself with Tommy Girl and put on some lipstick before leaving. "Like she was going to something else."

Narkeytah turned on her stool. "Why all the questions?"

Marian pulled out two business cards and handed them out. "I'm looking into her disappearance."

"Disappearance," Weezie whispered, her face sliding off into her plaid jacket.

"Mnh mnh *mnh*," was Narkeytah's comment, her brown eyes narrow and gleaming, seeing all manner of wiliness outside the light-flooded safety of the hospital lab. Then she turned calmly back to all the trouble she could handle clamped between two wafers of glass.

* * *

At a drive-thru on Cold Spring Boulevard, Marian ordered a papery roast beef sandwich slathered with wallpaper paste, a side of soggy Tater Gems, and a watery cola—her reward for avoiding Paulette Baron power-walking her way down a long corridor after Marian left the lab. Could only be her—gurneys veered off into walls, underlings shielded their eyes.

The glass doors to the main entrance slid open as Marian stepped out of the hospital into the sweet June air. Mercy was far enough out of town that the paper mill couldn't reach it, there on a hillside in all its blue glass and white stone splendor.

She found Jim Carney's general surgery practice in a small, freestanding building on a street called Hospital Way, next to a Taco Bell and Holiday Inn Express and within sight of Mercy. There were two cars in Carney's lot, a Focus and a Civic, neither of which looked like Carney material. She was right: the front office help told her it was one of his afternoons at "Quick," short for the Carthage and Wade County Clinic. "He consults," said Sherree with a dimply smile. "Mondays, always, Thursdays as needed. Yew have a noss die." Marian wished her a nice day, too, and drove side streets over to Quick, housed in the old county hospital.

It was a four-story brick building in an old residential neighborhood that was still trying to find its identity ever since Mercy Hospital siphoned off all the patients, the doctors, and the dough. Like any outmoded, abandoned building, it was only seen as a desirable piece of real estate by the government, who bought it, sank federal funds into it, and set out a bunch of health-related

CHAPTER THREE

services for the indigent and working poor, who probably couldn't quite understand why they didn't get to go up to Mercy like other folks when they came down with Old Timer's disease or very close veins.

Marian got off the elevator on the second floor and discovered that undiluted ammonia liberally applied to black and white linoleum really helped with the smell from the paper mill. Looking around, she tugged at her shirt to get some air going—typical of old buildings, the heat was on in June, and the windows were open—and then headed for a middle-aged nurse, dressed in blue scrub bottoms and a pullover top in a pattern of panda bears, leaning over some paperwork at the old nurse's station.

Her hair was teased into a state of shock, but the spit curls were nicely retro, and her eyes were sharp. Marian leaned toward her, slowing slightly. "Dr. Carney?"

She gave Marian a quick once-over, decided she wasn't a terrorist, a lunatic, or a walk-in, and did a big sweep with her left arm in the direction of the hallway straight ahead. "Three doors past the water fountain."

There, Marian knocked, then pushed open the door and poked her head around. "Hi, Jim."

"Marian!" Jim Carney was sitting at a metal desk in a room that had once been a semi-private hospital room, now a makeshift office for the local private docs who rotated through the clinic. He bounded to his feet and gave her one of those loose hugs that's as good as you get when you both happen to start sitting down at the same time. He hadn't changed—hair still that dense white color of middle-aged blonds, tortoise-shell half-glasses still slipped to the tip of his angular nose.

Today, he had on a blue Oxford button-down shirt under his rumpled white lab coat and a red tie. Aside from Cy and Barbara Hauser, Jim Carney was the third easiest person for Marian to see after the January disaster. Only this time, he wasn't in the morgue in the basement here at Quick, snipping threads from his quick-stitch job on the corpse from the Mission House. Jim pulled off his glasses and sent them sliding across the desk. "Well, hell, Marian Warner," he said, leaning back in his creaky swivel chair, "how are you?"

"Okay," she said with a tense sunniness even she didn't believe. "Quite, quite okay." They nodded at each other. "What about you—and Jen?" His round-shouldered wife, who thought Christopher Marlowe was a better writer than Shakespeare.

"Status quo. And Jen's fine, thanks. Still teaching. Although the school year's over this week," he said kind of momentously—one of those inconsequential things people say before they get down to the real conversation.

"Right," she said. "Right."

"How's Charlie?"

"Charlie doesn't know I'm here yet—" She knew where this was going.

"Talked to Girard?"

And there they were. "No," Marian said in one of those plummy voices kids suddenly have when you ask if they've sent Great Aunt Greta a thank-you note for the birthday money. It was all harder than she thought. Then she cleared her throat. "How is he?"

He's good, he's bad, no answer was correct, of course. "Also, okay." It suddenly occurred to her that Jim Carney, the coroner, must have been brought in after the shooting—witness to the most godforsaken mess she had ever created, which is certainly what happens when what you've got at the moment is a bellyful of terror, a loaded gun and a damn good aim. Jack Girard—and Jim Carney, M.D.—had been left with the mess. "What brings you back to Carthage, Marian?"

"Here on business."

The soft rocking stopped. "Namely?"

"Beth Prescott." His eyebrows went up. "Courier for the Mercy lab."

He nodded. "She picks up the pre-op blood work."

"She's been missing for nearly two weeks."

"That's what I hear. Any leads?"

"Car's gone, suitcase isn't, no one's heard from her. Not work, not family."

"Friends?"

Her smile felt grim. "Her phone messages are piling up."

"Not a good sign." Jim Carney shook his head slowly. "We say hello, talk

CHAPTER THREE

weather, trade jokes. That's it." But back in the fall, he added, he saw Beth Prescott professionally—for a lipoma, a fatty tumor, just below the clavicle. Small, benign, out it came, end of story.

That explained the Tylenol III in Beth's medicine cabinet. "So, she was under your care."

"Only in the event of a reoccurrence."

"Was there? Recently?"

His answer was slow. "There may have been. I don't know," he said. "I think she missed an appointment."

Marian downshifted. "Wednesday, two weeks ago."

He grabbed his desk calendar and checked the date. "Go on."

"How did she seem?"

Jim Carney squeezed his eyes shut, trying to remember, then shook his head slowly. He was in surgery most of the day. First, a hot appendix, then a bowel resection. He didn't get to the office on Hospital Way until after closing, where he read his mail, made a few calls, and did what he could about physician impairment with the help of his pal Jack Daniels. "Sorry, Marian, I can't help you. I didn't see Beth Prescott at all that day. Or much of anyone else." They sat in silence for half a minute. "She was friendly, pretty enough, stuck in a small town." His hands burst open like he was releasing captive birds. "Maybe she just—took off."

Took off. Some scatty, half-baked impulse that explained everything and wasn't worth a bit more of our attention. Beth Prescott just went out to the Dairy Mart for a pack of cigarettes and then stayed out drinking all night—all week—all right, all right, half a month—with the clerk. If they could convince each other that Beth Ann Prescott just "took off," then nobody left behind had to feel very bad.

* * *

Sometimes that was true. Twenty-two years ago, the man named Tom Warner, father of Joan and Marian, took off. He looked like Buffalo Bill Cody—claimed some relation on his daddy's side—with thick swirls of untamed, side-swept dark hair and a shapely moustache, the kind of look you see on old photographs of Union soldiers from Pennsylvania coal country. Marian knew she shared his broad shoulders and shaggy hair and the kind of riveting glower she uses when life finds her walking alone through Hell's Kitchen at two AM.

Tom Warner didn't leave home, he just never came back from a wilderness trip to Hudson Bay he was taking with some friends from Warner Lambert. He got the group all the way back down to Toronto, put them on the return flight, and then missed it himself. On purpose. He called home, told Penelope, Marian's mother, Joan's stepmother, he was going back up north for a couple of solo weeks, and that was the last direct communication they had from him.

For the next five years, they all knew where he was and told each other they didn't care. After all, Tom Warner had taken off. During this time, Penelope heard from their banker that Tom had cashed in his IRAs and had the money sent to a post office box in Timmins, Ontario. She also heard from their State Farm agent that Tom had called for information, about insuring a new wilderness retreat he was calling Nature's Way, which all three of them thought sounded like a laxative.

Then, twelve years ago, Marian got a call from Penelope, who said, "I'd actually like you to find your father." All that stood between Marian and Tom Warner, the man in question, was a charm called a PI license so she wouldn't be just a daughter wondering what the hell had happened to her Buffalo Bill daddy—she was a PI, and it was just a job. What she got was a license, but what she didn't get was a father. Which isn't to say she didn't find him. Nature's Way has a slick website that would never even occur to Penelope to check out—complete with a mission statement about fashioning itineraries for "worshipful adventurers," and a photo gallery. There stood "Shaman" Tom Warner, with a long gray ponytail and a paunch, with his partner Kiki and their two offspring, Namaste and Shantih. From what Marian could tell, it looked like he had lost at least one tooth, two fingers, and somehow an eyebrow.

From Buffalo Bill to junkyard dog.

CHAPTER THREE

Joan and Marian drove fourteen hours up to Nature's Way, making the final leg of the trip in a rented boat, and dropped anchor off the island site and fished. Under their wide-brimmed hats, they took turns with the binoculars, watching a drumming circle crammed on to the dock at Nature's Way. At one point, a silver pontoon boat flew by, carrying "worshipful adventurers" who looked extremely well-dressed for this wilderness gig, and Shaman Tom Warner himself, standing in the stern, at the wheel. Business was good. He actually waved. The women in the wide-brimmed hats waved back. He never knew who they were. And Marian guessed they never knew who he was, either. That day, she and Joan caught two bass and one perch.

They let all four of them go.

Chapter Four

William D. Rinaldi and David Barish shared an OB practice next to an upscale strip of shops called The Marketplace, where local artisans sold little hand-painted teapots and Longaberger baskets. Marian pushed open a black wrought-iron gate and followed the flagstone walk around a small courtyard, past a trickling fountain and green benches. The sign on the stone wall next to the waiting room door said Carthage Women's Health, William D. Rinaldi, M.D., David Barish, M.D., Obstetrics and Gynecology.

Inside was reproductive Hell, with women sitting around in various stages of pregnancy. The nine-monthers sat listless on one hip with a look of chronic heartburn, but the five-monthers were energetically flipping through magazines called *Child and Parent* and *Your New Baby and You*. Piped in overhead was the pumping disco beat of the *Flashdance* theme, some singer who never had hemorrhoids telling all the rest of them to take their passion and make it happen. Marian gave one of her business cards to a front office team member named Callie to take back to Dr. Rinaldi—*It's about Beth Prescott,* she wrote on the back.

Rinaldi was one of those men whose appeal lay in the fact that he couldn't give a damn about his looks. He had a mobile mouth, a dimpled chin, and skin that thirty years ago had seen its share of Clearasil. To find Marian a seat, he had to clear off an open tin of cookies and a load of obstetrics journals. "See this one?" He held out a magazine so shiny it looked like it had been shellacked. 'Dedicated to the Physician at Play' was the subtitle. The cover had one of those sharp, oozy pictures of a Greek island where

CHAPTER FOUR

everything is blue or white that makes you think you made a critical error in not being born rich. That issue promised articles on Shopping Shanghai and Trekking Tuscany.

"'The Physician at Play,'" Dr. Rinaldi snorted. "You know what I do with my free time?" They sat down. "I sleep." His fingers scraped through his short, graying hair. "If I'm lucky, I get to dream about trekking Tuscany. But mostly," he offered her a cookie and then popped one into his mouth, "I get a call at, oh, three in the morning from Labor and Delivery, telling me the tracing's showing some late decelerations." He slapped his hands clean. "I call it Rock Climbing in Carthage, Ohio." Marian looked at a sunny, framed photograph on his desk of two little blond kids wearing orange PFDs, maybe about the same age as Namaste and Shantih. Rinaldi grabbed her business card and tapped it against his desk. "Well, Marian Warner, tell me."

"Well, Dr. Rinaldi, you tell me."

"The subject is Beth Prescott."

"Right."

"She hasn't been around," Rinaldi said. "But then, I guess that's why you're here."

"That's it."

"To tell you the truth, I like the new courier better," he said, flicking crumbs from his Levis and green plaid shirt.

"Weezie Tiller? Why?"

He thought about it and shrugged. "I just do. Beth Prescott's hard to describe. She has this way of acting like she's holding something back. Like any minute you'll get an earful about Jesus." Rinaldi blew out air and leaned back in his chair. "What do you think? Is she dead?"

"I honestly don't know."

"But you think so." They looked at each other. "Too bad," he said softly. "Now I'll never know what she was just about to say." He smiled, which nearly improved his looks. The last time he saw Beth Prescott, he went on to say, was about two weeks ago—that Wednesday would be about right, he thought—maybe around 10 AM. It was a slow morning with a lot of cancellations. He was standing in the front office when Beth breezed in, taking the sealed samples from Callie. She told him thanks, the Bactrim's really clearing up "the bloody pee thing," and he told her to finish the course. Then he heard her say to Callie and Mary Jo that she was "hauling A," as she put it, what with a full day ahead and plans later, and she'd catch up with them next time. Then away she went.

"How long has she been your patient?"

"She isn't. She's Dave's, maybe for the last couple of years. I only saw her recently for a urinary tract infection on a day he wasn't in."

A stab. "Has she ever had an abortion?"

"That's confidential."

"I know."

He shook his head. "Sorry."

"A baby, then."

"Sorry."

"Any STDs?"

"Sorry, Marian."

"She could be dead."

"She *could* be dead." He sat up suddenly, nodding. "But for now, she's our patient, she's missing, and she sure as hell wouldn't want us blowing confidentiality five minutes after a PI walks in off the street." They looked at each other for a minute without saying anything, then William D. Rinaldi, M.D. rubbed his eyes. "We'll get along a whole lot better, Marian," he said, finally, "if you bring me a release from her family,"

"If that's what I have to do."

"It is. Only I think you're wasting your time."

Which was the closest thing to information Marian was going to get from him. "I'll think about it," she said, meaning she wouldn't, not now, but she could still play along.

He looked harder at her business card. "Funny I didn't connect you to Beth Prescott. I thought maybe you came about the Clemm kid, but then I saw your message."

"What Clemm kid?"

"Dave's case."

CHAPTER FOUR

"Dr. Barish?"

He nodded.

"I'd like to talk to him, but they said he's unavailable."

"Front office speak for coming unglued."

"Why's that?"

"He's being sued for twelve million."

"For?" What was he, Philip Morris?

"Kid he delivered four years ago who has cerebral palsy."

Things fell into place. "Right in town?"

Rinaldi plopped his elbows on his desk. She got a whiff of Calvin Klein for Men, which sure beat the hell out of anything else she'd smelled since she hit Carthage. "Right in town. The trial started today."

"I met his lawyer."

"Kemp?"

"We're staying at the same place."

A beat. "The defense is saying Dave's management of Jeannie Clemm's labor met the standard of care."

"Did it?"

"It did, but the Clemms wound up with a brain-damaged kid, so I expect they're saying standard of care be damned. Bad outcome must mean bad care, right? Somebody's to blame, somebody's gotta pay, and preferably not them. Preferably some faceless insurance company up to its boardroom in bucks."

Marian felt out of her element. "I guess what matters is whether he acted responsibly."

Rinaldi snorted. "What matters, Marian Warner, is what you can make a jury believe."

"Dr. Rinaldi, you're a cynic."

"You bet. I've been in practice for sixteen years. And it's Bill." He held up a hand and spread his fingers out wide. Five times, he'd had requests for records. Five patients had approached five different lawyers who "explored" the possibilities of suing him over common complications of common procedures. Nothing came of any of them. Nothing could.

Even a plaintiff lawyer could see that.

"You were lucky."

"I was lucky. I've never had a bad baby. There isn't a jury in the world who won't put aside their hankies long enough to throw millions at a bad baby. Forget the medicine. Forget the truth. It's the new lottery. You can go to 7-Eleven and spend a buck on a Superlotto ticket. Your chances of shopping Shanghai and trekking Tuscany are a whole lot higher if you try your luck with the courts, even *after* the plaintiff lawyers scoop out their take."

"Which is?"

"As high as forty percent." If Dave's jury awards the Clemms, say, two million for the lifelong care of little Courtney, their lawyer walks away with a cool eight hundred grand. "But with us doctors," he made a face, "it's fee for service. A total hysterectomy is ten grand. A tubal ligation, six grand. Prenatal care and vaginal delivery, around sixteen grand. Even then, insurers pay us what they think we're worth, the hell with the fees, which in some cases is less than you'd pay Roto-Rooter to ream out your sewer. And either we take it, or we don't get paid. But for personal injury firms like Crenshaw, Pike and Haberman there's no such thing as a fee for service, it's all contingency—meaning the higher the dollar amount awarded, the more they make. Talk about employee incentive plans." There was a soft, quick tap at the office door. "Maybe I'll start charging more for really cute babies. Come on in."

Mary Jo stuck her head in. "Next patient's ready, Dr. R."

"Thanks. Just one?"

"Well," she wrinkled her nose, "actually, the next three, but I didn't want to rush you." As he groaned, she rolled her eyes and disappeared.

Bill Rinaldi squinted at her. "Are you married?"

"That's confidential."

He grinned. "No, it isn't."

"Can't tell you. Sorry. Get a release. Maybe then."

"Come on."

"Okay, no. You?"

"Once. Presently I'm resting, otherwise I'd suggest dinner."

CHAPTER FOUR

"I'm resting, too."

"I can tell. From what?" Could this be the only man in Carthage who hadn't heard?

"Homicide." She scratched her ear. "And related messes."

"But, to your stomach, what of that?"

He was right. "I guess we can still eat."

"We could go in separate cars."

She pitched in, "We could get separate checks."

"Separate tables," he joked, but when they couldn't come up with a free evening between them, Rinaldi tossed his pencil in the air. "Hell, separate nights."

"Deal."

* * *

She found Buddy Bryson five doors down from the center of town in a shop called Carthage Camera. Buddy's place fell within that tiny square advertised as the "heart of the Carthage commercial district." It had one in a line of ornamental pear trees jackhammered into the sidewalk near the curb. Fairy twinkle lights had been strung up and clipped to the wires were cents-off coupons on film developing. The window display had the usual camera store Kodak cardboard stand-ups featuring blissful models who looked like they just walked over from a Xanax ad. The signs pretty much told the story of the lengths Buddy would go to lure people in off the street.

One-Hour Photo—We Mean It!

Instant Passport Photos—Why Go Elsewhere?

See Our Selection of Frames!

Video Transfers—Why Go Elsewhere?

Photo Restoration—Bring Us Your Fading Ancestors!

Buddy Bryson was alone in the shop, where vanilla-flavored Glade plug-ins did what they could to keep the paper mill from affecting the camera-buying public. He peeked around the wall of the back room, a drone with a broken propellor tucked under his arm. "Hello there." He ducked out of sight.

"Buddy Bryson?" When he came back out, he was drone-free. She waited for him at the counter.

"And you would be—?" His dark blond hair was moussed back in a look that said when he wasn't developing one-hour photos—We Mean It! —he was practicing his ten-meter dives. He wore two diamond studs in his right earlobe, a purple shirt buttoned up, and baggy grey trousers that were nice Armani knockoffs.

"Marian Warner. I'm looking into Beth Prescott's disappearance."

For a second, he got incredibly grave. "Heard it. So sad." Then he brightened, the way people do, when they can steal back the missing from their strange fates by filling in the pre-sad history. "Bethie," he launched, leaning against the glass counter, "is the original funkmeister."

Marian nodded as if she could possibly know what that meant. "So, she's —"

"A hoot!"

That explained it. Why Go Elsewhere? "You've been friends —"

"Since junior high, *and* —" He got coy and shot Marian the side-eye.

"And —?"

Buddy's eyes darted around the empty shop, and he lowered his voice. "We were each other's 'first' in the back of my mother's Caddy. Mom," he added, deadpan, "was not driving at the time." Marian laughed. "It was an act repeated a few times—without much success." He raised an eyebrow at her, which, unless she was mistaken, had been carefully tweezed.

Buddy Bryson saw Bethie last about a month ago, but not to talk to, really. He was leaving Gringos just as she was coming in with some girls. She was really liking that Girard job. "All that schooling's really paying off," she told him. "Well, that's classic Bethie," Buddy laughed. "Six months at a medical assisting school in Columbus was 'all that schooling.'" And she was always, but always, looking for things to pay off. Jobs, men, school. Like she invested so much.

Buddy put on his grim face. "She's a hard worker, but she has no savvy." Even when she takes a side, she can't argue it. He's heard her say, "Well, *that's*

CHAPTER FOUR

no good," about everything from a Ku Klux Klan rally to a rent increase. "It's not that she's dumb," Buddy said, two fingers polishing a spot on the gleaming counter, "she's just more of a trog than the rest of us. She puts on her shiny belted rayon dresses and never even knows she's in a mine. And if you're in a mine," Buddy cocked his head at me, "I say you might just as well dig."

* * *

By dinnertime, Marian was pulling into the gravel parking lot at Gringos, the roadhouse Rodie had told her was one of Beth's haunts. She locked up the Volvo, adjusted her bag, and looked around. Her phone trilled, showing only a number and no caller ID. "Hello?"

"This Maryann—" the voice on the other end seemed to be reading something, then went on, "Warner?"

"I'm Marian, yes."

"This here's Vince Varnum. You left me a card."

Beth's neighbor downstairs and diagonally across. "Right, thanks for calling me back, Vince."

"No worries. Beth Prescott okay?"

If he was feigning concern, he was good. She was buying it. "We hope so." Her standard line.

"She hasn't been around for a while." He sounded a little hazy on hours, days, weeks.

Marian put a small smile into her voice. "That's why the family's brought me in."

Varnum grunted. "I—don't know her for real-like, if you know what I mean."

"I understand you're busy."

"My little boy's half an hour away."

Which jibed with what Randy Gillison had told her. "Can I talk to you? Meet up for coffee?"

"How's now? We're already talking."

Man needed a vacation. Play it his way. "Good. Right. When did you last see Beth?" Marian worried that between double shifts and frequent son runs, Varnum would be weak on specifics. While he hummed his way through his last couple of weeks, Marian glanced overhead where the clouds were quietly bunching, working up a good rain. Across the curving country highway was farmland for sale—*Will Build to Suit*—and a number to call, but until that call came, someone was still planting acres of corn.

"Closest I can recall is the Monday maybe two, three weeks ago, around 5:30."

Two days before Beth disappeared. "How can you be sure?"

"Boy was sick. Stomach flu. My ex called just as I was leaving the warehouse to head me off. I was supposed to pick him up and we'd go for a bite out at Rally's, he loves Rally's, all the checks, so I came on home instead. She was parking—Beth Prescott, that is—same as me, and we headed in together."

"Did you chat?"

"I'm not much for chat. But she said beautiful weather. I said if you like it hot." He fell silent. "That's the last I seen of her."

Marian picked it up. "What about visitors, Vince?"

"Well," he got energetic, "I got day shift, overtime sometimes, and my boy. I don't know if she had any visitors, but—" he added reasonably— "it don't mean she didn't."

"Very true. Well—" The fact that Beth Prescott could make a minimum of small talk with a hardly-home neighbor wasn't much of a clue.

"Now, wait," Varnum added suddenly. "There's that guy. That one guy." She heard him snap his fingers. "Him I seen a couple of times, you know, just kind of hanging."

Marian felt a ping of excitement. "Tell me."

"Once he seen me looking out my window and acted like he was checking an address or something, then stepped clean out of sight. But he'd been looking up at A4, that's for shit sure."

"Can you narrow down the date?"

"Mm," he considered, "two days after I seen her that last time. Close as I

CHAPTER FOUR

can get. Sorry."

Putting the mystery guy looking for Beth Prescott on the day she disappeared. "Vince," Marian said, "sounds like it wasn't just that once, this guy looking up at A4, am I right?"

"I'll say. There was that other time, bit of snow left on the ground, same guy, carrying a package, or—" here he tried to be mysterious, "—leastways what looked like a package and heading up the stairs. A3 or 4, take your pick."

"I'm guessing A4." She let out a big breath. "Can you describe this guy?"

Vince Varnum sucked in the big breath she had just let out. "Hard to be sure, you know, what with only seeing the guy from my window, but I'm guessing my height, around 6 foot. What you might call thin, long arms, white hair—"

"White?"

"No, no, maybe light yellow, no particular cut."

"Young? Old?"

"Not either, especially."

"What kind of walk?"

"Well, when the guy wasn't slipping outta sight, kind of a half-run sort of walk, like someone who had to be getting somewheres."

"Dressed how?"

"Nothing that stood out. But the same both times I seen him."

"Dressed the same?"

"Yes!"

She was beginning to get the picture. "Could you have missed a UPS truck?"

"No, no."

"An Amazon truck?"

He scoffed. "I know those like I was born in one."

"Any sort of delivery truck?"

"Can't speak to any trucks, Maryann. But—" another finger snap, "a red vest. I remember a red vest. I remember thinking I may not be no clothes horse, but I'd be dead before I'd turn up in a red vest." He gave a laugh.

The vest. The package. "Describe the package."

"Oh," he cast his mind back, "looked cardboard, square, kinda flattish, you know, like—"

Marian rolled her eyes. "Like a pizza?"

A beat. "You're good," said Vince Varnum admiringly.

He had just described Flyboy from Pizza Shack. Flyboy with a regular order for Miss Elizabeth. Flyboy who, if she got the dates right, hung around on days he wasn't delivering a pizza.

She thanked Vince Varnum for his time—she wasn't quite sure she could call it help, exactly—and shoved her phone into a pocket. Still, she'd have to follow it up with a trip to Pizza Shack to get a lead on Flyboy. In the parking lot at Gringos, she took in the property. On either side of the roadhouse itself were dense woods with orange POSTED NO HUNTING signs nailed to every fifth tree. Gringos had a prime location, all right, and a parking lot big enough for the usual thirsty regulars as well as Road Scholar tour buses. But at 6:20 on a weekday evening early in June, she counted just eight cars and pickup trucks.

It was a low, sprawling, one-story place made out of logs and lined with clean white mortar. The towering sign for the joint was mounted on the roof and spelled out GRINGOS in orange neon in the shape of a horsewhip. Next to the name sign was a neon, two-sided caricature of a man with a mustache, each side blinking on and off, which made it look like he was winking and rippling his moustache in a Zapata sort of way. The music hit her—Kenny Rogers chewing out Lucille—before Marian even got to the front, where a tall, double door with metal sculptures for handles made her think of the entrance to the Emerald City.

Inside, she stood still while her eyes adjusted, and *after* her eyes adjusted, she stood still some more. Eddie Estremera's Gringos was the Ponderosa on speed, every bit of wall space clamped with yokes, sleigh bells, moth-eaten saddle blankets, stolen road signs. The county engineer's department in Intercourse, Pennsylvania, must have to keep a warehouse full of them. Eddie alone had three. Hanging from the rafters were tattered old Latin American flags, wagon wheel chandeliers, and, unbelievably, disassembled

CHAPTER FOUR

Model Ts.

The only thing that didn't make her want to run for cover were the vintage movie posters *en español*. *Los Tres Hermanos Marx! en Una Noche En La Opera!* Behind the bar were 8x10 framed glossies of celebrities who had stopped by Eddie Estremera's on their way to more important places. Lady Gaga told Eddie to keep his draft cold and his buns warm. Ray Romano reminded him they have a big one on Atlanta in five. And Leo DiCaprio wrote that the buffalo burgers were excellent.

Farther down the bar was a long row of draft handles lined up like chorus girls. On the wall behind the bartender was a blue neon sign: *Beer Is Slippery. Watch Your Step.* And what was probably the motto at Gringos tubed its way in orange neon across the top of the entire length of the mirror behind the bar: *The Coffee Is Hot. Deal With It.* As she eased onto a stool, Marian realized that down at the other end of the bar sat Chopper, who looked like he couldn't quite place her, but had found someone who pours drinks and keeps court orders out of it. He'd take his chances with hot coffee and slippery beer.

She watched the bartender close the book he was reading, slip it into a back pocket, and start toward her. When he got within ordering distance, Marian recognized him from the rooftop: Eddie Estremera. Immediately, she understood the entry on Rodie's list. *Eddie Estremera???* Is he sleeping with Beth? What's a man with this kind of sex appeal and business acumen doing in Carthage, Ohio? Is there any woman in town who *hasn't* been to bed with him?

"And for you?" Soft-spoken.

"Let me think."

He rotated a hip at her and set one hand on the bar. "Let me surprise you."

"Go right ahead." Pulling out her wallet, she showed him her license. "I'm Marian Warner." He looked at her in a *that's cool* kind of way. "And I'm here about Beth Prescott."

Nodding slowly, Eddie Estremera poured her a shot of something, saying she had come at a good time, "the lull between happy hour and alcoholic abandon."

"Yours?"

"Never mine. The first rule about being a barkeep. Never drink your own profits." He pushed the glass slowly toward her with one finger, the kind of guy who could make passing the salt a sexual encounter. "Chivas. It's on the house." Then he came around and joined her on the expensive side of the bar. Eddie Estremera was slim, just a slice taller than Marian, which put him at about 5'9", with light brown hair, a moustache edged with blond, and the kind of green eyes only the devil should have. That day, he was wearing 501 jeans and an old Banana Republic cargo vest over a black t-shirt. Knotted around one bicep was a red bandana, like a biker boy.

He pulled out a pack of crushed Winstons from one of the cargo pockets and flicked aside the warped paperback copy of *Fear and Loathing in Las Vegas* he had been reading when she came in. When Kenny got done with Lucille, Chopper howled, and Eddie Estremera pushed a little leather bag of change down the glistening bar at him. "Here, Chopper, you go play something nice. My treat." Chopper rose from the dead and headed to the jukebox.

Eddie went on to say that when he bought the place five years ago, it had been a derelict roadhouse that had never reopened after its last kitchen fire. He lighted a cigarette, between drags managing that steely look she pretty much associated with Texans and terrorists. "I picked the place up at a sheriff's sale with a loan from the SBA, and then a few of us did all the renovations." A sheet of late afternoon sun came through the windows, glancing off a scattering of salvaged, mismatched booths, tables, and chairs. "Rodie Prescott did the lathing. Still in high school at the time."

"How do you know Beth?"

Eddie looked at the ceiling, taking some kind of mental inventory, while some new music started up and Chopper steamed back toward the bar. "Customer, neighbor," Eddie started itemizing, "lover," he shrugged and looked at me, "pal."

"All at once?" And if he said no, he's a liar.

"There were times," he temporized.

"Recently?"

CHAPTER FOUR

He scratched the side of his nose. "I'm married."

"Recently?"

Eddie Estremera, Gringos??? looked at her narrowly. "Recently," he said with a slow smile, "just customer and pal."

"How long were you involved?" Marian blotted her lips with a cocktail napkin.

He raised his eyebrows. "If you mean sex, we met maybe a couple dozen times over…ten years." Eddie went on: "We're what you might call each other's spare—you only use it when the good one goes flat." And as spares went, Beth Prescott was perfect: discreet, undemanding, fun. It never went any deeper between them because she didn't like his sense of humor, and he didn't like her lack of one. Still, for the couple dozen times they needed a spare, the occasions did not require—Eddie raked at his moustache, looking for the right word— "repartée."

"When was the last time the good one went flat?"

"A year ago."

"How long have you been married?"

He stubbed out his cigarette. "Longer than that," he said, meeting my look. When I didn't say anything, Eddie's features stretched out into tolerant crinkles. "It happens," he told me. Like he was describing tidal waves that flatten whole fishing villages. Suddenly Chopper slammed the bar and bellowed along with Mary Chapin Carpenter on the juke, *It's been too long since somebody whispered, woo-oo-oo, Shut up and kiss me*, which, for the Chopper part of the duet, sounded more like a wolf gargling rabbit bones.

"May 25th," she said, turning back to Eddie, "a Wednesday evening."

"Beth was here."

"You're sure."

He nodded. "It was ladies' night. Drinks for a buck, come with a friend, and it's two for one. It brings in typists and salesclerks by the carload."

"Beth came for cheap drinks?"

"Nah. When Beth was dry, she came. Saving a buck was never the point."

"Then what was?"

She watched with a strange kind of clogged panic as Eddie Estremera reached slowly across the bar and laid just two fingers on her sleeve. "Refreshment."

And to some folks, that might actually mean a beverage. "How long did it take her to get refreshed?"

He shrugged. "Thirty minutes, tops, and I made her the usual, a Singapore Sling—she likes the sappy, umbrella drinks—and she mentioned she had to be somewhere in half an hour, which means she was cutting it pretty close."

"She talk to anybody?"

He smiled. "Not the way you mean it."

"How do I mean it?"

"She wasn't cruising."

"How do you know?"

He wrinkled his nose at me. "Visible panty line."

Marian laughed. "Seriously, Eddie."

"I am serious." The front doors opened, and four gals trying for the Betty and Veronica look—capris and twin sets—flounced in, checking out the place, laughing hard at nothing, whispering at everything, and dithering between taking a booth or bellying up to the bar.

"Anything else?"

"'Business or pleasure?' I asked her."

"And—?"

"'Not anymore,' was what she said.'" Eddie headed back around to serve the Jughead set, who, despite the nearness of Chopper Chapin Carpenter, had decided on sitting at the bar.

"What time did she leave?"

"Around eight-thirty." He tapped out another Winston and lit it. "I walked her out to the parking lot—"

"In case you were wrong."

"About—?"

"The visible panty line."

He laughed. "Well, the air felt good," Eddie leaned in to Marian, "and I hung around."

"And—?"

CHAPTER FOUR

He blew a line of smoke out of the side of his mouth. "She drove off."

"Which way?" '

"North," he said. "Straight up highway 8. What'll it be, ladies?"

One of the Bettys declared: "I'll have a—" she looked around like she was expecting to find signs with the treats at Ben and Jerry's, then shrugged, "—Harvey Wallhanger—"

"Hallbanger," one of the Veronicas corrected her.

"Ballwhanger," one of the others said, and they all seemed to think it sounded kind of dirty, so they shrieked. Even Chopper looked horrified and cleared off, clutching his glass to his mountainous chest and stomping toward a table. Eddie grabbed a cheap vodka with a siphon top and gave me a look that said, *I earn my money.* While the gals took turns shouting the names of mixed drinks—a Jughead kind of parlor game—Eddie motioned Marian closer.

"I'd say Beth's got something pretty regular going for herself, man-wise, Marian." He stuck a swizzle stick in the drink. "One Ballwhanger," he announced, setting it in front of the Betty in the yellow twin set. "For months now," he told me.

"How can you tell?"

"Sandy, my wife, says all the customers are here for one of two things. In for a drink or in for a wink."

"In your experience, is that so?"

"In my experience," Eddie tilted his head, grinning, "that's most definitely so."

"Bartender!" One of the Veronicas squared her shoulders. "I'd like a screw—"

"Driver!" the others squealed. "Driver! Omigod."

"Beth Prescott?" I had to yell over the noise.

Eddie had poured himself a Diet Coke, which he lifted at me in a kind of publican's toast. "In for a drink."

"And then there's me," Marian slipped off the stool, grabbing her bag. "In for a think."

"Marian, Marian, Marian," Eddie said, reaching for a plastic jug of OJ, "there's no third category, sweetheart," he chuckled, pouring. "Not even for you."

Chapter Five

Mrs. Viola Simms-Garber of Upper Arlington, Ohio, sat rigid in the high-backed chair in her room at The Briars. She had big blue eyes and a thicket of silver hair cut into a wedge. The skin on her face was folding in on either side of her lips, but it still wasn't enough to keep her from talking. The middle-aged daughter LaVerne was blowing into a tissue and staring out the window.

All the really worthwhile ancestry was on the Simms side of the family, Mrs. *Simms*-Garber was saying, and her seven-time great grandfather had fought in the infantry in the Revolutionary War. She and LaVerne— "a great pollen sufferer if ever there was one"—at this, LaVerne hurled the tissue toward the trash can and missed—were in Carthage for Tulip Time, where the D.A.R. always has a resplendent booth—

"Between the goats and the hogs," LaVerne put in.

"—where I'll be presenting the plaque for most active chapter to the Wade County Daughters." She had brought Flaggie.

"Mother names her jewelry." LaVerne pressed her lips together as if to say, how nuts is *that?*

"—to wear at the occasion."

"Would you show me where you packed Flaggie?"

"Yes, of course." She rose—most people just get up, but Viola Simms-Garber rose—and showed Marian her suitcase, a floral Samsonite, sitting open on her bed. Inside were layers of what looked like presents wrapped in white tissue paper. Marian stared.

"Mother wraps her clothes when she packs," LaVerne explained.

"Wrapping keeps them nice," Mrs. Simms-Garber explained.

"Show me where, please?"

She pulled the unzipped "lid" of the suitcase back up from where it touched the bed and showed Marian the one deep inside pocket—no zips, no snaps, totally unsecured. It was where, in her own suitcase, Marian jammed her rolled-up dirty underwear when she traveled. Not a place for carrying the Flaggie that almost cost as much as her annual income. She felt around carefully inside the pocket. "Did this pocket hold anything else?"

"Pearlie and Morris."

"And those would be—?"

Mrs. Simms-Garber stared at her. "Why, my pearl necklace and my gold and amber cat pin."

"And were they also—?"

"Dear God, no, not taken. I still have them." She indicated her neck, where Pearlie drooped, and LaVerne flicked at a shapeless gold and honey-colored brooch on her own lapel.

"What are their values?"

"Pearlie is quite dear—"

"Twenty grand," piped up LaVerne.

"—and Morris only around twelve, but I love him." Had Penelope Warner ever spent sums like those on anything that didn't also include a roof? Suddenly, Marian had to hand it to her mother, that P.T. Barnum of the Ivory Tower, there in her sweet, purring tenure at Rutgers. She cranked out pop cultural books called *Suburban Apocalypse* and *Dire Sexology*. There were waiting lists for all of her classes, and from the time Marian was old enough to know this woman was her mother, the only piece of jewelry she'd ever seen her wear was a copper MIA bracelet with the name of William G. Keenan USAF 6 Apr 71. In all of her 62 years, probably the only thing she had ever lost was Tom Warner, who, on the whole, was probably worth less than Morris.

"How were they packed?"

"In tissue, of course, like Flaggie, each separately. I'm very careful."

LaVerne spat out, "I told her not to bring them."

CHAPTER FIVE

"What's the point in owning these beauties if I can't—"

LaVerne rounded on her. "You left the damn diamonds at home, that's what happened."

"Oh, LaVerne, I'm not *senile*."

"And you gift wrap your pantyhose—"

Mrs. *Simms*-Garber's lip quivered. "I take care of things."

"No, you don't, you wrap them. That's not the same thing."

"It was that maid, that little brown person."

"Ladies," Marian outshouted them, then made them sit while she quickly covered the known ground. The investigating officer had checked the whole room—no Flaggie—and Marian was inclined to believe him. She had talked to the maid Esmé Culp, the "little brown person," who insisted she didn't go near the Simms-Garber suitcase and nothing else had gone missing from The Briars in the nine years she had worked here.

At that, Mrs. Simms-Garber opened her mouth as though to say, but what a temptation the dazzling, one-of-a-kind Flaggie would be, but Marian held up her hand and then gave them an assignment: call a friend back home who could go check the jewelry box. The two of them suddenly seemed breathless with a mission. "As for me," said Marian, heading for the door, "I will pursue other inquiries," which was the phrase she used before she had any kind of a plan. "By the way—Esmé Culp?"

Mrs. Simms-Garber's expression flattened.

Marian went on. "Esmé Culp is Esmé *Hemmings*-Culp. You'll know the name, of course. She tells me her own six times great grandfather *started* the Revolutionary War, and she's wondering if that makes her eligible for membership in the D.A.R."

* * *

Downstairs in the kitchen, Barbara Hauser was rolling out dough the size of an area rug on her marble pastry board. That thick brown smell of a fresh pot of coffee hung over the room, and if Marian could figure out where it was coming from, she would have flung herself at it. Standing next to

Barbara was a greasy-haired guy dressed in the kind of drawstring pants old hippies wear who have spent some time in Bangalore. His eyeglasses were patched in two places by adhesive tape—no, one patch looked like a Cookie Monster band-aid—and he was gulping down a lemonade and rattling on about the time he shoed the horse that came in ninth at the Kentucky Derby.

"The blacksmith," Barbara said meaningfully.

Marian could tell Barbara was fed up with him because tomorrow morning's scones were turning into tomorrow morning's crepes. As Marian shook hands with Jerry Vulcani, she walked him clean out of the kitchen before he even knew he was out of the room. When she unfolded a Wade County roadmap on the part of the island work space not taken up by dough, Barbara Hauser wiped her hands on her apron and moved closer.

Marian put it to her. "Beth Prescott had an appointment half an hour away from Gringo's, and Eddie Estremera said she headed north. Where would that put her?" They leaned together over the map. Barbara propped her chin on her elbows, setting her finger where Gringo's would be. While she looked around and tried to fill in places from memory, Marian ticked some flour off her cheek.

"No damn where at all," said the other woman, finally.

There's State Highway 53, Barbara pointed, connecting Dayton and Wheeling, West Virginia, which intersects Highway 8 about fifteen minutes past Gringos. Putting Beth Prescott exactly nowhere. A big green blotch just east of a burg called World Without End was a state park called Hopewell Range. Then, west on 53—but a few minutes past Beth's limits—were the Wade County Fairgrounds. Aside from spidery country roads, that was it.

Marian nicked some dough with her fingernail and stood up, nibbling. Then she circled her other hand over the spot on the map. "Barbara, think of where else you could go to meet someone. Not on the map. Just—a spot. Another Gringos, say, or a movie theater, a B&B—"

"Hey, hey—"

"Not as good as The Briars, fewer lawsuits—"

She flicked flour at me. "Like a driving range, or a U-Store It place—"

"You got the idea."

CHAPTER FIVE

She narrowed her eyes. "Public?"

"That's my hunch."

She scoured the map again. "Have you talked to Jack yet?"

"No."

"Don't get defensive."

"Then don't put me on the spot."

"It's all this stress."

"You?"

"You."

"Keep thinking."

She suddenly looked straight ahead. "Well, wait. There's Trillium."

"Which is—?"

"A country inn, pricey rustic, you know the type. Stone fireplaces, venison. They've got a few rooms upstairs, so if you're having an affair with someone rich and married from the big city, it's a thought." She tapped a spot on the map outside the northeast entrance to Hopewell Range State Park—clear on the other side.

"But how far is it from Gringo's?"

Barbara Hauser shook her head and looked grim. "Fifty minutes," she said softly, meeting my eyes. "Sorry. Fifty minutes."

"It's too far."

"Marian, there's no place. There just isn't." She pushed away the map. "Unless what Beth Prescott was looking for in a pair of britches—" she widened her eyes, "was straw."

※ ※ ※

Marian dumped everything out of the Prescott folder onto her bed. Beth's bills, bank statement, date book. The *Aida* CD. The sealed envelope with the retainer. A scrap of paper with Rodie's number she'd have to put in her phone. If she couldn't figure out where Beth went the night she disappeared, then she could at least see how she shopped. On her Visa credit limit of $2,500, she had charged a meal on April 22nd at The Gleaner, the Carthage answer to fine dining. There was a fill-up at Highway Shell on May 12th, groceries from Kroger's on the 19th, and something from Express for $98.00. Maybe a shiny belted rayon dress.

The bank statement from Third Carthage Trust showed less than $1,200 in her savings and just over $800 in her checking. There were canceled checks covering rent, utilities, haircut, and dry cleaning. Four ATM withdrawals for a puny $20 each time were made from machines around Carthage and one in Columbus.

Marian called Rodie. "Who's she seeing?"

"What makes you think—?"

"Eddie Estremera."

Rodie groaned. "She's back with *Eddie?*"

"No, but he says there's someone." She went on to tell him that the evening Beth disappeared, she had an appointment with *someone* at approximately nine PM. Chances are she made the plan just that morning, what with the uneaten ribeye in the fridge and no mention of it in her date book.

"Well, whoever it is, Beth didn't tell me."

"Which means—?"

"Which means it's pretty heavy."

"Heavy how?"

"Oh, someone important, or someone married—or someone embarrassing." I had a quick image of Beth meeting up with Chopper for a tumble behind a haystack. "That sort of thing."

"Does Beth like opera?"

"God, no."

"Art?"

"Not really." His voice sounded small and sad as another day had gone by with no sign of his sister.

While Rodie launched into a memory of Beth skipping school the day of the field trip to the art museum in Cincinnati, Marian felt a kind of low-level dread seep into her as she came to the conclusion there was no more avoiding the Girard part of Beth Ann Prescott's life—which meant that tomorrow she'd probably have to chase Jack down at a work site. At least that would

CHAPTER FIVE

pry Barbara Hauser from her back. She'd drop the Girard piece into the next day somewhere between the other doctors on Beth's route, Lila Ketchum the tanning salon lady, Pizza Shack—and Charlie. Her Charlie. Her wired, funny, glorious Charlie. Marian slid her one decent fingernail through the envelope Rodie had given her and peered at the check. The amount was right.

The signature wasn't.

Jack Girard was paying her fees.

* * *

She and Nan Kemp ran into each other outside the bathroom at their end of the hall. Marian was tired, pretty close to cranky, and at that moment didn't need to be the bad half in a Before and After shot, but there Nan Kemp was, wearing white silk pajamas and carrying a Sonicare dental hygiene system that cost as much as Marian's Volvo. Marian herself was wearing her moth-eaten robe and was carrying a toothbrush with splayed bristles and a travel tube of Colgate.

After thirty seconds on the subject of the missing Beth Prescott, she told Nan she needed twenty minutes tomorrow with David Barish, M.D. Nodding, Nan suggested, "Come by the courtroom before the noon recess." She narrowed her eyes. "Have you ever been to a trial?"

A beat. "Nothing criminal."

"A civil suit?"

"My mother." How could she have forgotten? She stood silent for half a minute, slowly twirling her toothbrush. "Intellectual property case."

"She was—?"

"The plaintiff."

"Ah."

"My mother's a full professor at Rutgers. About twenty years ago—" she heard her own voice slow with the memory of those days of drama, more drama than usual from Penelope Warner— "a colleague lifted concepts and whole lines out of the book my mother wrote that had landed her tenure."

Nan leaned against the wall. "You sat in?"
"With my sister. I was fifteen."
Nell prompted, "And...?"
"What did I think?"
A nod.
Marian cast her mind back. "It felt bloodless." But was that all? "Open and closed."
"Cut and dry."
"Well, very clear the poor old prof had stolen Mom's stuff."
"Old prof?"
"Helen Weskind was eighty-six and still teaching and just wouldn't retire. Despite the bad student evaluations. Which—" Marian smiled, "the Dean of Faculty didn't have the heart to show her." And she was still writing—"just one more book" became her slogan—but with no new ideas. She forgot where the holiday party was, forgot who her TAs were, forgot she was the foremost Eudora Welty scholar. "Who? What? You must be mistaken," said Helen Weskind once when someone reminded her. Penelope Warner and Helen Weskind nearly came to blows over which of them was first in what came to be known as Reactive Mimesis Studies, whatever that was, and pretty soon, lines lifted from Penelope Warner's *Suburban Apocalypse* showed up in the slim monograph called Mediocrity as American Phenomenon by Helen Weskind. It was what Marian's mother called a screed of stolen phrases.

The dinner table, those days, was all about warmed-up Lean Cuisine with a whopping side dish of Helen Weskind. Joan, nineteen and very Olympian in her judgments declared the old prof pathetic. "Pathetic, hell," roared Penelope Warner. And when Marian softly offered up some pity for what her mother called "that miscreant," the table got very quiet until Penelope erupted, "That crafty old crone knows exactly what she's doing." It seemed to Joan, Marian, and the Dean of Faculty that the department's resident plagiarist was showing signs of senility.

Nan leaned in. "But not to mom?"
"Ah," said Marian. "Mother is a purist." And Professor Penelope Warner, PhD from Princeton, decided then and there to make an example of what

CHAPTER FIVE

she called "this arrant theft." Phrases like "slippery slope," "not stand for this nonsense," "nip it in the bud" got fumed around the house until Marian's mother hired a lawyer and filed a lawsuit.

Marian was achingly proud of her.

In the end, the trial was short, dry, packed with boring linguists on the stand, droning through ossifying charts of Old English verbs. Finally, the jury recommended a token judgment against Helen Weskind in the amount of $3,500 and damages to the tune of $1.5 million. On that, all three could agree—Helen, Penelope, and the judge: "Asinine." Helen couldn't pay the money, Penelope didn't want the money (although it would have come in handy with Joan and Marian's college bills), and the judge wouldn't formally decree the money.

What Penelope Warner wanted was public vindication.

What Helen Weskind wanted was public vindication. She tottered a bit in the center aisle as the jury was dismissed and drew on a pair of white kid gloves with a victorious tug, as though she had won the case. And there, in the emptying courtroom, she raised her voice. "If what academe now wants is the kind of claptrap tossed about by Professor Warner, then by all means, let me provide it." Just as Marian was wondering what else Helen had in mind, she watched her mother lope over to her adversary. "You should have asked, Helen," chided Penelope, the way she chided Joan for signing her up to speak to her Future Spies of America club, and with a flip of her hand, mumbled, "Or maybe just used quotes."

The old professor did a slow quarter turn and looked her square in the face. "Damn right, and I apologize."

Both women pulled themselves up as straight as they could get. "Lunch?" said Penelope Warner with a lift of her chin.

"Dutch treat?" A second chin lift. No multi-millions had changed hands, and it was a way of keeping the strange comradeship fair.

And Marian remembered her mother's high, breezy laugh. "What a day we've had, you old darling," she said, as they left the courtroom arm in arm, leaving her daughters behind. Fifteen-year-old Marian watched them go, wondering what peculiar magic had turned the "crafty old crone" into an old darling. While Joan talked to the bailiff about job opportunities in the justice system, Marian stood still in the aisle and slowly looked around. A courtroom was a place to air disagreements. A fine, temperature-controlled, lofty spot where combatants could be heard. Views were expressed, Old English verbs had their day, order was followed, decisions rendered, lunch pursued. Altogether a fine experience.

Nan Kemp whispered to Marian, "You were fifteen." And just as Marian was about to ask her what she meant, Nan went on. "Believe me," she said, "Dave Barish is not. If you come before the noon recess tomorrow, he can use the diversion, now that he's had a look at Kelvin O'Malley, the plaintiff lawyer." She added with a grim smile, "The guy we all call the Paid Piper." Any day now, Kelvin Connor O'Malley will turn up on TV for the firm of Crenshaw, Pike, and Haberman during the afternoon soaps, looking sanctimonious, saying nonsense like, *Injured? We can help you collect.* The buzz in the law bars around town says O'Malley goes on some combination of Gatorade and four hours of sleep a night. He's in his mid-thirties, he's unmarried—who has time?—and he grew up in Toledo, where his dad worked for Conrail, and his mom was an LPN.

He got first-rate grades at a second-rate law school and tumbled into a clerkship for a federal judge whose granddaughter he just happened to meet at the Athletic Club of Columbus. His clerkship lasted two years until the old boy shot himself to death with his bailiff's gun—which pundits believe really had nothing to do with O'Malley, who had long since broken up with the granddaughter.

Kelvin Connor O'Malley had found himself available for work at a time when an ad for The Crenshaw Blight hit the highway billboards, and the response in the injured community was so great you had to wonder how the local economy could survive given the number of wounded it apparently had. O'Malley joined Crenshaw almost five years ago, spent the first couple of years mopping up victim spillover from the ad, and went on to make medical malpractice his bailiwick. He'd do wrongful death—nursing home accidents and surgical slips, that sort of thing—but what he really loved were birth injury kids, especially if they came decked out in a fetal monitor strip

CHAPTER FIVE

he could work with.

"It took us half the day to impanel eight jurors—" Nan went on, "—a machinist, an Avon lady, two homemakers, a bagger from the Kroger's, a retired street cleaner, a manicurist, and a pig farmer." That's it, the jury of peers for David Barish, M.D., with his twenty years of schooling and four years of postgrad training in Philadelphia—not to mention the year's fellowship in Houston in Maternal/Fetal Medicine. By the looks of the bunch, she figured the one who had the best shot at understanding periventricular leukomalacia was the pig farmer.

The afternoon was taken up with opening statements and Jeannie Clemm's testimony, said Nan, "...and already Dave's looking like he's been shot, stuffed, and mounted. Nan held her battery-op toothbrush up to her temple and pulled the trigger. Then, on an impulse: "Come to my room, Marian. We'll down some cognac and dream of—" she looked quizzical,"—what did you call it? Oh, yes—" she smiled, "a fine experience."

Chapter Six

Whatever happened to Ban-Lon? At nine AM, Marian was parked outside the medical offices of George Patton Briggs, M.D., waiting for the peckerhead to come to work. Barbara had sent her off with a tankard of coffee and two cranberry scones, and Marian was working on both when she suddenly realized she hadn't seen Ban-Lon around for a while. Like maybe two decades. When she was a little girl, Tom Warner had a lime green shirt with salmon-colored stripes—*Ban-Lon*—that was soft, thin, bright, stretchy and cheap, and there was nothing else quite like it. Unless you counted the black socks—also Ban-Lon—he pulled halfway up his legs that she and Joan got him for his birthday with some of Penelope's money.

And Penelope herself had a top with big pointy lapels and a pattern of lavender and brown psychedelic hoops—no question, Ban-Lon—that she wore a lot for a while there when she was a Teaching Assistant in the History of Western Civilization classes at Rutgers. It was a very likable fabric, which, now that Marian realized it had turned up missing, made her suspicious it had met with foul play. Were bolts of uncut Ban-Lon warehoused somewhere out in Utah? Were used Ban-Lon socks and shirts and tops "disappeared" whenever they turned up in secondhand shops? And what about Orlon? She was becoming a fabric conspiracy theorist, and her money was on OPEC. Hell, if she couldn't find Beth Prescott, she might as well look for Ban-Lon.

Maybe Jack Girard would pay her for that one, too.

Marian picked up a copy of the day's Carthage *Toiler*, Charlie's paper. *Local*

CHAPTER SIX

Doctor Sued was the headline. There was a shot of four-year-old Courtney Clemm in her wheelchair, her head twisted up at her lawyer. Kelvin O'Malley had one hand on her little bony shoulder and both eyes on the camera. A smaller, inset photo showed Nan Kemp and David Barish, M.D. To look at them, you'd think they knew what happened to Ban-Lon, and they damned well weren't telling. At 9:40, a green Lexus with BABYDOC for a license plate swung to the curb in front of Marian, so she sat up and brushed off crumbs. Nice wheels for a peckerhead, except for the *I'd Rather Be Flying* bumper sticker, which couldn't be reassuring for a woman in labor at nine centimeters going *hoo hoo hoo*.

George Patton Briggs, M.D., got out of his Lexus and set down a leather attaché case. With an electronic remote, he locked up and engaged an antitheft system that gave off a strangled blare as a free sample of what a car thief could expect. Then he frowned and rubbed briefly at a spot near the side view mirror, completely ignoring the fact that he'd parked two feet away from a fire hydrant.

Marian came up behind him. "Dr. Briggs?"

"Yes?" He was no more than forty, with a baby face and thick black curls, and he was wearing a blue blazer and a necktie crammed with the history of aviation.

"I'm Marian Warner," she said as she flipped open her wallet to her license. "I'm here about Beth Prescott."

"Who?"

"Beth Prescott, the courier for the Mercy lab."

"Oh, the fat little thing that comes around?"

"No, the woman who *used* to come around."

"What about her? I've got office hours."

"She's missing."

"Missing." He grunted. "Well, I guess you'd better come in." He opened the door to the ugly old brick Victorian and sailed through the crowded waiting room, scanning the group like it was the produce section at Kroger's. The ones who started to smile gave it up and went back to well-thumbed articles on Harry and Meghan and things you can do with strawberries.

Marian followed him through another door, where he came to a bored stop at the front desk, his fingers flexing on the handle of his briefcase. A gal about 55 dressed in whites with a nest of springy curls around her little face looked up, small and brave. Her nameplate said *Denise Frey.* She wet her lips and said good morning.

"Anything?"

Denise checked her notes. "Malva Price—"

"Who?"

"You delivered her six weeks ago?"

Briggs picked up a stack of mail. "If you say so."

"She was in for her postpartum check on Monday?"

"Okay," he said, thumbing through business letters.

"She wants a note to get off work longer."

"Reason?"

"She's just not ready."

"Write her the note."

"Betsy Stevens."

"Go on."

"She's on for a TL next month, but her insurance is changing."

"When?"

"In two weeks."

"Do we take it?"

"No."

"Then get her in sooner."

"Well, she's got this vacation—"

"Get her in sooner."

"Well, what if she can't—"

He flung a hand. "Then ship her out. I'm not running a free clinic here."

"I *guess* I—"

"Tell her to call Rinaldi. He takes anything."

* * *

CHAPTER SIX

Either George Patton Briggs was a whole lot craftier than Marian was giving him credit for, or he really couldn't tell the difference between Beth Prescott, the courier for the Mercy lab, and the FedEx driver Denise Frey thought might be called Buster. Briggs saw one patient every seven minutes, all day long, with twenty minutes for lunch, so forgive him—he said in a way that meant he didn't give a shit whether she did or not—if he couldn't remember "incidental people who wander in and out of here." With a flip of his hand, he made all the rest of them sound like a bunch of roving stoners. By the time she left Briggs, Marian felt pretty sure that by quitting time, he couldn't tell the difference between Beth, Buster, and Marian.

By 11:45, she had finished working her way down the list of doctors on Beth's route, and she still hadn't called Jack Girard. Marian had, however, killed off two perfectly good fingernails in the process. And as she pulled into a parking space across from the Wade County Courthouse, she was wondering whether she could call in all of Charlie's emotional I.O.U.s and have him take on the Girard interview. Over nearly twenty years of friendship and debt, she had saved him from the Scientologists, the Libertarians, and the Levitans (his parents). Surely, he could do just this one little thing for her.

She stood in front of the Wade County Courthouse.

The ornate windows just below the roof line of the courthouse were draped in black hardware cloth, which made the only building in Carthage that you could truly call an "edifice" look more like the cafeteria lunch lady. All that hardware cloth must be a deterrent to pigeons, because she realized a neighboring building had the hairnet, too. The smell from the paper mill the Chamber of Commerce let flourish—but a dozen pigeons, this they go to great expense to foil. Maybe because they can.

A couple of teenagers in Grateful Dead t-shirts and torn jeans sat smoking and kissing on the front steps of the courthouse. No truant officer to shoo them back to school. No ramp to comply with the Americans with Disabilities Act. Twelve gritty steps up to the front door. Inside, Marian peeked into the single courtroom on the first floor—empty—then she sprang up the winding marble steps to the second floor, where she slipped inside

Courtroom 2 and found a seat two rows behind the defense table. The courtroom had the kind of soundproofing that swallowed sound. No windows, lots of fluorescent lighting, beautiful cherry paneling that sucked away at sounds like a mosquito magnet. The jurors were looking a little like the teacher had just started a unit on quadratic equations.

Kelvin Connor O'Malley was walking his expert witness through the fetal monitor strip from Jeannie Clemm's labor four years ago. The witness had to be a doctor named Barrett Rance that Nan had mentioned, so the Paid Piper was meeting the Hired Gun. Rance was one of those mannequins in pricey men's retail stores and country clubs. Color was cheap. Color was tacky. The goal was a sublime rich man's monochrome—clothes, skin, hair, eyes—and if there was some slinky elegance to the mix, all the better.

Rance had it all, including a medical degree, and he sat on the witness stand with his legs crossed like he was fielding questions about estrogen on *The View*. Well-bred, he'd have you think, meant being comfortable everywhere, even fifteen feet away from an Avon lady who didn't get the thing about color, or the retired street cleaner who didn't know that the only piece of jewelry a man of class was allowed was a Patek Philippe wristwatch, not three heavy gold-plated chains ordered off the Home Shopping channel.

Nan was paging through a medical textbook and scratching at her hairline with a pencil eraser, going for a look of polished indifference to the Rance testimony. Next to her was Dave Barish, dark gray suit, average build, thick auburn hair. Nan was right: he looked bagged, stuffed, and mounted as he managed to sit there completely motionless, listening to a colleague he had never in his life met tell the court that David Barish, M.D., had been negligent in his management of Jeannie Clemm's labor.

To Marian, already this case felt very different from what she remembered of her mother's suit against the colleague who claimed Penelope Warner's words as her own. Suddenly, that long-ago trial seemed more like a matter of extreme inconsequence, more an elegant "show" trial than anything else—despite the fulminating efforts of those linguists to show that life as they knew it depended on the jury's understanding the difference between two Old English verbs.

CHAPTER SIX

She found herself staring hard at the alarmingly still back of David Barish. No tiny rise and fall of his suit jacket, even in some sign of life.

How can pain be quite that invisible?

Penelope Warner and Helen Weskind went to lunch.

What if David Barish was just a good doctor with a bad jury?

He could lose his practice, his license, all of his assets, his reputation, his life in this community, his ability to find work elsewhere, and maybe—at the end of the day—finally even his sanity. Marian heaved a sigh. Now here she was to grill him about the disappearance of a lab courier. She hoped Nan Kemp was right, that whatever information he could contribute to Marian's case would be a distraction for this man—otherwise, she felt embarrassed just to be piling on.

She glanced at her watch. Past noon. When would the judge call the lunch recess? All around her, even the smallest things seemed ponderous. The court reporter's fingers. The bailiff's hanky. O'Malley's haircut. A shoe scraped. A cough fizzled. The small things that happen alongside someone else's pain. She got off easy, at fifteen, when her mother and her old adversary left the courtroom together. There was no ruin in their wake. And sometimes, life does go on.

But here. Here.

Terms like *decelerations* and *bradycardia* and *scalp pH* hung in the air. Barrett Rance called the monitor strip "unwieldy," and O'Malley was ingratiating without saying a thing. Rance was his witness: if he wanted to call the monitor strip sweet potato pie, fine with him. Rance noted a place where the fetal heart rate was looking fairly decent, then suddenly dropped to 120 beats per minute for forty-five seconds. He sat back in the witness chair. "Severe fetal distress," he opined, letting go of the strip. As it fluttered toward the carpeted floor, O'Malley scrambled to catch it to show he was just a helpful kind of a guy who wanted to stall for dramatic effect.

Nan Kemp looked unconcerned and jotted down a note on a yellow legal pad. At the table across from her sat what had to be the Clemms, a skinny, good-looking woman with long, dark blond hair and a burly man with military shoulders who sat with his knees apart, holding his wife's little hand on his thigh. She wore a floral dress and had pastel clips holding back hanks of hair. He wore a brown suit that fit his massive legs like shrink wrap. In the aisle between O'Malley's table and the jury box was four-year-old Courtney Clemm, in a wheelchair. Her placement was no accident, thought Marian—the child looked like the ninth juror. Hovering behind her was what had to be Grandma, an older version of Jeannie with a loose perm and the kind of overbite that photographs well.

O'Malley gathered up his exhibit and narrowed his eyes at the witness in a feint meant to look like grilling. "Based on your training and your education," he raised his voice, going for oratorical, "your experience in the field of obstetrics, and your review of these various materials, do you have an opinion, Doctor, within a reasonable degree of medical probability, as to whether Dr. Barish fell below the applicable standard of care in caring for Jeannie Clemm and her unborn daughter Courtney?"

"I do."

"And what is that opinion, Doctor?"

"I believe he was negligent."

The cherry-paneled walls sucked up a cough and a gasp.

"Doctor—and I know it's always difficult—but do you have an opinion within a reasonable degree of medical probability, had Courtney Clemm been delivered by cesarean section one hour earlier, would her condition have been normal?"

"I believe she would have been normal."

When O'Malley paused in front of the jury, taking a moment to look grimly at the little girl in the wheelchair, Marian finally got a good look at him. He had big bovine blue eyes, the kind called candid just because so much of their whites were showing, and a large head with side-parted brown hair and a golden-brown moustache like a whisk broom over a very wide mouth. He was broad-shouldered and long through his torso, but he seemed to end at his waist, held up by short, skinny pins. Plop a big brown Stetson on his head and what you had was Yosemite Sam. Just then, he turned, smiling at something Barrett Rance said, only Rance hadn't said a thing. It was off.

Then, it was Nan's turn to cross-examine Rance. As she rotated a hip

CHAPTER SIX

around the edge of the defense table, her elegant, copper-colored silk skirt moved like koi in a fishpond. Nan spent a few minutes at arm's length from Rance, establishing that a Dr. Joel Heller, who had more specialized training than Barrett Rance, held a contrary opinion. She got it right out there, let it sit unexplored and ticking—like sweeping your queen diagonally halfway across the chessboard—and still managed to seem non-threatening.

While she and Barrett Rance, M.D., chatted—all that was missing were the lattés—she extracted a few facts for the court's perusal. Over the last six years Barrett Rance had reviewed six *dozen* cases of possible physician negligence. Seventy-five percent of those were on behalf of plaintiffs. (Bias? Better pay?) And although he still practiced office gynecology, he had stopped delivering babies over eight years ago. Marian understood Nan Kemp's strategy: When is an OB not an OB? When is an expert witness not an expert?

Then they reviewed Jeannie Clemm's prenatal record like they were deciding between swatches for the new couch covers, touching on things like the possible relation between alcohol—Jeannie drank—smoking—Jeannie smoked—and placental insufficiency. When she drew on info from obstetrics journals, Nan phrased a whole bunch of questions to Rance in such a way that he had to respond, "I'm not sure" or "I'm not aware of it." At one point, the pig farmer exchanged a look with the Avon lady that said, *well, shouldn't he be?*

Nan got Rance to agree to the statement that on the basis of fetal heart rate patterns alone, definitive cause and effect relationships between those patterns and long-term outcome couldn't be made. And she got him to admit to the possibility that a fetus can experience asphyxial "events" days, weeks, or months before labor even begins. Pretty soon she'd have him saying he wore black lace panties. Like O'Malley before her, Nan took Rance through maybe a mile of fetal monitor strip for what seemed like an hour. Out popped terms like *hypovolemia* and *acute brain syndrome*—by that time, Marian's eyes swept the room, everyone was thinking, *forget the truth, all I want is a ham sandwich*—followed by some chit-chat about whether Baby Clemm had truly been acidotic.

Nan moved away from Rance. "I believe you testified in direct examination that you characterize this infant as severely asphyxiated because she had severely depressed Apgars—"

Rance shifted. "I felt this baby was severely anoxic and depressed. Correct."

"But in the opinion of the American College of Obstetricians and Gynecologists," Nan said, holding up a wad of papers, "and I quote, 'the term asphyxia is imprecise and should not be used.' Do you agree with that?"

"Asphyxia is more or less a wastebasket term meaning not getting enough oxygen."

Nan set down her papers on the defense table and turned back to the witness. "Would you agree with me, Doctor, that there is a body of medical literature out there that expresses a completely contrary opinion to the one you've expressed in this courtroom today?"

O'Malley rocketed up. "Your Honor, I'm going to object. I don't think there's an array of publications on—on—" he had to take a quick peek at his own papers, "—Courtney Clemm or Mrs. Clemm *and*—" here came his most persuasive argument, "—I don't know what she's talking about."

The judge overruled the objection and instructed the witness to answer the question. Everyone forgot about the ham sandwich as Rance looked straight at Nan. "Restate the question, please."

"There's a body of literature out there that expresses an opinion contrary to yours; is that correct?"

Rance thrust out his lower lip and thought about it. Do we want mallard wallpaper in the lounge at the club, or fox and hounds? "I think in medicine there are opinions contrary to what anyone would say, correct." Fox and hounds. Definitely.

"Because medicine is an imprecise science."

"Medicine is an art and a science *both*, correct." *I've got you there, my good woman.* "It's imprecise, correct."

"Would you agree with me, Dr. Rance, that not all asphyxia—whether it's the asphyxia that occurred before Ms. Clemm ever got to the hospital or while she was there—not all asphyxia is preventable?"

He tugged at his cuff. "Possibly."

Nan moved toward the jury box, giving her skirts ample time to slink and

CHAPTER SIX

sway. "Finally, Doctor, any physician, whether it's you or Dr. Barish or any other obstetrician, does need to make his own clinical assessment in order to come to a decision based upon all the facts and circumstances as they might exist, right?"

"That's the usual standard, yes."

"The usual standard." Nan swung around. "No other questions," she said with a smile.

The judge called O'Malley and Nan to the bench to tell them he decided to recess for lunch before redirect, then he instructed the jury not to form or express opinions about the case.

When Marian stepped back out into the hall, where she figured she'd wait for Dave Barish, she realized her heart was pounding. She had walked heavily up the aisle, looking for all she knew, as bagged and stuffed as Barish himself. What the hell was wrong with her? Twenty years after her mother had won a case against a plagiarist, here was a case where Marian could hardly get her mind around the stakes. Were multi-millions at stake here, won or lost on slippery phrases like *the usual standard* and *would have been normal* and *a contrary opinion*. These were no boring linguists rolling out charts with Old English verbs that could never destroy anybody's life—Rance and Nan and O'Malley were engaged in a dangerous game. Did anybody else feel it?

Marian quickly scanned the hallway for anyone else staring at the walls, but all she saw was a man built like Stonehenge decked out in creased cotton twill coming toward her. Hank Khartoukian. At something over six feet and two hundred pounds, the Wade County Sheriff was one of those stiff, graceful guys with bristly gray hair and a face all slits and excrescences like a tiki.

It was Khartoukian who had picked her up out of the snow in Jack Girard's front yard after the shooting in January. First, he slathered a big old blue handkerchief all over her face like she was a five-year-old who had fallen into a chocolate ice cream swoon. Then he wrapped her up in a wool blanket he kept in the back seat of the cruiser and packed her off to the station.

Hank Khartoukian stopped in front of her. "We got the car."

It took her a second. "The Kia!"

69

"Beth Prescott's."

"How have you been, Sheriff?"

"Getting along." He gripped the hand she held out. "You?"

"The same. You've been tracking me down?"

"You might say."

Marian looked down the hall. "Where is it?"

"Cleveland Hopkins Airport, third level of the long-term parking garage." He crossed his arms. "A drunk in a Navigator sideswiped it, so the locals ran the plates and came up with Beth Prescott. We got lucky."

Cleveland. A whole lot farther away than that half-hour ride Beth had mentioned to Eddie Estremera. She lifted her hands. "Blood? Hair?" Suddenly, the door to the courtroom swung open wide and out came the Grandma pushing Courtney Clemm in her wheelchair. "Here we go!" She said in that sing-song way adults use to hype things to kids. Khartoukian stepped in close to Marian to let the wheelchair pass. She grabbed his arm. "Blood? Hair? *Prints?*"

His voice came at the top of her hair. "A lot of nothing."

"You call that lucky?"

"I can smell your adrenaline."

"Sure beats the paper mill."

Then they moved aside for Barish, Rance, the Clemms, and the lawyer. Barish, who looked like the only thing keeping him upright was muscle memory, headed straight for the steps in a daze, but O'Malley and Rance lost no time lighting up, like they had flowed out to a lobby during intermission. "Where are you staying, Doctor?"

"I'm not staying over, no, indeed." An elegant drag. "You?"

O'Malley jerked his head. "Days Inn."

Then Barrett Rance just stood around looking pained and patrician with his hands in his pockets, waiting for something more from O'Malley—praise, a smoke, further persuasions about why he's selling his soul for these—these—hayseeds. Kelvin O'Malley just blew a scrill of smoke and said something about thundershowers later on.

"What about the parking garage ticket?" Marian asked Khartoukian.

CHAPTER SIX

"No mention of a ticket."

"Did they check the glove box?"

"Registration, tire gauge, owner's manual. That's it."

"And no ticket. Too bad."

"The ticket's the only way we know for sure—"

"—when the Kia arrived."

"Prescott stuck it in her handbag and did a bunk to Aruba."

"When the Kia pulled into the parking garage," said Marian, slowly shaking her head, "Beth Prescott wasn't driving."

He looked past her. "Maybe she was next to the driver and they both did a bunk to Aruba."

"If that's what you like."

"It's what I've got."

"Beth Prescott is somewhere between Carthage and Cleveland, Sheriff." Marian slung her bag over her shoulder. "And she hasn't got her thumb out."

He grunted. "We've got the airlines checking their flight manifests."

"I think you're wasting your time."

"In this business, you only know you're wasting your time," he said, "after you've wasted it."

"Sign me up."

"You know," he said, and his eyes got really narrow, "I think I've missed you."

"Not enough violence for you lately?"

His eyes softened. "You were cleared."

She suddenly dug around in her open bag for nothing at all. "So you say." Nan Kemp came out, finally, set down her attaché case and unbuttoned her suit jacket. With a quick smile to Marian, she took in Khartoukian and raised her eyebrows. When Marian introduced them, Nan gave him a frank look and a slow handshake. If Jerry Vulcani wanted to get anywhere with the lady lawyer from Columbus, what he needed was a uniform.

Chapter Seven

The three of them found a Subway sandwich shop one block away from the Wade County Courthouse. A boy who looked like Sean Penn in a black visor and green polo shirt slammed, trickled, and splashed their sandwiches together and rang them up. Sliding into a booth next to a long wall covered with the history-of-the-New-York-City-subway, they started unwrapping lunch.

"I've got yours."

"This looks like the combo."

"Mine's the no mayo."

Nan, who sat across from Dave Barish and Marian, started picking the onions out of a six-inch cold cut combo on whole wheat. Between the white tissue wrappers, the handful of thin napkins, and the tissues Nan dragged out to dab an eyelash out of Dave's eye, they looked like they were all face down in a lily pond. "The way I figure it," Nan was saying, "over the last six years, our friend Barrett Rance has pulled in two hundred grand just whoring for plaintiffs. And that's in addition to the Gyn practice he still has."

"Mmh," Marian said, munching, "think what he saves on his malpractice insurance."

"While he makes everyone else's go up." Dave Barish was staring at the ice in his Pepsi.

Nan shot her a look that said, *do something, change the subject,* so Marian sang her old song. "Beth Prescott."

He looked at her, interested. "Okay."

"Missing for two weeks."

CHAPTER SEVEN

His mouth thinned out. "Not good."

"Not good."

"What can I tell you?"

She grabbed a few napkins and wiped the mayo off her veggie sub. "Bill Rinaldi tells me he saw her at work that Wednesday morning. What about you?"

His eyes narrowed at Nan, who was pushing shredded lettuce back into her bun while she bit at it and still looked elegant, then he shook his head slowly. "It's my surgery morning, Marian. I'm pretty sure that's the day I had back-to-back D&Cs, so I didn't hit the office until after lunch that day."

Another dead end.

Was she missing something?

Then he went on. "But I did see her the day before. Tuesday."

"Did you talk?"

He shrugged. "Oh, little stuff. I told her when she stops by Jim Carney's—he and I have this baseball rivalry—tell him I said maybe the Reds should try T-ball instead. Beth said when she saw him on Thursday, she'd give him the message. Then Callie in the front office said something about tornado season, and we all argued about where you're supposed to hide in your basement." He gave Marian a wry look. "These days, it's all I can handle."

"Nothing from Beth about any sudden vacation plans?"

"No—" He seemed unsure. "Although, you know, Callie was leaving the next day for a week in Myrtle Beach, and Beth said she'd see her when she got back."

"So she seemed herself."

"Absolutely."

"Candid." She sipped her Pepsi.

"Well, I wouldn't go that far. Maybe Beth Prescott can keep a little secret, but she can't—" he opened an empty hand, looking for the words, "plan a big one—" he turned to her, "if you know what I mean."

Marian did. "When she told Callie she'd see her when she got back in a week—"

"I'd say she planned on being here." They went quiet for a while, thinking.

The day before she disappeared, Beth Prescott had no plans to take off. Add that to the ribeye she took out of the freezer Wednesday morning. What we take for signs are so pathetic. Nan started thumbing through what looked like a deposition, scribbling marginal notes. Dave Barish took a bite out of his sandwich and then forgot to chew it. Finally, his eyes were on Nan. "Did you see their faces?" He wrenched a napkin across his mouth, then balled it up.

"The jury?"

"They're lost."

"You don't know that."

But he was right. Marian had seen them, too. Forget the fetal monitor strips and the charts showing the timetable of Jeannie Clemm's labor. Forget the medical reference books and the verbal gymnastics. All the bagger from the Kroger's and the pig farmer understood was a four-year old in a wheelchair. Barish knew it, Marian knew it, and probably even Nan knew it, although she'd rather be disbarred than admit it.

He pushed away what was left of his lunch and leaned toward Nan. "Four years ago, I didn't do anything wrong. Can you make them see that?"

Nan sat back. "If we can cram enough medicine into them."

"In a week?"

"You've got it."

"It's not going to happen."

She wiped her mouth. "No."

"What you're saying is—"

"Maybe we can give them the possibility of the truth."

"The *possibility?*" He looked around the Subway sandwich shop like he didn't know where he was. "Hell, I'm sunk."

"It's the best we can hope for."

"Then what are we doing here?"

"We have to try cases—"

"*You* have to try cases."

"—because just going after a quick and easy settlement isn't going to make the O'Malleys go away—"

CHAPTER SEVEN

"This Clemm case is my whole goddamned life."

She overrode him. "Then I say make them sweat, make them have to haul in their visual aids and their expert witnesses—"

"And I say fuck making them sweat, Nan. I've got two million dollars' worth of coverage—" he leaned toward her, "and the Clemms could get twelve."

"You knew that when you pushed to take it to trial."

He leaned even closer. "The Clemms," he said slowly, "could get *twelve*."

"Okay, David." She dropped her hands on the table with a thud, then pointed at him. "You tell me why you're here."

He was silent.

Nan waved a hand. "Come on, come on, tell me."

Marian watched the muscles in his jaw tighten up, but he didn't take his eyes off his lawyer. "Because I know the medicine, and I know the truth, and settling this case is the same thing as losing it."

"Maybe that's why I'm here, too."

"Only where the hell am I supposed to get ten million—"

She got nearly lighthearted. "We've still got a whole defense ahead of us." Who needs pickle relish or ten million dollars when you've got Nan Kemp?

"I'm still paying off my student loans—"

She heaved a sigh. "It won't happen."

"The hell it won't."

Nan looked down. "PQA could settle at any time."

It was like she had hit him upside the head. "What are you saying?" He sat back. "Not without my okay, they can't."

"Actually, David," she said, "they can."

"Now that we're in trial?"

"At any time."

Dave Barish was pale. For this kind of pain, Marian thought she might as well go take a long walk with Jack Girard. She started to rustle wrappers and napkins. "Nan," Barish kept shaking his head, "I did nothing wrong."

"David, listen to me—"

"And I'm as screwed as if I did." It wasn't often Marian got to look a

75

painful truth square in the face, but there it was, and she had no help to give. Nothing to say to make it better. No one did, not even Nan, finally. Compared to what Dave Barish was facing, Marian felt an odd relief to be hired simply—simply—to locate the missing Beth Prescott, who, for all Marian could tell, was done facing anything unspeakable ever again. Finding her felt sickeningly easier than anything unfolding in Courtroom 2. All three of them sat frowning silently at their garbage.

Marian jumped when her phone trilled. She gave it a quick look. Joan. She'd let it go to Voicemail. Things suddenly seemed bleak right there in Carthage, Ohio, where buildings wear hairnets and peckerheads thrive. Maybe she couldn't make the Clemms or Rances go away, and maybe she couldn't make Beth Prescott come back, but as she sat there staring at the lunch trash, she had a pretty good idea what had happened to Flaggie. Before heading toward The Briars to test her theory, she sat in her car, cracked open the windows a couple of inches, and when the Voicemail turned up, listened to a pumped and impatient version of her half-sister. *Okay, then,* her sister said by way of greeting, *when can you be back? Something's come out of left field.*

Without going into any more detail, Joan Fleck had simply finished with a curt *Call me*, and disconnected. Recently, when art crime seemed to be either particularly slow or particularly good, Joan had been getting worked up about fake Chinese porcelains making it past Customs. Marian stared uncertainly at her phone. Would just more of the same silly imports qualify as "out of left field"? Doing a quick U-Turn, she headed toward The Briars. She'd call Joan, but she had no answer to the question about when Marian would be back in New York, where she had honed her garbage-sifting skills on a particularly tough case two years ago.

Chinese restaurant.

Chinatown.

Broken disposal.

Garbage strike.

Dead rat.

Crispy duck gone bad.

CHAPTER SEVEN

Fried rice that moved.

Half an hour later, the Wade County Waste Management truck was churning toward her up the street, and she was waist-high in a week's worth of garbage in the dumpster behind Cy and Barbara Hauser's inn. Cy kept anxious tabs on the progress of the garbage truck, loping back and forth, telling her to hurry—*hurry!*—like they were trying to tunnel their way out of a stalag. Hair pulled out of brushes, nonrecyclable cottage cheese containers (for her, on a par with the writhing fried rice), various hunks of fat and gristle she really didn't think was human, black banana peels, stinking teabags, worn-out men's socks from worn-out men, tissues wadded up with all sorts of viruses, cold cream, phlegm—and Flaggie.

Another *pro bono* high.

***

If anyone ever asks, the fabric of the gods is cotton jersey. It breathes, requires very little care, and just likes to be near you—making it altogether better than a boyfriend. After a long hot shower that freed her up from any lingering blue-green nubs of cottage cheese, Marian put on her jersey pants, her cocoa-colored jersey top with the very flattering boat neckline, and her tiger's eye pebble earrings in a silver coil that are really better on a blond, but what the hell. Then she raked her hair, called it combed, and set out for the Wade Lake Country Club, where she was meeting Charlie Levitan at six for drinks and dinner. He said to come find him wherever inside the clubhouse the Greater Carthage Growth Association was meeting.

What Marian had with Charlie was twenty years of funky adoration that always managed to keep its feet on the floor. Literally. This was a matter of some occasional regret, sometimes on his part, sometimes on hers, but never at the same time, which is why the feet stayed on the floor. Over drinks, he'd remind her of the time in high school when he helped her stuff her tortured love sonnets under the Manhattan door of Al Pacino. And she would remind him of the time in college when she pulled him out of his trashed newspaper office just minutes before the cops lobbed in the tear gas to scatter FIAT, the new generation of the Weather Underground. Then they'd remind each other of all the dateless Saturday nights they spent together at midnight movie marathons followed by bacon and eggs at an all-night place on Broadway. Followed by shared toothbrushes and last-minute futons and the kind of loony 4 AM observations you chalk up to alpha waves and caffeine.

Charlie Levitan was better than any girlfriend Marian had ever had, and they had made it through their twenties without sex slinking around the friendship like some hollow-eyed spook from an Ingmar Bergman film. Even when he'd been shaving in his boxers in her bathroom while she writhed into pantyhose, wondering to each other why the hell they had agreed to those particular dates with people named Doreen and Abu. Maybe all these years Marian and Charlie had really been dating each other and never knew it.

The Wade Lake Country Club was east of town by about twenty minutes along one of those roller-coaster country roads that jack up the anxiety level, considering the speed limit was a baffling 50. And everyone did it, church ladies, DUIs, kids with temps, Wade County cowboys. At one point, it was Whistler's Mother who passed Marian on a blind curve, doing sixty in a purple Taurus. She pulled shaking into the country club's driveway—the Volvo was whimpering—and puttered down the leafy lane to the parking lot, which had a fair amount of takers for a mid-week evening.

Marian sprang up the stone steps of the sprawling Tudored clubhouse and waited for her eyes to adjust. Exposed beams, wine red wall-to-wall, discreet Muzak, same old Wade Lake Country Club she remembered from January. There was the line of Audubon prints she could never look at the same way again ever since she found out that the way James Audubon studied birds was by killing them. (The cedar waxwing, he claimed, was particularly tasty.) In the lobby bar was a great framed black-and-white glossy of Bogie and Bacall on the flagstone terrace at the Wade Lake Country Club. Next to them was an unidentified photo of a man at the bar in a white dinner jacket and a nimbus of smoke who looked a lot like Tennessee Williams.

Marian checked out the sign on the tripod while Julio Iglesias sang to

CHAPTER SEVEN

her about all the girls he's loved before. *Welcome Greater Carthage Growth Association, Room 2.*

The meeting was just letting out as she legged it down the carpeted hall. A woman in a lime green, wrinkled linen suit passed her, breezing off to another meeting, and by the time she got there, she'd have picked up another dozen wrinkles. Cotton jersey is the fabric of the above-ground gods. Linen is the fabric of the underworld. You can iron it, put it on, stay completely vertical and inert, and within five minutes, you will have wrinkles. Behind this poor, wrinkled soul came two men, following kind of hotly, one with glasses and a satchel the size of Rhode Island, the other a Brooks Brothers kind of guy with a stack of wiry white hair and an old preppy droop to his mouth.

And then, barreling out of the doorway to Room 2 was Charlie Levitan, doing his usual multi-tasking thing—half-running, pulling a cotton sweater over his head, chewing a sheaf of papers.

"Marian!"

"Hi, honey," was as far as she got. He pulled her in, landed a kiss near her nose, and shoved all the papers at her. Turning quickly, he said he had to call the office, high winds, fritzy computers, nobody but the local parakeets would notice if the *Toiler* didn't show up, but hey, order them both something, he'll find her wherever—and he was gone. For some reason known only to the Fates, Marian turned into Room 2, where a lipsticked blond in a blue silk sheath was slipping papers into a plastic portfolio—fingernails the size of scarabs were clicking all over the place—and a balding Catholic priest celebrated getting up from the conference table by doing some neck rolls.

They weren't alone.

Jack Girard was standing across from the clicking blond, listening to her say what a good ah-dea this here Streetscape plan is for the dan-tan district, and she, for one, was gawn to do her level best to sell it to the good people of Carthage and Wade Canny. But he wasn't listening. He had looked up and seen Marian, mainly because she couldn't dive for cover under anything, and inside her head, she was ripping into Charlie for not mentioning the fact beforehand that there was a possibility that Jack Girard might also be at a meeting of the Greater Carthage Growth Association.

Girard was wearing jeans and a faded work shirt. How could she make any sense whatsoever if that's what he was wearing? The same, wonderful short dark hair and military shoulders, no different from January, the same beautiful brown eyes. He'd have to be a whole lot closer for her to see the lines in his clean-shaven face. Closer still to see the scar at his hairline from falling through a glass door in a playground fight at the age of nine. The clicking blond sensed something, shut up about Streetscape, and dimpled at the priest, who had started on waist bends.

As Jack Girard started toward Marian, all she could remember was the feel of his hand on her ribs, pulling her close under the scratchy Army blanket—yes, *yes*, this would be the perfect topic at the dinner table later with Charlie. Girard didn't say anything. Neither did she. Maybe he was remembering standing devastated in the snow at the DOI work site. Then Marian couldn't stand it anymore. "I can't work for you."

"I didn't ask you to."

"You signed the check."

"The Prescotts are broke. It's a loan."

"I have to think about it."

"Don't do that, Marian. They need the help—and my father needs Beth."

"I've got to talk to you." Who said that?

"Let's go outside."

She was determined to be the professional he had basically hired, no matter what he said about loans. "Beth Prescott's been working for you for two months—"

"Three months."

"Good." Why good? *"Three* months. And her hours are—"

"Three to seven, weekdays."

"I see." See what? It was all old stuff, but it was all she had. "Her duties include—"

He held open the terrace door. Ah, the outdoors. Many more possibilities. She cheered up. As she passed him, Marian was weighing the chances of outsprinting him to the car, only from where she was standing, she couldn't

CHAPTER SEVEN

find the parking lot. "Taking care of my father. Period."

The sun was low and heavy over Wade Lake. She whirled on Girard. "Which means—?"

"Washing, feeding, dressing." He was sounding baffled that she apparently needed a definition of "taking care of." He bit off a smile. "Spending time."

"Wednesday, May 25th." Marian realized she was Nan Kemp cross-examining Barrett Rance.

"The last day we saw her."

"How did she seem?"

He leaned against the low stone wall and crossed his arms. "She was a lot like you, Marian—rushed."

"Did she mention any—any—"

"Marian, what are you saying?"

She blurted, "Why didn't you call?"

"You didn't want it."

"How do you know?"

"Did you?"

"Yes, but I didn't know what to say."

"Start somewhere."

Marian could tell him how she suddenly stopped right in the middle of reporting to the Maersk shipping people exactly why she and Joan had to break into the Red Hook warehouse in their line of work and thought, *I didn't have to shoot*. And, two weeks later, it came to her with more conviction: *I didn't have to shoot*, as she looked at her gun hand hailing a cab on Avenue of the Americas. Then she ran down pee-soaked subway steps and took the F train all the way to Brooklyn, but Joan wasn't home. Marian then spent half the afternoon walking around on what felt like boneless legs.

She could tell Jack Girard that what she's had on the doorstep of her cabin has been everything from an eight-foot black snake to a schizophrenic handyman, when all she really wanted to see on her doorstep was—Girard. There was nothing she didn't want from this man—except to have him tell her she did exactly what she had to do in the dead January daylight. When Marian was sure that's what he'd say, she gave up wanting to see him on her doorstep.

The sun was setting over Wade Lake, laying gold streaks across the water. It was beautiful. She could tell Jack Girard all those things—even the part about the sunset—but all she said was, "Since January, I've had maybe a total of twelve hours' sleep."

He looked closely at her. "And not a whole lot of thought."

"It hurts too much. What about you?"

"Me? I came to one conclusion, Marian."

"What's that?"

"That I can't do this by myself."

"So you got Beth Prescott."

"I wasn't talking about my father." It hung there. "Call me about Beth," he said, pushing himself off the wall. "If that's what you want."

* * *

"Are the scallops fresh?" Charlie looked up from his menu at the pockmarked kid in a bow tie who had told them his name was Gerald.

"Yessir, nice and fresh, you bet."

Right: fresh from the walk-in freezer. Marian looked at Charlie, where they sat hundreds of miles from any scallop-yielding coast. She knew the drill: Charlie would quiz this kid on everything not covered by the menu and then order the least expensive thing. It's not that he's cheap; it's that all the preliminary stuff kills his appetite. She always knew he was winding down by the time he started grasping at inedibles like the candles on the tables or the art on the walls. Gerald was still cheerful.

The swordfish and mahi mahi were also fresh.

The house red was a nice little Nay-pa burgundy.

The dinner rolls had seeds.

The prime rib was, oh, Jews.

The spring water was Evvie Ann.

The menus were printed locally.

On acid-free paper, yes, he was almost totally sure, but he could ask.

CHAPTER SEVEN

Charlie closed his menu. Her cue. "The salmon, please," Marian told the poor kid.

"I'll have the Caesar salad." Charlie handed back the menu and ordered a merlot. Shell shocked, Gerald backed into another waiter, whose name pin said *Sergio*, struggling with a magnum and a champagne bucket. Sergio muttered "asshole" and turned to his own customers with a beauty pageant smile.

Marian kicked off her shoes and listened to Charlie start to tell her about the crater in his life, what with his daughter Hannah having left to spend the summer with her crackpot mother in British Columbia, while 101 strings floated "Blame It on the Bossa Nova" around the ceiling. If it's ever known for sure that a meteor is going to slam into the Earth, Marian's own disaster plan consisted of a BarcaLounger, a liter of martinis, and a headset with an endless loop of "Blame It on the Bossa Nova." No news is so bad that it can't be cured by grooving to the sound of cabasas.

Call me about Beth, if that's what you want. The look on Jack Girard's face, some kind of disappointment in her, his back as he left by the terrace steps— all they ever really had between them was a distance that never grew shorter. All Marian wanted from dinner with Charlie was to stop wondering whether it was time to rev up the BarcaLounger.

Over Charlie's shoulder, she caught the last trailing purples of the sunset, backlighting the white sails of an FJ as it slid over the water toward the dock. No one replaced his murdered girlfriend Derry, he was saying, which was why he joined the Wade Lake Country Club at the social membership level late in February and started to plot how he could get the hell out of Carthage, where apparently the only single women between the ages of 25 and 50 were Eloise Timmler at the bakery who winked at him and called him Chuck, and Lila Ketchum who—never mind the source—had venereal warts the size of bocce balls. No, it was time to get himself into a larger Gannett market. His exit strategy consisted of getting HQ's attention by rocketing the *Toiler's* circulation.

Marian sat back. "Today's piece on the Clemm case."

"The first in a series."

"A whole series?"

"Marian, there's nothing on Earth folks like to read about more than their neighbors' hard luck."

"What about Beth Prescott?"

Charlie shook his head, lighting the stubby candle at the center of the table. "She's not some cute ten-year-old yanked off the street by a creep with a Hershey bar." He replaced the glass globe. "I ran a small item on her a couple of days ago. Frankly, we've had more calls about the 4-H squirt who was abusing his pygmy goats at Tulip Time than we've had about Beth Prescott. If she turns up," he leaned back, "now, that's news."

"One way or the other."

"No, not one way or the other." He looked wry. "Only one way. Alive she gets half a column, bottom of page three. Dead, I can get ink for a week out of her." There's the devastated family story, Charlie went on. There's the history of the victim story. The scene of the crime story. The shocked neighbor story. The compassionate pastor story. There's the handgun control story and the rebuttals from the NRA. There are the letters praising the coverage as thorough and the letters calling the paper a bottom-feeding scandal sheet. And the letters from the Rape Crisis folks, not to mention the local Nazi crank. "For a week, the *Toiler* will be sold out by ten in the morning, guaranteed." He rolled back his cuffs. "Not enough to get me to D.C., you understand, but at least to the Atlantic seaboard."

"Pack your swim fins."

"Chasing a corpse?"

"And so far, she's outrunning me."

Gerald sidled up to their table, flourishing a bottle, proving it was the cheap little wine Charlie had ordered and not some other cheap little wine instead. He hastily poured two glasses and set the bottle on the table, sidestepping Sergio on his way back to the kitchen.

Marian sipped her wine and sat back. Sometimes, she thought it was just a matter of time before she and Charlie ended up together in a condo in Savannah. Her mysteries and his biographies would work it out on the bookshelves. His socks and her bras could form a laundry support group.

CHAPTER SEVEN

There would be a line about them in the Rutgers Alumni Bulletin, and all of their friends would say it was about time.

They'd go to minor league ball games together and have what she imagined would be pretty fair sex every other night. Charlie, with his broad shoulders and glossy black hair, Charlie who cooked Thai and read everything published in the English language including Chaucer and the Congressional Record, Charlie who talked her head off. It would be so easy. Even Joan liked him.

"What's funny?"

"Oh, I was just thinking about the future."

"Whose?"

"Yours and mine."

"It was funny?"

"It was natural."

He raised his hands like he was warding her off. "Ah, no. Don't do this."

"What do you mean?"

He shook his head. "Don't use me. We go back too far."

"I wouldn't."

"Sure you would. Only you wouldn't know it."

Marian lifted her wine at him. "Well, thanks for that."

"All the times you held my hand, all the times I bailed you out—"

"Bailed me out?" What was he talking about?

"I figure at this point we're just about even. And it feels good. So don't use me. Not like that." Charlie pushed around his silverware, then suddenly pointed a fork at her. "The trouble with you, Warner, is that you keep moving the line in the sand."

"'Warner'?"

"Where the hell are the dinner rolls?"

She pushed the basket at him. "Since when do you call me Warner?"

He slumped. "Since you gave up journalism," he said, finally, "and took up construction work."

Jack Girard.

There it was.

There it was. Charlie had gotten it out. She downgraded him to a tropical storm and unfolded her napkin. She watched him flick seeds off a roll and then butter it, humming. Filing a 1040 form with Charlie seemed like a truly sensible idea. No more solitary dinners at the cabin with just NPR for company. No more wondering whether what she discovered in the January snow with Jack Girard was the thing they write bossa nova songs about. "It would be so easy, Charlie."

He stopped chewing just long enough to say, "I'm not a hospice, Marian."

Chapter Eight

The tinker, the tailor, and the candlestick maker sat in a line down at the other end of Barbara Hauser's breakfast table. Only the blacksmith was missing, and he was probably holed up in a bathroom with a Q-tip stuck in his ear. Marian hid behind a wide-open wall of that morning's edition of the Carthage *Toiler*, adjusting it just enough now and then to watch three guys dressed in brown suede get-ups and white muslin shirts overturning every piece of china and silver on the table to see the pedigree. One waggled a long piece of bacon between his teeth while he shoved a porcelain jam jar over to the others to inspect. One of the others managed to dredge his beard through the maple syrup on his pancakes while he pushed a silver pitcher over to his pals. *"Plate,"* he intoned, propping up the tents that passed for eyebrows.

"No surprise," waggled the bacon, which got two inches shorter.

Cy Hauser, wearing a pink polo shirt and his usual khaki shorts, came banging through the doorway carrying a basket of pastries and a coffee carafe. These he set down, whistling a George M. Cohan medley, near Marian, she thought, because the "artisans" on the other side of the table intimidated him. Or maybe because she had gotten the two of them through the barbed wire at the stalag, recovered Flaggie, and left him enough time to sprint the garbage out to the street for pickup. Life was good. For whatever reason, Cy was giving her first crack at the baked goods. And he poured her coffee, gave the tinker and tailor an arch look, and headed back toward the safety of the clatter in the kitchen, but not before Marian smiled at him.

Sipping her hot coffee, she read the coverage of Clemm versus Barish.

Today's photo: little Courtney smiling at her long-haired mommy, who was kneeling beside her wheelchair. Clutching a briefcase on the courthouse steps in the background was Kelvin O'Malley with a chin so high you'd think he was defending John T. Scopes. The "staff writer" went on to say that according to Dr. Barrett Rance, engaged in the practice of obstetrics for thirty years, the management of Jeannie Clemm's labor fell below the standard of care, and had little Courtney been delivered by cesarean section an hour sooner she would have been normal. Marian skimmed the rest of the piece but didn't find any mention of opinions contrary to Rance's, a point Nan had brought out. Suddenly nothing appealed, not even the raspberry cheese danish she had set on her plate.

Nan Kemp walked in, dressed for the day in a midnight-blue silk suit with a cropped jacket and a street-length skirt, toting her black leather attaché. Classic pumps in place, French twist in place, only worked into one side was a tiny little braid that said fairy tale princess. Still no makeup, but one ear had two little crystal studs lined up. She gave everyone kind of a general "Good morning"—here the candlestick maker dragged his beard back across his syrup-soaked plate as he ogled her, but the tailor elbowed him, whispering, "Jerry turfed her."

Nan looked over Marian's shoulder at the paper as she sat down next to her. "More rot?"

Marian bit her lip. "That's really what it is."

Nan poured herself some coffee. "Who's the editor of this rag?"

"Charlie Levitan."

"He's dangerous." She indicated a need for the cream pitcher, and the candlestick maker moved it closer to her. *Plate,* he mouthed at her, wrinkling up his nose, looking for some way into a conversation. She nodded, smiling, leaning toward him, and said, "I don't care." The tinker snorted a laugh that came out in a spray of orange juice.

"Charlie would probably thank you. He's always wanted to be dangerous."

"Oh, friend of yours?"

"Old."

"What's his background?"

CHAPTER EIGHT

"A master's in journalism, if that's what you mean," I told her. "Columbia."

Nan grunted. "You'd expect higher standards."

Marian put down the newspaper, feeling sicker by the minute. "They used to be." Just how badly did Charlie want to get to the East Coast?

Nan pulled the breadbasket toward her and eyed what was left. "Now he just wants to sell papers."

"And the Clemms want twelve million."

Nan looked at her. "And O'Malley wants a partnership."

"And the jury wants to go home."

"No," Nan said, holding up one finger and then choosing a cranberry scone, "the jury wants to do the right thing," she said. "And then go home."

"What about you?"

"Me? I want to run as many docs past the snipers as I can before I drop dead."

"Why?" At that moment someone in the kitchen turned on the radio, probably to drown out the clattering of dishes, and jerked the tuner around until it found an Oldies station. Perry Como was right in the middle of telling them to catch a falling star and put it in their pockets when Jerry Vulcani walked into the room. The good news: shampoo. The bad news: clown pants. He actually licked his purple lips when he spied Nan and swaggered around the table like he'd spent the night in her company *without* the clown pants.

Since she was sitting, he must have thought she was fair game, so he came around behind her. "Have dinner with me, and I'll tell you my tale," Nan was saying to Marian, smoothing apricot jam over her scone as he brushed against her in a remember-last-night sort of way, trailing his hand along the back of her chair. "Better yet," she went on with a nibble, "make it lunch." Just as he reached for the chair next to her, her free hand heaved up her attaché and landed it squarely on the seat, leaving Jerry Vulcani nothing to do but take a hint the size of the Queen Mary and move on down the line. His pals suddenly hunched over their plates and started babbling about Tulip Time.

"Come early and catch the testimony of Eve Terhune," Nan went on, "another expert witness for the plaintiffs. Like Barrett Rance," she lowered her voice, "who hasn't delivered a baby in eight years. Only *this* one's a neurologist whose patients are virtually all adult epileptics. O'Malley's using her," Nan looked at her over the rim of her coffee cup, "because I think he couldn't find a pediatric neurologist willing to say Courtney's condition is a result of physician negligence—"

"Which is huge—"

"Which is huge. He's slipping in Eve Terhune and hoping some combination of her legs, his balls, and a sudden fugue on my part will make it fly."

"And the chances of that would be—?"

Well, she had no control over Eve's legs or Kelvin's balls, Nan mused, licking at the apricot jam, commanding the attention of every tinker tailor in the room, "but on the subject of myself, I can assure you I'm feeling alert."

"And punitive."

"Terhune's never testified before, and I intend to see to it that she never testifies again, because," she carefully dabbed at her lips, "she has no earthly business appearing for these plaintiffs. If you come by the courtroom, Marian, think of what you'll be seeing—" Nan looked up with a smile "—as a cautionary tale."

Marian's two stops that morning: Ketchum Rays and Pizza Shack. "I think I can work it in."

"Besides, Dave Barish has no family here. If you show up again, even for a little while—"

"I'm a witness for the defense."

Nan looked at her. "In a manner of speaking."

Marian folded her arms on the table. "Dave Barish says he didn't do anything wrong, but he's as screwed as if he did." She pushed some crumbs into a crooked line. "I think the same's true for Beth Prescott."

"And that means something to you."

"It means something to me."

"Then I guess we're in the same line of work. Only you get them deader."

Suddenly, Marian remembered the way Dave Barish looked at lunch

CHAPTER EIGHT

yesterday. "I'm not so sure."

* * *

Lila Ketchum had her very yellow hair pulled up to the top of her head in a pink scrunchy, but it was short enough to stick up like a crown-rump roast. Gooey blue mascara ruffled over close-set eyes the color of the Caribbean and the white-pink lipstick nobody does better than Yardley overfilled her lips. Lila's shoulders were narrow, which made her breasts look even more startling, and the tie-dyed caftan she was wearing flowed everywhere except around her middle, where she was tubby. She studied Marian's business card, which she held in both of her small hands with a motherboard of veins and unpolished nails. Marian could only continue to wonder about the bocce balls.

Lila's tanning parlor was set up in an old white clapboard house about three blocks out of the prime business district in downtown Carthage, where the zoning laws got sketchy. Ketchum Rays was keeping company with eighty-year-old bungalows with Little Tikes wagons and trikes in front of them, two doors down from a German brick church called *Doers of the Divine Word, Unaffiliated*. It was a dry day, a pleasant day, and the heaps of brilliant white clouds looked like they had nowhere to go. On Lila's little patch of lawn was the closest thing to a psychedelic sign Marian had seen in nearly twenty years—a big, sturdy wooden half-moon on railroad tie "feet," *Ketchum Rays, Lila Ketchum, Prop.*, etched with a round, androgynous face with yellow electrified hair zooming straight out to the borders of the sign, maybe Lila herself, maybe Medusa on Zoloft.

The whole first floor— "my business establishment," Lila explained, adding that she lived upstairs—was done in sixties time warp, all except the ornate white French provincial desk in the front room where Lila scheduled clients and kept the Mr. Coffee flowing. "Four rooms have tanning beds, and all the amenities," Lila pushed aside a beaded wall hanging and led Marian down the small hall, "stocked, dorm-sized fridges and French chaze lounges for the *ah*pray tan." The piped-in music was a mix that wound its way through the usual late sixties stuff from Bob Dylan, the Beatles, the Stones, and Motown. As they got to the first tanning room, "I'll show you two," she said, as the Fifth Dimension airy-fairied, "When the moon is in the seventh house, and Jupiter aligns with Mars—"

"Have you got a juice bar?"

She took my question seriously. "No, not for this crowd," she said, then leaned closer. "Honey, you get people in here riding the melanoma express. They're not the sort of folks who wonder whether they're getting enough beta carotene." Lila had done away with every single door in the place and replaced them with wooden folding screens découpaged with everything from *New York Times* clippings about the Tet offensive to *Newsweek* shots of the stoned denizens of Haight-Ashbury. There was even a titillating chance when you're there to Ketchum Rays that you might glimpse or get glimpsed somewhere in the process. Stick incense spiraled up in little terra cotta holders in each room, sending up a funky cross between patchouli and Catholic Church.

In the first room, painted the most shrieking shade of orange Marian had ever seen, a poster of Huey Newton stood guard over the general nakedness, wearing a Black Panther beret and cradling a couple of semiautomatic weapons. In the next room, painted a creamy green the color of a Jello that had once made Marian throw up on a train when she was ten, Dustin Hoffman was watching patrons strip, looking straight through the flexed leg of Mrs. Robinson. Each of Lila's rooms had a silver tanning bed, a lava lamp blooping away, and quaint little bongs— "just decorative," Lila crinkled her nose. Then she had an inspiration. "Say, would you like a freebie?"

My heart sank. "You mean *tan?*"

"Sure." She continued to be inspired. "You're helping with Beth. Some UV is the least I can give you."

"Thanks, Lila, but—"

She clutched Marian's arm. "To tell you the truth, honey, and I think I know you well enough to say this, but you're, well," she uttered the P-word, "pasty."

"Pasty, huh?"

CHAPTER EIGHT

"Like maybe you haven't taken advantage of the nice weather we had last month?" Like maybe Marian hid her creamed peas in a pocket.

"Right, Lila, that's true, but—"

"I'll give you Huey—"

"Oh, orange is my favorite, but—"

"—and he gives you the softest warmest nuttiest *hint* of—"

"—I've got this claustrophobia thing going on."

"You're afraid of dogs?"

"No," Marian's hands came up like claws, "small, closed, coffin-like—"

Lila smiled serenely. "Then how about some coffee?"

Back at the front desk Lila offered Marian a mug of chocolate raspberry Mr. Coffee. "Fifty years past Nehi and Bubble-Up," she said gravely, "and welcome to it. The sixties had shitty drinks." Cultural history at its finest. Penelope would be interested. "Oh, yeah," Lila breathed, giving Marian a sidelong look, "and there was the war."

"Yeah, that."

"Bummer." She sipped.

"Totally." They both sipped. How old could she be? "You were born in—?"

She was pleased Marian asked. "I was born the day after Alan Sherman got back from outer space." Oh, it sounded vague and spooky and historic all at once, so privately meaningful, and her Caribbean blue eyes glistened.

"You mean Alan Shepard."

"Whichever."

"Like, 1961?"

"I didn't get to the sixties, really, until the seventies," she explained. "When I went to a boarding school in Connecticut."

"Oh," said Marian with some energy, "that must have been fun."

"Well, no, because, really," Lila lifted one caftaned shoulder, "I didn't get much of an education, and I'm pretty sure I didn't get laid."

"Seems like the sort of thing you'd remember."

"Seems like." She licked her Yardley lips.

"Tell me about Beth Prescott."

"A real little sweetheart."

This was a first. "How so?"

"She doesn't know jack about who's on the Supreme Court, or who won the World Series two years ago. But I've never seen anyone softer than Beth Ann Prescott." The phone rang, a burbling little trill like someone was suffocating it with a pillow, and Lila went around the desk and answered it. "Ketchum Rays Tan Your Way to Success, this is Lila."

She went on to book someone named Arthur—*the mayor*, she mouthed at Marian, who smiled—for tomorrow at ten in the Bridget room—"Bridget *Bardo*," she whispered with her hand over the receiver, making the French sex symbol sound more like an Irish colleen, "white cowboy hat, topless, half-zipped jeans, end of the hall." Her other hand flapped at Marian like *weren't those just the silliest times, but Hizzoner just loves that poster.* She hung up, wrote him in the daybook, and went back to Beth. "This home health aide gig is a good fit for Beth. Giving old Mr. Girard a bath and coaxing him to eat his carrots would all be just swell to her."

"What about her lover?"

"You know about him."

"Can you give me a name?"

Her chest heaved. Lila was stumped. "Damned if I know who he is, but I can tell you when she sees him."

Marian hadn't been that still since Eddie Estremera laid two fingers on her sleeve. "When?"

"Well, Thursdays for sure."

"Evenings?"

Lila shook her head. The crown-rump slid to the side. "Between jobs."

"Between the hospital and the Girards?"

"Yeah." Like, who wants to work *that* hard?

"How do you know?"

"Because she threw me over for it." Lila laughed. "That used to be the time she'd tan, Thursdays at two. Then, over the winter, she told me she couldn't come any more at her regular time. Well, I kept after her about it just to tease her, and all she said was that it's her standing date with someone special, and he has a hard time getting away other times. What is he, married, I asked

CHAPTER EIGHT

her, and she said she couldn't tell me anything and I shouldn't ask her again."

"What about recently?"

"Meaning, are they still together? I guess so since she still isn't back to Thursdays, and she pretty much only comes every few weeks on a Saturday when the tanning traffic is steady, and I don't really have time to talk."

Marian set her cup down on the desk. "Where do you think she is?"

Lila looked sad. "Well," she said softly, "I'd say she's gone where she never thought she'd be going this soon." Lila pursed her white-pink lips. "Only I'd really rather not know about it for as long as I can. I guess," she said, turning away. "I'm really a lot like Beth."

* * *

Marian stepped out of Ketchum Rays into the kind of warm, light rain she liked. There was even some sun, which stopped her in her tracks. Everything suddenly seemed sweet and small, and backlit, the silent rain lent a bright, optimistic mist to the case. No thunder or lightning, no slipping on drenched sidewalks, no flood warnings, maybe even no Beth Prescott dead in a ditch somewhere. Maybe she had just taken off with the Thursday boyfriend, after all.

Making more of a dash toward her car than she really had to, she figured on a quick stop at Pizza Shack to get the lowdown on Flyboy. Too early to say whether he was a stalker—but if he was, she knew the statistics put prior stalking definitely in the picture of something over 90% of the cases of murdered women. Would Beth Prescott be that unaware if the pizza delivery guy was shadowing her? Well, Marian thought as she turned off Scioto Pike into the parking lot of a mall anchored by a Big Lots, now she had a new angle to add to her interviews.

Flanked by places that promised pet supplies and math tutoring, PIZZA SHACK wore large block letters in white on a red background. On the front window was the motto: Shack Up With Us! Only the exclamation point was shaped like a slice, with a pepperoni as the dot below. *Mancha! Mancha!* ran misspelled along the bottom of the windows on either side of the glass door, followed by a phone number the size of a great Dane. Inside, where she counted just two seen-better-days café tables, it became clear Pizza Shack was strictly a takeout or delivery operation.

Swiping the counter with long, quick strokes was a woman, Marian was guessing, in her late sixties. She wore the red Pizza Shack vest over a black turtleneck and sweatpants, plus the visor worn by fast-food workers everywhere. This one was green, and the message was machine embroidered across the front: I'm Rose. Shack It to Me. "Hello," said Rose, who seemed oddly happy with her job. Marian stepped up. Rose's rag was suspended over the counter while they took each other in. "Margharita pizzas are on special today."

Marian rummaged in her bag. "You've been working here for a lot of years, Rose?"

"Oh, my. No, no, no, this is my retirement job. I taught eighth-grade math for thirty-two years." Marian followed her as she moved like a sprite toward the computer where she'd entered the nice lady's order. "Practically lost my pension in that Silicone bank mess," she said over her shoulder to Marian, covering the reason for her Pizza Shack visor in fewer than ten words. Her mouth twisted for a second, then Rose looked straight at Marian and added brightly, "Well, spilled milk, I always say." When Marian nodded, Rose topped it. "As my late husband used to say, 'It is what it isn't.'" The two of them laughed, and then, crossing her arms over her chest, Rose glanced wistfully at a bare corner of her workplace. Thinking either of lost money, husband, or dreams. "Now, what can I get you on this lovely June morning, Miss?" Either Rose didn't see the rain, or she saw it, and the June morning was lovely anyway.

Marian set her business card on the gleaming counter. Rose picked it up like she'd been presented with a puppy. "I'm here about your employee Flyboy."

"Oh," said Rose, delighted to set the record straight with a couple of steps backward, "no, no, I'm no higher up the corporate ladder"—at that, Marian blinked— "than Flyboy, you understand. We're co-workers." She made a begging gesture. "Colleagues, you might say."

CHAPTER EIGHT

"I see. Well, I'm hoping you can help me, Rose. Flyboy may have some information I can use in my investigation."

"Oh," she breathed, "investigation. That must be very important work."

The only thing she could think of saying was no answer at all. Then: "Can you tell me where I can find Flyboy?"

"I surely can." A sudden inspiration. "Can I get a pizza started for you?"

Marian winced. "Too early for me, Rose," she said, clapping her hands over her stomach. "Another time. Right now, I just need the information."

"Of course, of course." She leaned closer. "I can't eat tomato sauce in the mornings, either. Too acidic." She finished confidentially, "Must be our age."

Marian had to be thirty years younger than Rose. "It is," she intoned, "what it isn't."

Delighted, Rose snapped the rag at her customer. "Oh, you. Too clever by half. Flyboy doesn't come in until the afternoons, you know."

"All right..." she pressed. "Where can I find him this morning?"

At that moment, the bell over the Pizza Shack door tinkled, and Rose slid sideways to see. "Be with you in a minute," she called to the young woman with a bandana threaded through her upswept hair and tattoos ranging across her collarbone. "He cleans at the Catholic church in the mornings. St. Lydwina's, over on, well, Church Street."

Marian made a note on her phone. "And his address?" She narrowed her eyes at Rose.

"Oh, that's his address, too. You can't miss it. Go east on River St., past the Kroger's, then right on Church."

"You're saying Flyboy lives at the church."

To Marian, Rose looked a little troubled, like this was yet one more bright-side silver lining she was trying hard to find. Suddenly, there it was, and she beamed at Marian. "As you and my dead Harry always say, it is what it isn't."

Chapter Nine

Since the sheriff's department was in an old annex attached to the Wade County Courthouse, Marian stopped by to see if there was anything new on Beth's Kia, only Neva Jean the dispatcher told her the sheriff was out on a homicide. Marian left a message for Khartoukian about where he could find her if he came back anytime soon, then let herself into the weighty hush of Courtroom 2.

Dave Barish saw her right away and smiled thinly.

Eve Terhune, M.D., wearing a grey satin blouse over a crinkle skirt with a fleur-de-lis print, sat on the witness stand. Her black hair was streaked with gray and cut to droop elegantly around her cheeks. O'Malley, leaning on the witness stand, squinted at the flag behind the bench and asked Dr. Terhune to share her opinion as to the cause of Courtney Clemm's cerebral palsy. He was wearing yesterday's suit and he had gotten the part in his hair just off enough that a new cowlick was putting in an appearance. O'Malley smoothed at it.

Eve Terhune looked at the jury—they were still sitting ramrod straight, determined to pass the quiz on quadratic equations—and explained that in her opinion the Clemm child's "neurologic deficit, the spastic quadriplegia, was due to a hypoxic ischemic insult shortly prior to the time of birth." Mr. Gold Chains juror was lipsynching to the word *ischemic*, trying to keep up, looking like if he could *say* the words, he would somehow also know what the goddamned things *meant*.

Kelvin O'Malley then acted like he was hearing for the very first time what he already must have heard plenty of times from Eve Terhune on the phone,

CHAPTER NINE

in his office, and in her deposition—that at the time of birth, Courtney was a very abnormal child neurologically with diminished tone and significantly delayed Apgar scores. Marian looked at the jury: *abnormal* they got. But then Eve Terhune warmed to her subject, and the Avon lady started chipping quizzically at her nail polish, like she just couldn't understand why the pink tones wear better than the reds.

Terhune expanded on Courtney Clemm's birth record, saying she was quite acidotic, which is certainly compatible with hypoxic-ischemic insult (Gold Chains mouthed *ischemic* again), and before birth, there were significant drops in the heart rate that are compatible with the diminished Apgars and acidosis occurring with cerebral palsy. She and O'Malley chatted comfortably about the causes of cerebral palsy, went over the efforts to resuscitate the newborn Courtney, and came to a stop at Terhune's belief that although Courtney Clemm would continue to progress with regard to speech and awareness, she would never be able to read, write, walk unassisted, or live independently.

She would need speech therapy.

She would need physical therapy.

She would need occupational therapy.

"Will Courtney," O'Malley paused and then said momentously, "ever be able to ride a bike?" *Bikes* they can all understand. O'Malley had just taken every human opportunity and aspiration and reduced it to a Schwinn.

"No."

The jurors sat with their mouths open. You would have thought every single one of them was a bike dealer.

O'Malley said softly, "Thank you."

Nan waited until O'Malley sat down next to the Clemms—Jeannie was looking undernourished in a powder blue cardigan, and her long hair was pulled back in a clip—before fixing the witness with a cool look and pushing back her chair. She wished Dr. Terhune a good morning and quickly established where in Cleveland she had hospital privileges, making the point that she was neither a neonatologist nor a pediatrician.

"When it comes to making judgments about an infant, you would not come into a neonatal intensive care unit as a neurologist and make an assessment of that child?"

"During my residency training, I would, yes. I would not now."

"I'm talking about *now*, Doctor."

"Now, no."

"And with respect to obstetrics, you don't practice that branch of medicine either. Correct?"

"No, I do not."

Nan seemed to be remembering. "Am I correct that you had about two months' worth of obstetric training in medical school?"

"Yes."

"And you did not have any obstetric training at all after those two months in medical school."

"No, I did not."

Nan maneuvered her, then, into reviewing the fetal heart monitor strip from Jeannie Clemm's labor. At first, Eve Terhune resisted, telling the court, "I don't critically evaluate those," but then she went right ahead and did just that when she added that she noticed drops in the heart rate—called *decelerations*—were present, which helped her reach the opinions she expressed today.

Nan pointed to a place on the strip. "Is this an early or late deceleration?"

Terhune was ready. "I'm not an obstetrician. I don't comment on early or late decelerations. No." I won't dance, don't ask me.

"Well, I'm confused," Nan stepped back, not at all confused. "If you don't know how to interpret them, how then can you say they play a role in the opinion you just gave the ladies and gentlemen of the jury?"

Terhune shifted. "Based on my review of the neurologic literature, including—"

"Excuse me, Doctor, we aren't talking about the literature. Right now, we're talking about the drops in the heart rate that you mentioned. Do you know whether or not the infant had good beat-to-beat variability as you look at this tracing?"

"I'm not an obstetrician. I can't comment on good beat-to-beat variability."

CHAPTER NINE

Nan cocked her head. "So you don't know whether or not the infant had a good beat-to-beat variability that would undermine your opinion?"

Terhune licked her lips. Still coral. Still coached. "I'm not an obstetrician."

"I didn't *ask* you if you were an obstetrician, Doctor. I asked whether or not the infant had a good beat-to-beat variability that would undermine your opinion that an asphyxial event occurred between four and five o'clock in the morning of Jeannie Clemm's labor?"

Eve Terhune rallied. "I'm just commenting on the absolute decrease in the heart rate as far as it relates to asphyxia and cerebral palsy."

"And how long does the heart rate have to be down for you to reach this opinion?"

"It's variable."

"How long in infant Clemm did it have to be down for you to reach this opinion?"

Terhune threw up her hands. "There are—no absolutes in medicine."

Nan paused, smiling, then she paged through the folds of the fetal monitor strip and bent over one section of it. "Would I be correct in assuming that you noticed a diminishment here—" pointing, "and saw that it's a decrease from the baseline fetal heart rate?"

Terhune hardly looked. "I don't consider myself an expert at reading them."

Nan refolded the strip. "Well, if you're not an expert at reading them, then I take it you would agree with me that your interpretation may not be the same as an obstetrician's. Correct?"

"My interpretation was based on the records from the hospital."

"I didn't *ask* you about the records from the hospital. I'm asking whether your consideration of what is or is not on the fetal heart tracing might differ from that of an obstetrician."

Terhune straightened up. "I would never make an interpretation of the tracing. I would never do that."

Nan inclined her head. "If I asked you—no matter what other things might be occurring on the tracing—whether normal beat-to-beat variability would suggest that the fetus is *not* suffering from asphyxia—" she raised her voice, "—you couldn't agree or disagree with that statement, could you?"

Terhune inhaled. "I'm not an obstetrician."

By then, everyone in the room was clear on that point.

"And if I asked you whether or not you agree with the proposition that the incidence of cerebral palsy since the use of fetal heart monitors has not diminished over the past twenty years, you would not either agree or disagree?"

The witness blinked. "I've seen that article, yes."

Nan was quick. "Then you agree with it?"

Rattled, Terhune made a helpless gesture. "I haven't been in medicine for twenty years. It's really hard for me to, *you* know, assess." She was beginning to remind Marian of the Bettys and Veronicas at Gringos. "I really don't have that, *you* know, wealth of experience as far as incidences of cerebral palsy and changes in obstetric monitoring, er, go."

At that, she recrossed her legs.

Nan held up the fetal monitor strip. "But you do know the cause of *this*—" she shook the strip until some of it fluttered out— "infant's cerebral palsy, is that right?"

Eve Terhune looked straight ahead. "I expressed my opinion, yes."

"And you've related that cause as an asphyxial event that occurred sometime during labor, is that right?"

"Yes."

Nan stood still. "Are you aware of the fact that Dr. Constantine Berger, the very first neonatologist who treated this infant, has said in his deposition that, based upon his training and experience as a neonatologist, *he* doesn't know the cause of the asphyxia?"

O'Malley was on his feet. "Objection. I don't believe that was Dr. Berger's testimony, Your Honor."

"Page 84, line 13, Your Honor," Nan said. The judge thumbed through the deposition, found the page, and gave Nan permission to read from it. "'Question, so you have no opinion as to the cause of the asphyxia in this case, is that correct?' Answer, 'I can tell you the baby was asphyxiated at birth.' 'Question, you've said that, Doctor. I'm asking you, you don't know the cause of that asphyxia, though, do you, Doctor?' Answer, 'no.'" Nan set

CHAPTER NINE

the deposition down on the defense table and shifted gears, chatting with the witness about the texts she did or did not consult to help her form an opinion about the case. Exactly which authoritative books, exactly which articles. Eve Terhune gave her hair a soft toss and seemed to relax. This was a gal whose dog never ate *her* homework.

Nan Kemp moseyed over to the defense table and stacked up a bunch of textbooks and medical journals, making a show of scrutinizing the titles, and then—*fwack!* — landing one on top of the other. She somehow got her arms around this pile and, with a little helpful laughter from the jury (sheeee-it, they wouldn't want to come within a horseshoe toss of any of *that* stuff), half-stooped her way back over to Terhune. Nan opened the textbooks willy-nilly and lined them up along the rail of the witness stand, like she and her pal Eve were going over some wallpaper samples. Then she fanned out the journals in a sloppy way meant to show just how much of this stuff there was, and when two journals flopped to the floor, she left them.

Nan folded her hands and looked at the flexed toe of her left shoe. "Now, it was based upon this literature that you formed your opinion today, is that right?"

"Yes, and my clinical experience."

Nan held up a finger. "Well, you don't *have* any clinical experience treating neonates, do you?"

"I see a lot of children and adults with cerebral palsy."

"I don't think you've answered my question, Doctor. You don't have any experience treating neonates," Nan stood over her, "do you?"

Quietly: "No."

Nan gestured to the mass of information. "Can you point to where in any of the material you see here you formed your opinion as to when the asphyxial event occurred that definitively caused infant Clemm's cerebral palsy?"

Eve Terhune moved closer to the books with a look like she suddenly thought maybe her pantyhose was a size too small, tried turning a few pages, then gave up. "It's not—" she struggled to express the idea, "one isolated event that causes the problem."

"Do you agree with me, at least, that episodes of asphyxia occurring *in utero* long before labor begins can result in fetal brain damage?"

"Long before, you mean, months before?"

"Months, weeks, days."

"Months before," Terhune conceded. "There's a theory that asphyxia can occur idiopathically."

"What does that mean?"

"Of unknown cause."

Nan plucked a journal from the pile. "Isn't that what Dr. Neiswander said in this article you said you reviewed?"

"Cerebral palsy can have many different causes, and that can certainly be one of them."

"Do you recall if, in fact, Dr. Neiswander said that episodes of *in utero* asphyxia, which occur long before labor begins, can result in fetal brain damage?"

"Yes."

O'Malley half-rose. "I'm going to object, Your Honor."

"Overruled. She's answered the question 'yes.'"

Nan flashed the judge a brief look. "Thank you, Your Honor." Back to the witness. "Do you remember if Dr. Neiswander said that immaturity of the brain can cause central nervous system damage, yes or no?"

"It's been a while since I—"

"Or that maternal stress can, yes or no?"

"I looked at a lot of—"

"You don't recall?"

She let out a little *tsk*. "I can't remember one particular sentence from one particular article." *Just pass me a Ballwhanger, please.*

"This isn't a test, believe me." With great deliberation, Nan stacked the texts and journals—all except one, which she held up. "When you read the article by Nelson and Ellenburg that appeared in this issue of the *New England Journal of Medicine*, do you remember this opening statement?" Nan found the page. "'Despite earlier optimism that cerebral palsy was likely to disappear with the advent of improvements in obstetric and neonatal care,

CHAPTER NINE

there has apparently been no consistent decrease in its frequency in the past decade or two.'"

Nan closed the issue and set it all by itself in front of Eve Terhune. "Do you remember reading that opening statement?"

"Yes, but I—"

"Thank you, Doctor." Nan walked over to the jury box, where she stood with her back to the witness. "Finally, Doctor, when it comes to the asphyxia you've been telling these ladies and gentlemen about, would you agree with the statement that not all asphyxia is preventable?"

Eve Terhune had to lean forward in her seat, not sure she had heard the question. "Not all asphyxia is preventable?"

"Yes." Nan turned with a casual shrug. "Would you agree with the statement that not all asphyxia is preventable?"

Terhune's eyes narrowed while she thought it over, then out it came. "It depends on what the cause is. If we're talking about an infant damaged at birth, some of it is not preventable." The suck-it-up feature of the cherry-paneled walls seemed to get cranked up a notch as the room got absolutely quiet. Nobody moved. Even the bagger from Kroger's stopped cracking his knuckles.

Marian watched Dave Barish take a deep breath and just tap once on the edge of the defense table. More than anybody, he knew the significance of what Nan had gotten Eve Terhune to admit. But Jeannie and Craig Clemm kept expecting more, like they were waiting out a commercial break on *America's Got Talent*. Not O'Malley. O'Malley's head was turned so the jury couldn't see his face, but what she caught was a frozen, adversarial smile. *Damage control* was what it looked like he was thinking.

Unaware that she had torpedoed her own ship, Terhune sailed on: "If there's an infection that occurs, say, at five months *in-utero* and the child is significantly handicapped, it is not preventable."

"Thank you, Doctor. I have no other questions." Nan was careful to avoid eye contact with anyone as she quickly sat down at the defense table. All she allowed herself was the kind of little smile you get when you're in a public place, and you just remembered a joke that rushes you right to the edge of the sort of lunacy you'd really rather not share with total strangers. She lost no time reaching for her notes. Dave Barish leaned toward her to say something, but she cut him off with a tiny shake of her head.

"Re-direct?" the judge asked.

O'Malley was up, wetting his lips, wondering how to maintain the illusion of seaworthiness. The answer seemed to be to draw no attention to the wreck. "Thank you, Your Honor," he said robustly. He hunched his shoulders, working his suit jacket back into place, and approached his witness. To kill the sudden picture of his strangling Eve Terhune with the fetal monitor strip, Marian had to gnaw on the inside of her cheek.

O'Malley started to ask Terhune something about idiopathic causes—it seemed to Marian he was just exercising his vocal cords, waiting for something dazzling to occur to him—when she became aware of the door to the courtroom opening, and Hank Khartoukian stepped halfway inside. He was looking right at her, so she raised her eyebrows at him. When he jerked his head toward the hall, Marian slipped out, grateful for normal human sounds of phones and copy machines and shoes clacking on marble.

Khartoukian took her by the elbow and moved her around a beat-up metal chair and an old, standing ashtray. She got a whiff of Old Spice. Then he spread his hand out high against the wall. Not even noon, fully air-conditioned halls, and the sheriff already had a crescent of sweat in his crisp uniform shirt. With his other hand, he rubbed his eyes, tired. "You were right."

Marian felt herself sag. "Beth?"

Her voice felt little. She felt little. He nodded. "She never left Wade County. A couple of Eagle Scouts doing some orienteering in Hopewell Range State Park found her this morning—or what was left of her after two weeks out in the heat and rain." The Eagle Scouts got oriented real fast and puked their way back up to their van and phoned it in. It's the highest point in the park, along the ridge, where you can pull over and take a short trail. Pretty, all right, forested ravine everywhere you look—too thick for cold chicken or hot dates, but just the ticket for the scouts, who had hiked down maybe three hundred feet.

CHAPTER NINE

"Looks like she was strangled and dumped—" Khartoukian moved aside for two fluffy old gals who came out of the court reporters' office. They'll know more after the post-mortem—he gave the gals a fissure of a smile and touched the brim of his hat—only when that'll be is anybody's guess because Jim Carney's having fits, saying he won't autopsy someone he knows. And Khartoukian just left Rodie Prescott back at MHC Construction, wailing over the hood of his pickup. Jack Girard's got him for now.

"In which case, Marian," he finished, "if you plan on adding to the general hysteria, I can give you five minutes, and then I've got to go find me a deputy coroner."

"No."

"Are you still on the case?"

"If Rodie wants me."

"Then you've got to come across."

"How?"

"Give me what you've got." They both watched the door to the courtroom swing open, and Khartoukian leaned into her to get out of the way. Eve Terhune came out, blinking and looking pale, like she couldn't put enough miles between her and the hot seat fast enough. She stumbled into the ashtray and kept going. Khartoukian turned back to Marian. "I won't have you running after some asshole by yourself."

"I'll tell you what I can, Sheriff, but I don't want you all over me."

"This is a homicide."

"I know what it is." Next came the Clemms, shoulders slumping with some crazy kind of relief, Jeannie smiling at nothing. They were followed by a lieutenant lawyer whispering to O'Malley, a staff reporter from the *Toiler*, Grandma Clemm pushing Courtney, and a couple of street people who had wandered in for the air conditioning. Marian tried moving out of the way with Khartoukian, but she was blocked by Grandma Clemm jawing to Craig that the judge fella is the spittin' image of the fella used to be on late night TV, you know the one I mean, the one with the *hair*.

Khartoukian got closer to Marian. "What lines are you working?"

"Beth's lover."

"What else?"

"The business contacts."

"The docs, the Girards, who?"

She felt herself stiffen up. "The docs."

"Not the Girards."

"Oh, come on, Sheriff." Like it was preposterous. Suddenly, she understood what Rodie had meant. She watched O'Malley clap his long arms around Craig and Jeannie and tell them he wanted to catch up with Dr. Terhune to thank her for what he called "her good work"—still messing with the general perception even when the jury was out of sight. The Clemms looked bewildered. O'Malley and the reporter started to push through the crowd, making Khartoukian sway into Marian like a strap hanger on the subway. "Go on," he said to her, rolling his eyes. If he got any closer, they'd have to give some serious thought to birth control.

It all started to come down around her head. Old Spice, Beth rotting in a ravine, Ted Koppel. "Beth's former employer," she threw in, pulling it out of nowhere, feeling her voice rise—maybe she was adding to the general hysteria, after all— "the Columbus gig. Beth Prescott was there for two years. Who was with her? What work did she do? What files did she have access to? Where did she get that Thayer Coggin furniture? You can't buy furniture like that from schlepping blood. How did she come up with the tuition for medical assisting school? What favors did she do?"

Khartoukian squeezed Marian's shoulder, less to calm her than to keep her up on her own two feet. "You're saying blackmail—"

"Right. Blackmail." It sounded as good as anything else. "Blackmail gone bad." How the hell could she have spent four days in Carthage and have nothing better to give Rodie Prescott than his sister's corpse with a note—*sorry!*—pinned to what's left of her shiny belted rayon dress. All Marian wanted was to get the hell out of there, stick her retainer in an envelope, and fire it back at Jack Girard.

Suddenly, Nan Kemp grabbed her arm and pulled herself in close, but her eyes were on the sheriff. "No lunch for me," Nan said. "I have to call the office. Let's try for dinner tonight, Marian." Then she cocked her head and

CHAPTER NINE

grinned. "You eat, Sheriff?"

"Oh, every other day."

"Well, if this is one of those days, why don't you join us?"

"I'll give it a thought."

Nan gave Marian the once-over. "You're looking like my client," she said. "What's up?"

"They found Beth Prescott."

A beat. "And not playing the slots in Vegas."

"No. Strangled." And if you don't like blackmail, Marian felt like grabbing Khartoukian's collar, what friends did Beth Prescott betray? What busty lunatic in a prom dress did Beth Ann Prescott nose out for third runner-up for Tulip Time Queen? What scrawny homicidal babe in white cowboy boots did Beth edge out for a second-place twirling ribbon? How far back did Marian have to go—the playground in first grade?

"Shitty deal." Nan gave her back a quick rub.

"Yeah." She felt choked up.

"There are lots of those around," Nan said, peering into Marian's face. "And they don't all end at the graveyard." The three of them watched David Barish come walking toward them with his hands in his pockets. "Truly they don't."

Chapter Ten

Marian opened the windows of the Volvo, lurched her seat back, and watched a man in a Panama hat and yellow pants stroll by with two Jack Russell terriers completely uninterested in walking a straight line. She wanted to tear right on out of there, right out of Carthage, Ohio, right off Planet Earth altogether, to some starless place that didn't include strangling and dumping young women who came ever so close to being crowned Tulip Time Queen. Only Marian wasn't at all sure she could steer herself out of the parking space. At that moment, her phone trilled, and she glanced at it.

Joan, calling her again.

"Hey," said Marian dully.

"Hey?" her sister laughed. "Honey, I'm telling you, this is what happens when you go west of the Hudson River."

"We grew up in Jersey, old girl, remember? Check your map."

"Yes," Joan came back strong, "and it's all I can do not to slide into barbarisms like Jeet and Noork."

"You'll manage," said Marian, loving her boss sister bestie inordinately.

Joan pondered. "Forget the Hudson. I'll give us the Delaware grace. Anytime we go west of the Delaware, we're at risk of—of—"

"What?"

"Making casseroles."

Joan Fleck could always make her laugh. "In Crock Pots," Marian added. After the squeal that started when they were kids together, and Dad was still around, Joan got quiet for five seconds, which was about as long as it

CHAPTER TEN

ever took the Director of the Artifacts Authentication Agency to get back to business. Marian preempted her. "What have you got, Sis?"

When Joan sighed and growled, Marian knew it was big. Or particularly delicate. A confiscated shipment of faux Chinese porcelains was all in a day's work. Joan could handle that with one of her three-shot lattes and a couple of phone calls. "It's a Poe."

"A Poe?"

Joan rattled off as much of the case as she was willing to tell Marian, who was presently very west of the Delaware. "Hitherto undiscovered manuscript by the Crown Prince of Creep, what, two hundred years old, rolled and tubed, arrived yesterday by courier."

"And you've got to authenticate it?" There were three or four scholars they could tap. Then: "Who's the sender?"

Joan snorted. "There's more. Anonymous sender. And it's a photocopy of an original, which—" she said, raising her voice, "is being held for ransom for two million dollars. Deadline, one week."

Finally, Marian said, "Already there's a crime."

"You might say. Set aside the intellectual property slant."

Marian knew they were both thinking of Penelope Warner's lawsuit twenty years ago. Where it was easy to show theft, easy to show intention, easy to show mercy, grace, understanding. Easy to go to lunch arm in arm. "Not Penelope's case at all, eh?" The trial was a chance to see eye to eye, finally. To do the repair work that simply needed the light and air of the courtroom. Before damage seeped in too deep ever to be anything other than bottomless. She wondered whether, down the road, David Barish would be able to see things that way.

Joan made a sound. "I'll say. Hell of an end, that."

Marian's head jerked. "What are you talking about?"

"Penelope's case. You were there."

"You were there, too. They left arm in arm."

"Helen Weskind was convicted."

"Yes, but the judge skipped the award and the damages."

A beat. Then: "Marian," she said softly, "do you really not know?"

111

Two grey-haired gals in sneakers and cardigans ducked into a place called Princess of Wales Tea Shoppe, just across the sidewalk from where she was parked. Today, the paper mill was fainter. Or maybe Marian was just upwind. What was she about to learn? "I guess I don't." And Joan went on to tell her that, based on that conviction, the university fired tenured professor Helen Weskind on ethical grounds. Apparently dazed at the news, she left the chancellor's office and stepped out onto College Avenue, where she was hit by the campus shuttle bus.

"Why didn't Penelope tell me?"

Joan thought she had. "Maybe you just weren't around."

"The term at Hotchkiss, maybe."

"That'd be about right. Besides—" she added, "you know Penelope."

Marian sat nodding. "She'd be sad, but—"

"She wouldn't see her own connection to the way it played out."

"And then she'd just forget."

"Dad all over again."

Marian straightened up. "A kiss and a sandwich together—"

"Helen and Penelope?"

"Should have been the end of it." The damages had nothing, really, to do with money after all.

After a moment, Joan asked, "How soon can you get here?"

The tea ladies in their cardigans and sneakers didn't know Beth Prescott. For them, it was just a pretty day in June, little bit of rain, little bit of sun. Hell, for that matter, even Marian didn't know her, but she knew Rodie and it was Rodie she felt she had failed. She had to keep telling herself that Beth Prescott was dead long before she even got to Carthage. It's not like she fumbled a save. "Joan," she said finally, her voice free of any doubt or regret, "I've got a homicide here." She heard her half-sister suck in air. "My missing person was found strangled and dumped."

She couldn't help with the Poe ransom; no way she could wrap up the Prescott case in time to get back to New York and put her mind to work on the extortion attempt in Joan's lap before the anonymous sender's deadline. "Call John Clevenger," she added, putting her pressured boss onto the barely

CHAPTER TEN

semi-likable rich man who sat on art museum boards, made world-class omelets the morning after, and directed a powerful, low-profile organization that wouldn't appear on any Google search and made any threat to cultural heritage its zone of operations, and wore bow ties. Marian could deal with any of it except the bow ties. Clevenger called her position on his sartorial choices a deal breaker. But she could count on him to help Joan Fleck.

Disappointed, they ended the call.

Marian pressed in another number.

He picked up right away. "Girard."

"It's Marian, Jack."

A silence. "Khartoukian catch up with you?"

"Yes. Is Rodie there?"

"Ernie Diodakis came and took him home."

"What's his address?"

"She took him to *her* home."

"Where's—"

"Providence Lane. Ernie's my next-door neighbor."

They quickly disconnected, and she set out for Providence—only she wasn't ready to drive past the OK Corral of January's disaster, so she went down the cobblestone street from the opposite end, avoiding Jack Girard's house altogether. Providence Lane is just one short and narrow block long, lined with more houses listed on the National Register of Historic Homes than any other single street in America. It's one of those time-warp streets where, if nobody's SUV is parked out front, you can almost imagine a horse-drawn ice wagon clopping along. Things like fraud, murder plots, and shootouts don't happen on Providence, unless, of course, Marian Warner comes to town.

She parked two doors up from Ernie Diodakis's blue-frame century home, cutting across lawns, paying elaborate attention to someone's bearded irises, shading that side of her face where her eyes might roam, and her mental health said they shouldn't. She felt like a celebrity dodging the paparazzi. Ernie had wisteria vines winding over her long, flat wooden porch—nice shield from the neighbors—and a quick jump up the single step landed

Marian at the double door, where she rapped on the fanlight until Ernie opened up. She was wearing checkered capris and a black v-neck shirt with *Ernie's Neighborhood Bar* embroidered on the pocket—today the big hoops were silver. Her pretty face looked pinched. The smirk was nowhere around.

"Hi, Ernie."

"Hey, Marian." She closed the door and the two of them stood kind of lamely in the hall with their hands in their pockets, shaking their heads, for a few minutes. From where Marian stood, Ernie's was a beautiful little place, with long windows that nearly touched the gleaming hardwood floors, a baby grand piano standing in a sliver of sunlight.

"You came from work?"

Ernie bit her lip, jerking her dark head to the front door. "My mom's filling in for me. She took early retirement from the water department." A thin line of tears slid down Ernie's face and dropped off onto her shirt.

"My mom's a teacher."

"Oh, nice. Crayons and things?" Ernie found a crumpled tissue in her pocket and went at her nose.

"Not anymore. Bigger—" Marian made kind of a circle in the air, wondering why they were talking about mothers. "—bigger things."

"Can I get you a lemonade?"

"No, I—"

Ernie blew her nose, her eyes wretched over the top of the tissue. "It's just that Beth was all he had." Marian gave her a little push toward the stairs, where they sat next to each other. Their mother died a few years ago, and the dad, that piece of work Neal Prescott—Ernie rallied at the mention of this name, a flash of her old Chopper-at-the-gates self—moved away to Zanesville and started a whole new family. Like Beth and Rodie got buried right along with the mom, she guessed. Piece of work, piece of shit Neal. Rodie was practically a kid still, just thirteen, and it was Beth who got him through high school. And got him through a boatload of community service hours he racked up at fifteen when the cops caught him smoking a joint on school property. Then others pitched in later, like for a while when Beth lived out of town, Jack Girard kept a lookout, giving Rodie a job and a place

CHAPTER TEN

to sleep.

"What about you?"

"Me?" She dangled her arms over her bent legs. "Me, I married that piece of shit Neal Prescott when I was sixteen. Took me all of six months to come to my senses and call it quits, but poor Lorraine Kogan—Beth and Rodie's mom—lasted nineteen years until she just couldn't take it anymore and figured out dying was easier than walking, I guess. I always liked the Prescott kids. I always liked Rodie—and *now—*"

She gave Marian the look of a woman who knows she's only got the guy she loves, the guy she takes into her bed, until someone a whole lot younger comes along for him. "Go on up, Marian, but I made him take a sleeping pill—" The reason came roaring back to her, and Marian watched the petite Ernie Diodakis teeter on the brink of another meltdown.

"What's so bad about Neal Prescott?"

Ernie snorted. Crisis averted. "He's the two worst things a man can be." She ticked off the sins on her fingers. "He's mean," she said with a violent sniff and a toss of her thick black waves, "and he's cheap."

Upstairs, Marian tapped softly on Ernie's bedroom door and then just walked in. "Rodie?" In bright daylight, not a hair of him was showing under the pale green comforter on Ernie's queen-sized bed. The white wooden shutters were wide open, and she thought about closing them, but hardly anything is more depressing than a dark room on a beautiful afternoon where others got to be happy walking little dogs and having tea cakes. What she thought was the sound of air moving through the vents in Ernie's house was really Rodie, every breath a soft wail.

Shit, she hated this job. What had she been thinking, taking the Prescott case like some real-ass private eye? What made her think her license was anything more than a wallet stuffer like her Starbucks card? When she got out of there, she'd by God call Joan and beg for an assignment gathering intel on the Red Hook docks. Whatever happened there, it had to mean less pain than this moment. Suddenly Marian felt like she woke up and found herself the first Mrs. Neal Prescott. Or the second. Or the third. "Rodie?" She sat down on the edge of the bed. He stirred and then poked his head out, his eyes half-shut from tears and Ambien.

"Marian?" He flung himself at her, sobbing, and she caught him in a hug, and she knew in a flash he didn't blame her for anything. He didn't blame her for not being faster, not being smarter, not being able to change Beth's fate. Marian knew in her gut she would find the killer, oh, the thought became more savory by the minute, she would find the killer—she owed it to this very lovely twenty-two-year-old in her arms who didn't seem to think she owed him anything—and she would find his sister's killer with or without Khartoukian, and with or without Girard. Then she'd drive straight to Montgomery Place in Brooklyn and hole up at Joan's, and they'd play Snap five hundred times until Marian could forget about it all. But for now, she shushed Rodie Prescott, settled him back down, and tucked the comforter in at his sides.

"You didn't even know her," he sniffed.

"But I know you." He nodded like it made all the sense he needed in a world where sisters get strangled, and for some reason Marian could never account for, she started in softly singing what Penelope Warner used to sing when Joan and Marian were sick. "There's a burlesque the-AY-ter where the gang likes to go, To see Queenie the cutie of the burlesque show—" By the time she got to the part, "Take it off, take it off, all the customers shout, Down in front, down in front, while the band beats it out—" Rodie Prescott was fast asleep.

***

Marian let herself into Beth Prescott's apartment with the keys Rodie had given her. Something was here, something had to be here, and she was damn well going to take it away with her before Khartoukian descended on the place. The apartment was darker than Ernie's bedroom—someone had pulled the blinds shut—and it smelled two days blanker, staler, than the last time. She opened the blinds. Mid-afternoon at Coconut Palm Estates. No banana-clip moms, no Flyboys with pies, no Beth—no cops. Maybe this was a full-employment building. And here she was, standing in a dead girl's

CHAPTER TEN

closed-up living room where she felt like she was trying to breathe through concrete.

Marian gave a quick look around. Someone had cleaned the joint before word came that Beth had been found. Rodie? Ernie? The ribeye was gone, the dishes done up. One of those useless, hopeful things people do who are decked out in denial. Jesus. She didn't want to be the one to explain to Khartoukian just why the victim's place looked better now than when she lived there. Loping to the bedroom, Marian discovered that Beth's dirty laundry had been washed, including the two-piece white uniform Beth had flung aside when she'd gotten off work at the Girards' the night she was killed. It was all folded and set in neat piles on the waterbed. She was tempted to offload it all into drawers but decided against tampering with anything—anything she wasn't actually planning on taking away with her, that is. Charlie was right: she kept moving the line in the goddamn sand.

She pulled out the Rubbermaid bin with all the memorabilia, and in the end unplugged Beth's answering machine—covering up the dust-free rectangle on the nightstand with a paperback about the same size—and threw it on top of the stuff in the bin. With the backs of her fingers, she pressed down a slat in the miniblind and saw a cruiser pull up to the back of the building. Since she didn't recall any second set of stairs out of the building, Marian was going to have to brass her way past Khartoukian's gang. She grabbed a scarf, tied it around her head like a babushka, tucked some of Beth's clean laundry around the stuff in the Rubbermaid bin, and legged it to the front door, elbowing the light switches as she went.

With the bin angled against her right hip, she got out onto the landing, pulled the door shut with the merest of clicks, and started the improv in front of Beth's neighbor's door just as the sound of heavy shoes hit the stairs. "Now, Harley, I told you I'm coming back just as soon as I get these here things to Ivorine for the church jumble." She tugged at the already shut door as two deputies came into view, who were too busy flipping through a set of keys and talking about the specials out at Eat 'n Park to pay Marian any attention. She cracked her fake gum a few times, gave them a stiff nod, and slunk by them down the stairs and out to the parking lot, feeling for some strange reason like Wile E. Coyote making off with a box of Acme gizmos.

* * *

After three days in court, Nan Kemp told Marian all she wanted was to get the hell past the city limits, so they shot out to the Wade County Fairgrounds in her Saab to prowl the gyro and fried dough stands at Tulip Time. Steeped in murder and judicial mayhem, they agreed that what they needed were some serious slippery fried things. The late afternoon was one of those strange, warm, calm, overcast days where anything can happen—a cooling rain, a rib-rattling storm, a clearing wind.

A grim old gal with gray braids who was wearing a gold pinnie swung a Maglite to guide them over a crumbling curb past her five-foot PARK $10 sign into a rocky field, where Nan jerked to a stop between an old VW bus and a black Caddy with a dented hood wired shut. Two more tens got them past the admission booth and into the Fairgrounds, and they tagged along behind Wade County families with strollers and bare midriffs. When it came to heading for the fun, they figured ten-year-old boys with hi-tops and shorts slipping down to their knees, jumping backwards, pointing and shouting, were the best guides. Who needed a map?

The two of them followed the clanging calliope music to the midway, not being able to make any sense of the non-stop spunky announcer on the PA system who was inviting them either to the Norelco Shave-off in the Alarm Tent or the Pez Shoot-out in the Barn of Men. All the screamers on the midway rides sounded like twelve-year-old girls. All the losers at the midway shooting galleries sounded like sixteen-year-old boys. Caps, pings, dings, splashes and roars—Marian looked around for the dunking booth—over all of it, barkers pitched games involving guns, rings, darts, water pistols, and basketballs, damn near promising a stuffed pink lion prize just about the right size if Marian decided she didn't want to shell out for that end-of-all-time BarcaLounger. Tempting. As she and Nan scanned the elephant ear and Philly cheesesteak trucks, they passed a couple of two-year-old red-faced tantrums. Parents screamed at their kids. Parents screamed

CHAPTER TEN

for their kids. Kids screamed, period.

They slowed by the rides, where lines of pushing, leaning, dirty-dancing young people waited for the fun of being flung upside down in locked cages at high speeds. Nan and Marian dared each other to try the one called the Demon's Revenge, but then they both decided it was old hat since it couldn't be any worse than what they already did for a living.

"Guess your weight? Guess your age?" called a guy in a derby at a kiosk. "You! Red!"

Nan didn't even slow down. "You can keep your damn guesses to yourself," she shot back, and he laughed. A fling at self-preservation made them stumble into the Grange building, where it looked like they could eat a burger sitting down. The Grange is one of those names Marian had heard practically all of her life without ever really knowing what it was. Like actuaries or magistrates, or FDIC. From what she could tell, the Grange was like a farmer's support group, slicing up enough pies to meet any emergency, including flood and drought.

Since it was cafeteria-style in the Grange eatery at Tulip Time, Nan and Marian grabbed trays and joined the line, ending up with what the overhead menu called B-B-Q Beef sandwiches, paper cups filled with shoestring fries, wedges of blueberry pie (*Home Made!*), and Cokes. The bevy of Grange Ladies dishing up the eats were a fine bunch of rosy-cheeked fairy godmother types who, behind their flinty giggles, were seriously running the country. And lucky for all the rest of them.

No one looked at them over the counter and asked if they wanted to Biggie size that—although one, Jonelle, when Marian tried to get a read on whether what she really wanted was a medium or a large Coke, said, "Honey, we got but one size — *ours*," and Marian spent a few moments wondering why David Barish didn't have the good fortune to draw Jonelle as a juror. As long as there are Grange Ladies to plunk shasta daisies into little glass vases and sling tasty B-B-Q Beef onto buns, you know you can forget all about pesky worries like the national debt.

They nabbed two seats at one of the long metal tables covered with red-checkered plastic tablecloths, sat down across from each other, and dug into their B-B-Q Beef. While they did their part for farm relief, all they could manage to talk about in a tooth-sucking sort of way were the county fairs they had been to as kids. Finally, even the pie was history, and Marian watched Nan scrape her fork across the blueberry smear. "For a cup of coffee," she said, "I'll tell you my story. How's that for cheap?"

Marian went right back up to Jonelle and, forgetting everything she had ever learned about venti, grande, small is medium, and tall is small, ordered two decafs, hoping she'd say exactly what she did: "Honey, we got but one kind—*real.*" Marian steered her way back around wandering babies in draggy diapers, feeling chipper, all of a sudden, about things like tanning beds and Jack Girard and the prospect of putting a face to Beth Prescott's killer, who could right this minute be winning the Pez Shoot-out in the Barn of Men.

Nan blew gently across the rim of her Styrofoam coffee cup. "My dad's name is Alexander Kemp. He's an OB in Philadelphia, where I grew up—well, he's retired now. But he graduated fourteenth in his medical school class at Johns Hopkins, and in thirty-five years, he's delivered around seven thousand babies." She sipped. "I'm his oldest kid and his only girl." He taught her chess when she was eight and took her to a place called the Alcazar Ballroom when she was eleven, but not before she was passable at the waltz and fox trot. Whenever Nan had a fever, he played Chopin downstairs on the baby grand piano until she dropped off to sleep. Whenever Nan was bored, he took her with him to make rounds at the hospital, where she tapped the glass on the nursery windows while he checked his patients.

When he was sixty, he did a routine laparoscopy for pelvic pain on a thirty-year-old woman named Celia Dean and perforated her bladder without realizing it. It wasn't his fault, she had an anomalous bladder—an oddity—that extended almost to her belly button, and through a laparoscope an empty bladder, looks like the rest of the abdominal wall. After three days at home, Celia Dean showed up in the ER with abdominal swelling, fever, and chills. A general surgeon took her to the OR for an exploratory laparotomy and damned if *he* didn't perforate the bladder, too, when he made his midline incision.

He repaired the bladder and expected she'd recover completely, but Celia

CHAPTER TEN

Dean did not get better. A week later, she was taken back to the OR for unexplained fever. Whether it was the necrotizing fasciitis—what *National Enquirer* calls "flesh-eating bacteria"—they discovered when they opened her up, or complications of anesthesia, no one knows, but while she was on the operating table, thirty-year-old Celia Dean unexpectedly went into cardiac arrest and died.

Of all the doctors who had taken care of her—a gynecologist, a surgeon, an internist, an infectious disease specialist, and an anesthesiologist—Alexander Kemp was the only one who went to the funeral, where he was met with shouts, threats, and even a few stones. He left. Six months later, the lawsuit came, naming him, the general surgeon, the anesthesiologist, three different nurses, and the hospital itself negligent in the matter of Celia Dean.

The case settled for $735,000—Mr. Terrence Dean, the widower, received more than half and remarried eight months later—and, for the purpose of the payout, a faceless peer review panel had to carve up the various doctors' responsibility for this medical disaster and express it in percentages. They found Alexander Kemp, M.D., thirty-four percent responsible; the remainder divided equally among the other defendants.

Some of his colleagues set the bag of blame squarely at his feet, because blame is the sort of creature that really prefers a single host. Other colleagues—you can't quite call them friends—people whose lives he had shared for twenty years—called him into a closed meeting at the hospital and censured him. He sat there and listened to talk about whether they should put him on probation. It didn't happen, but the talk was enough. For all of them, including Alexander Kemp.

There were days when he couldn't get beyond the insurance company's lack of faith. Days when he couldn't get around wanting to ask the members of that peer review panel how they came up with those figures—thirty-*four* percent responsible? It seemed as random as picking the lottery numbers—especially since, to talk to them, each of the doctors involved had felt the full measure of that horror show that was the final week of Celia Dean's life. There were days when he couldn't get past the sight of those colleagues he had called his friends censuring him, because even as he sat there in front of them without a lawyer—he refused to believe he needed one: these were his *friends*—he could see what was behind it.

He was sixty and close to retirement; they were younger and had things like the hospital's image and public opinion to consider—they had to be perceived as *doing something*, no matter how damaging, if only to preempt any kind of unpleasantness coming at them from the community. It never came, but neither did an apology. These colleagues had dressed themselves in the rags of Alexander Kemp's reputation, and they discovered they liked the fit.

His malpractice premiums doubled.

At no time did anyone say what was extremely clear to her father: that what had happened to him looked very much like what had happened to Celia Dean. At every step in the parallel cases of Alexander Kemp and Celia Dean, what could go wrong went horribly wrong. Her fate was his. Only Celia Dean had simply died. Nan's father grew paranoid, and, after a couple of sullen years, he suddenly quit what was left of his practice. There were days he felt those stones all over again, bruising places inside him that had nothing to do with anatomy—nothing, even, to do with the family and friends of Celia Dean.

He stopped playing Chopin. He stopped playing everything. He cleans the piano three times a week, which takes him most of the day. He likes Jimmy Kimmel. He eats fried bologna sandwiches while he dances a paper clip up and down his knuckles. Her mother says sometimes he drives to other hospitals in other places and just stands outside the newborn nursery windows and looks at the babies. Nobody knows him in these places—they just think he's a grandpa. An ambling, shambling old grandpa. "Marian, I ask you," Nan pushed away her cup, "who do I sue for the loss of my father?"

Philip Morris?

No lung cancer.

General Motors?

No airbag head-butt.

American Airlines?

No breakup, no freefall, no boxcutters.

CHAPTER TEN

Dow Corning?

No breast implants.

McDonald's?

No lap full of coffee.

Frito-Lay?

No tight pants.

Smith & Wesson?

No suicide.

"Where can I set my bag of blame?"

At the feet of all the Kelvin O'Malleys who stink up a courtroom? At the feet of all the Barrett Rances and Eve Terhunes who never turn to look at the mess they leave behind? They sat looking at each other. Then Nan shot up an eyebrow and opened her hands wide, waiting. "I don't know, Nan," said Marian, jerking her head toward the counter at the back of the Grange eatery, where burgers and brats and dogs and kraut were still getting slung onto plates, "but I think you should ask Jonelle. She'll know."

Chapter Eleven

They turned down the volume on the clanging calliope music by getting past the midway, where the 4-H animal barns were lined up. Without looking at the signs over the barn doors as they strolled along, they tried to guess the occupants based only on snuffling, clucking, lowing, and just how bad the smell was.

"Pigs."

"Cows."

"Chickens."

"Goats."

"Guess again."

"Sheep."

"Correct."

"Nothing."

"Guess again."

"Rabbits!"

"Hey, you can take the girl out of the Main Line, but—"

For a buck, they could milk a goat. For ten, they could buy a floppy-eared rabbit. Baby strollers chewed over the straw strewn in the open doorways, where kids pleaded with their slack-faced parents—a gyro sandwich just before the Demon's Revenge will produce that look—to buy them a baby goat, a baby rabbit, a baby pig, a chick. They got to the last barn, far enough away from the carnival rides, where everything slowed down.

The animals were going nowhere, none of them, standing for hours in their pens and stalls, turning to the silly fairgoers what really seemed like

CHAPTER ELEVEN

a single face of calm acceptance. Marian could tell them about Beth Ann Prescott, and they'd listen and continue nibbling on her sleeve in a way even the wise Jonelle would admire. Nan stopped to watch a goat get milked by an eight-year-old boy while Marian waited just outside the barn. Late afternoon shadows cut the heat by a little bit. The air was changing in some way she couldn't figure, but if she were a barnyard animal, she'd know better than to try.

Just past the barns were the show rings, where the Junior Fair was in the middle of a horse competition. Some spectators sat in the stands on the far side of the show ring, but there were a few lined up along the weather-beaten split rail fence. One was Jack Girard, in jeans and a white oxford shirt with the sleeves rolled up, leaning against the rail. He was alone. When Marian drew alongside him, he planted a kiss on her right cheek. "*Marian*," he said in one of those tones you use when your pup has peed on the kitchen floor.

"Jack."

"I told Tom Minnifer, my foreman, I'd watch his girl Annie ride." Then they both turned to the show ring, which was empty. The conversation stalled.

Her hands, clutching the rail for no good reason, looked tiny. "It's good to see you," she squeezed out.

"You sound surprised."

She gave him a sidelong look. "Only that I said it."

"In that case, thanks." Over a raspy PA system, an announcer with a folksy monotone garbled that next up was rider 141.

"I'm sorry about Beth."

"So am I. Did you catch up with Rodie?"

Rider 141 trotted toward the ring. "I sang him to sleep."

"Lucky him."

He said it pretty straight, which made Marian nervous, so she cranked up the Warner Deflector Shields and did her conversational ploy of making no sense whatsoever. "If I don't turn up something pretty soon, I'll get out the trawler and the big nets."

Somehow, she didn't shake him off. "If you need any help—"

"I don't. Not yet. I really don't."

"Okay."

"Look, I'm sorry." She kicked the fencepost. "I'm in the damn dark, that's all."

"Oh," he said. "You mean Beth." He was actually trying not to smile. There were sweet little hollows—in Wade County, they're called hollers—under his cheekbones, and she was liking the way his skin was kind of tight across his jaw. She could count just about every pore where he shaved off a hair every morning, and she smelled the warm, vague drift of patchouli she thought of when she thought of him; only her damn dumb hands were like cudgels, and she couldn't lift so much as one of them to touch his wonderful face.

"What are you going to do without Beth Prescott?"

"Dad's going into respite care tomorrow."

"Can't you find someone else?"

"When I get back from Denver, I will."

"You're going to Denver?"

"I'm leaving Saturday for three weeks."

Why did she feel like shrieking?

Girard tipped his head toward the show ring. "There's Annie Minnifer." Riding a large dapple gray, a young teen in a black cowboy hat cantered toward the first barrel.

"Is it business?"

He shook his head. "I'm seeing some old friends, including my ex-wife. Claire."

"Lucky her," Marian said before she could stop herself. All she had to do was look at him, just turn her head and look him in the eye, and her time in Carthage would suddenly become very different. It might even include some sex. Instead, she tried to look offhand, like she had grown up in Montana, where girls jumped over barrels every damn day of the year. With or without horses. She felt Girard give up on her and lean against the rail, watching Annie Minnifer take her horse through the course, the silver bangles around the crown on her hat shining.

As the girl finished her run to applause—which was more than Marian

CHAPTER ELEVEN

knew she herself would ever get based on how she ran her love life—she felt so sad she wanted to kick a few more fenceposts. It had something to do with where the sun was bleeding out all ragged and white through the haze and something to do with the soft, trusting look of all those farm animals penned in the cool barns behind them. After four months of overwork and bad sleep, she had Jack Girard just inches away from her, and she couldn't close the gap. In the order of things, a sissy pants private dick falls somewhere below the farm animals, that was for sure. So far below, in fact, not even Jonelle could find her with her ladle full of baked beans à la Grange. Because there wasn't a farm animal worth its little cloven hooves that didn't look at the hand that feeds and the hand that slaughters with the same unchanging eye. It was a bravery, Marian told herself, she would never know anything about.

Nan came over, she and Girard shook hands, and Marian explained to him that Nan was defending David Barish in a civil suit. Girard was interested, making supportive noises. Nan got all modest and said something about how it's a living she'd really rather not make, and in an ideal world, she'd be defending parklands against polluters, but so it goes, and just then a funnel cake—she said, turning away—would hit all sorts of spots. And at that moment, as the rain started, Marian did the worst possible thing she could do: she went with Nan.

On the way home from Tulip Time, she had fallen into a kind of lethargy that had something to do with complete fatalism about Girard, magnificent futility about Beth Prescott, and that second funnel cake. Maybe tracking down Flyboy would justify her existence. She Googled the Catholic church the cheery Rose had mentioned and headed across town.

* * *

St. Lydmila's was a small, trim brick church tucked into a sleepy residential street. The walkway was shaded by young maples, and urns of pink and red begonias flanked the front steps. Off to the right was a wide, gently sloping ADA ramp. Marian took the steps two at a time in soft splashes left over from the rain. Inside was the ponderous silence she remembered from her Catholic girlhood. Bells just fading, incense just lingering, the air just cooling, statues caught in the stillness of the ages. It all came back, how quickly everything in church moved off into mysteries she could never quite penetrate. Did something linger, like frankincense, or was it only a memory? When does the pitch of a bell fade for good from the Mass? It's the air, the air, Marian stood with her hands in her pockets, looking around. The air keeps it all: the smells, the sounds, the sins, the histories—sometimes even the quiet heroics.

"Can I help you?"

The voice startled Marian, and she whirled. A middle-aged priest, black shirt, gray pants, clerical collar. He was carrying a Target bag with groceries. She liked him already. "I'm Marian Warner."

"Father Pete."

"I'm looking for Flyboy."

"Ah." He shifted the bag, then squinted at her. "You from the county?"

A beat. "Do you mean social services?"

He gave her a quick nod. "Flyboy's new job coach?"

Marian smiled. "No. Although, from what I hear, you might be Flyboy's new job coach."

He lifted the groceries just high enough to give his cheek a scratch. "Well," he said cheerfully, "our Flyboy needs the job, but he doesn't need the coach. Not any longer." With that, he set the bag down in a pew and out tumbled a green bell pepper. Ignoring it for the moment, Father Pete shook Marian's hand. "You know he lives here?" he said softly.

"Yes. Is he here now?"

"No. More likely, you can catch him here in the mornings, when he cleans for us." Then: "What's up?"

She blew out air. "I've been hired to investigate Beth Prescott's...death."

His head drooped.

For a moment the two of them stood there, adding the stillness of murderous ages to the full, unseeable air. It felt oddly companionable to Marian. What two people do when they agree there are no words. "And," said the priest finally, "Flyboy can help?"

CHAPTER ELEVEN

"Possibly." How much should she tell him? Flyboy's strange familiarity with Beth Prescott? The neighbor's catching sight of him hanging around her apartment?

"Are you private?"

"Yes."

"Is he a suspect?"

She couldn't bring herself to say "a person of interest." Instead, she lifted her shoulders slightly. "He might have some information. At this point, that's all I can tell you for sure."

The priest started back toward the narthex, late afternoon sunlight slanting down toward them through the high windows. Motioning for Marian to follow him, he said, "Let's just see if he's home. Although, from what he tells me, rain leads to pizza deliveries." While they walked, he told her that Flyboy's a little slow, takes pride in his work, keeps a lookout for lost cats and dogs, and has friends in the Carthaginian Club who keep a lookout for Flyboy, "if you know what I mean," he smiled.

Through a frosted glass door and into the gentle gloom of a stairwell. "What's that?"

"The Carthaginians? A hiking club."

They clattered together down the steps to the basement, where Father Pete brushed a wall switch, overhead lights flooding the small hallway that led straight into the church social hall—and, to the left, to what he explained was the old custodial quarters. "Still," he said, "really. It's Flyboy's home—" and he went on, "rent-free." The closed door was clean and well-polished. On the wall next to the door frame was a small nameplate: LUCIUS BARKER, Custodian. Underneath, a small hanging sign on blue-washed wood with flowery script: Welcome Friends.

Father Pete knocked.

Nothing.

"Flyboy hikes?"

"More his natural element, I can tell you—" he knocked again— "than Mass." He grinned. They waited, Marian with her hands clasped behind her back. Finally, the priest shrugged. "Not in."

She'd give a lot to be able to look around Flyboy's apartment without either him or the lovely Father Pete keeping her company. "I don't suppose—" She eyed the door.

Smiling, the priest held up a hand. "You understand I can't let you in. But listen," he added suddenly, "when you catch up with him, ask him about the Carthaginians."

"Thanks for the tip."

From the look on the priest's face, she could tell he was puzzling over something. "You know," he said, shaking his head, trying to get clear, and then he said something extraordinary. "I think it might be how he met poor Beth Prescott."

* * *

Eddie Estremera was a lot like life: where you got to wasn't where you were headed. He called just as Marian got back to The Briars and said yeah, he heard about Beth, it's a bitch, and he's got someone there Marian might want to meet. She went off to her room to change into a gold bandeau she then pretty much covered up with a midnight blue satin and organza wraparound top. Jeans kept her humble. The millefiori glass earrings Charlie had brought back for her from Venice kept her happy. She felt incognito. At 10 PM, she climbed into the Volvo, lowered her window, and eased down side streets in the direction of Gringos. She thought she even dozed at a stop sign.

By the time she got to Gringo's, where Eddie's ten-foot neon mustache was blinking away up on the roof, the parking lot was full. Marian parked down toward the dark end. Tomorrow, she'd turn up at St. Lydmila's—hopefully, before any early bird hikes were booked with the Carthaginian Club—and find Lucius Barker, Custodian, at home. Somehow, it had never occurred to her that the pizza delivery guy might know Beth Prescott outside his world of pizza delivery. She could lay out the whole international trade in fake Chinese porcelains, but Flyboy with a life outside of mopping stone floors or making change from pizzas—not so much.

Inside Gringos, the joint was a smoky gauze that made her eyes water,

CHAPTER ELEVEN

and she looked around at typists and truckers yelling to be heard over the jukebox, where even Reba McEntire was really no match for them. Pushing her way through the bimbo blockade, Marian tried hard to keep herself from touching the bustières and bodysuits, the tanks and tattoos. She hadn't rubbed up against that much naked flesh since the eighth-grade gym showers. Relieved to get to the bar, she practically hurled herself at Eddie Estremera, who had been watching her make her way over, his arms angled out stiff on the bar.

Eddie was talking to a big, classy white woman with red dreadlocks that made her look like an Irish setter. She dipped to the side to make room for Marian, but the bar stool next to hers was occupied by a guy in his twenties who resembled a marmot and sat facing out toward the crowd with his little arm crossed. Looked like he'd scrounged a basket full of beer nuts he then didn't pay to wash down. Eddie tapped his shoulder. "Hey you, what's your name?"

"Me?" The guy goggled. "Brandon."

"Brandon, did you pay your cover charge?"

"There's a cover charge?" He reared his head back, skeptical. "There's no cover charge. There's no band!"

"Is that what you think?"

Brandon looked at the Irish setter for help. She was unreadable. "Yeah."

"The cover charge," Eddie went on, "*covers* the time you spend taking up space on one of my bar stools hoping to get lucky without standing anyone a round. That'll be ten dollars—guy by the door with the dog collar and chains, see him?"

"Yeah."

"His name's Lucifer, and he collects. Go take care of it."

Brandon slunk off toward the door, struggling to get his wallet out of his back pocket.

The Irish setter patted the empty stool—Marian slid in place—and gracefully settled her hands back around a glass of blush. "When did you hire Lucifer?" Although she had the kind of low voice that happens to women in their sixties who smoke, she didn't look more than ten years older than

Marian.

"I didn't." Eddie grinned. "I don't know who the guy with the dog collar is, but he looks like he could use ten bucks." The general bar noise suddenly swept over in their direction as Eddie, dressed in a purple cotton shirt, gave Marian a creasy smile and said something by way of introducing the Irish setter that ended in *Toole*. She was wearing a lime green cocktail dress and black fishnet stockings—the kind Tom Warner would actually use to catch fish—that came to an end in a pair of three-inch black patent leather spikes. On her, it looked good.

Behind them, three violently drunk girls with nose rings and naked bellies suddenly appeared, swaying arm in arm, shouting down Reba, "The sunlight," they screamed, "the moonlight, are beyond my control—" The sunlight and moonlight were the least of it, by the looks of them.

As Eddie stretched across the bar, Marian leaned back— "Don't move on my account," he whispered to her in a wisp of Halston For Men, "leastways not in that direction"—and he gave one of the girls a shove. "Take it on over there, ladies. Out of my face or out of my place." Two guys with tattoos the size of placemats saw their opportunity, blew smoke around the girls' faces like it was some kind of foreplay, and herded them off to a far corner.

Marian waved the air. "Have you got a nonsmoking section?"

Eddie looked her in the eye and then down at her feet. "You're on it," he said, lighting up. "What are you drinking, Marian?" His lip moved around his cigarette. "It's on the house. This is a wake." When she didn't answer, Eddie pulled down a bottle of The Dalmore single malt Scotch for her consideration, landing his other hand on his hip. "Sherry cask," he added in a way that made Marian think that was a plus.

"Sure."

"Rocks?"

"Sure."

He poured. "Beth."

"Beth." She drank.

Leaning his elbows on the bar, Eddie opened his hands. "Makes me realize I haven't made nearly enough love yet in this life to wind up a stinker in a

CHAPTER ELEVEN

ditch for some Boy Scouts to fall over."

All three of them sat staring at nothing for a couple of minutes, then Marian heaved a sigh and looked up. Duty called. "What have you got, Eddie?"

"Tell her."

The Irish setter, Ms. Toole, turned her beautiful green eyes on Marian. She was at Gringos that Wednesday night, only she didn't know it was Beth Prescott she saw—she and Eddie only put that part of it together just a little while ago. When she went to fix a run in her pantyhose, the ladies' john was taken, so she went into the kitchen, where there was just Jorge, who's the cook, and this brunette in a blue dress on the phone.

Marian pulled out the picture of Beth and Rodie and set it on the bar. Ms. Toole leaned over it and nodded, saying how she had pulled out a bottle of clear nail polish and was dabbing at the run in the pantyhose while Beth Prescott talked. *We're meeting in an hour, and I don't know how long it will take. I'll call you tomorrow,* she said, then the person on the other end did some talking. *Look, it's two weeks away,* Beth said then, *a lot can happen, and I just want it dropped. You don't have to look at him every day.* Then Beth listened some more. *I'll keep your name out of it, don't worry. I've got enough to say without bringing you up.*

Marian looked at Eddie. "Where were you?"

He made a face. "I guess Beth came in before I got here."

She looked at the Irish setter, at the beautiful, straight nose and full lips that didn't need any help from Botox. "Are you sure about what you heard?"

"It wasn't that much."

"What did you think?"

The woman raised her blush and chuckled. "That someone was about to get the shove." Some poor asshole was at that very moment gargling with Scope and stuffing condoms in his wallet and checking his watch. Meanwhile, the lady was sick of seeing him every day and was just an hour away from dropping him. But by the time he got to her, all he ended up using were his two strong hands around her neck, and for that, he didn't need Scope, and he didn't need Trojans.

133

Eddie stubbed out his cigarette. "Who was she talking to?"

Ms. Toole lifted her wine. "The new quarterback?"

Two things for sure: the person Beth was talking to wasn't the one she met later, but the one on the phone knew the name. "Anything else?" I asked her.

"She told Jorge she owed Eddie for the call. Let him know her phone had died."

Marian found herself wondering exactly what on that Wednesday night was two weeks away— back to Beth's date book—and who it was she saw "every day."

Her lover.

The doctors on her courier route.

Clayton Girard.

Jack...

She knocked back the smoky Dalmore and shuddered, chalking it up to murky college memories about Scotch and nakedness. Just then, a brawny guy in a ponytail came up behind Marian. "Dance?"

Oh, God, as if the day wasn't bad enough. She twisted around and saw that it was Ms. Toole he was asking. The guy was wearing a ratty suede vest over a patch of grizzled chest hair and black spandex biking shorts under leather chaps. The elegant Ms. Toole looked him slowly up and down. "You must be new," was all she said, and with a quick glance at Eddie, legged it slowly with Chaps to a corner where the juke was the brightest thing around and three other couples dance-groped each other to Patsy Cline's going to pieces.

Marian watched Eddie pull a few drafts for the nose rings—whose designated drivers had their hands all over the girls—and slip the bills into the till. Then he came back over. "Helpful?"

"Yes. Thanks. There's one more thing you can do for me."

"Only one?" When he smiled, his cheeks pushed his eyes into crescents.

"Let me see your phone bill." He nodded, his eyes slipping from her face to her neck, mapping her. Strategizing. She let him. It felt just about as good as anything else and a whole lot less complicated. "How's tomorrow?"

CHAPTER ELEVEN

He leaned closer. "How's tonight?"

"Sorry."

"I'm wondering," he said, drawing his finger slowly along the palm of Marian's hand, "what would happen if I followed you out to your car."

"You'd watch me drive away." Snappy, Warner.

"That might depend," he said, looking straight at her lips, "on how close I get."

"In that case, you'd watch me drive away—" she smiled, "over your feet."

He lit a Winston, his eyes never leaving her face. "I don't think so."

"I'm here for information, Eddie."

"For information you pick up the phone."

He was making her nervous. "You're selling more than Mai Tais to typists, aren't you?"

"At the moment," he said, rolling the tip of his cigarette on the edge of the ashtray, "yes. Only what I have in mind is more like your company," he said, "out back."

"Where you'll show me the stars and planets."

Oh, those crescents again. "Only you won't remember what they're called."

"Eddie," Marian sighed, "I'd have to be a whole lot younger—" she pushed away her glass, "or a whole lot older."

"And less depressed."

"No," she said. "More." She told him she'd be by the next day to take a look at his phone bill. "Night, Eddie." As she pushed her way back through the bimbo blockade, Randy Travis was offering to make love to her in a New York minute and take his Texas time about it. When the door to Gringos closed behind her, all she could hear was the thump of an electric bass guitar. Everything else was just a mild, moonless night. Marian headed out across Eddie's parking lot, past all the pickups and Challengers in the pink floodlights.

Crunching across the gravel, she looked past the old split rail fence along the back of the lot, clear into the black fields, where Eddie Estremera proposed to show her the Big Dipper. Then she stopped where the parking lot tapered off at a road swinging down toward a railroad trestle. Somewhere along, there was her car, and she'd have to mention to Eddie that he could use better lighting at this end. When she bumped into the trash can, her foot clinked the empties that had been dumped on the ground.

Marian was just thinking how good a pocket flash would be, when she was suddenly pulled back in a choke hold. "Eddie," she grunted, pissed off. But then the grip tightened—she could just about make out the sleeve of a dark nylon jacket—and she knew it wasn't Eddie. Because the object was to kill her. Sometimes, things are just that clear. She started tearing at the arm angled against her throat, but it was like trying to shift a steel beam. Then she thrashed, jabbing with her elbow, hitting something, maybe ribs, but that only made him yank her free arm up hard against her back, fast, like cracking a wishbone.

Marian cried out, but it got cut off into a gurgle. Then she tried grinding her heel down his shin. *Who taught me these half-assed self-defense moves, anyway?* She flung her leg over the top of the metal trash can and tugged, rattling bottles and cans. He slipped, and they went down. As they hit, he flipped her right under him, and she landed hard, glass empties exploding against the side of her head and arm. She went kind of blank with pain and felt herself seeping into the gravel. The fucker wasn't even breaking a sweat. He was on her, heavy, driving the glass into her like blades, tightening his choke hold. *Let him.* Let him do it before he grinds your eyes into the broken glass. Because it wasn't clear which would come first. Something inside her was loosening, and she was all out of moves.

Chapter Twelve

"Jesus, Marian, look at you."

Someone was rolling her over, someone else lifting her shoulders. Marian's left deltoid felt twanged and floppy. She groaned. "Call the sheriff," she heard herself rasp.

"He's on his way." It sounded like Eddie crouched next to her, holding a bar towel to the side of whatever was left of her head. She couldn't open her eyes and was afraid even to try—they felt swollen with fright or beer dregs, damned if she knew which. "Now I won't say this wouldn't have happened if you'd taken me up on my offer," dab, dab, press, swipe, "but there's a pretty good chance."

"Don't be funny." Marian started to swallow and clutched at his hand. "I've got glass in my mouth."

"Looks like Styrofoam, love, piece of a coffee cup."

She flailed at the Styrofoam in her mouth and started to cry, which sounded a whole lot like gagging. "My arm and my head?"

"Sorry, honey, that's glass. You're a mess."

Marian's hand flopped around on her chest in some kind of inventory and came away smelling like blood and beer—the gold bandeau top was a whole lot more revealing than before—and then she touched her ear. Her earring. No millefiori earring. Her eyes flew open. "Where's my earring?" she wailed.

Eddie shifted on the gravel. "Oh, it's probably around here somewhere with the rest of your ear."

By then, she was blubbering, half-rolling deeper into the lap of— "Who the hell is this?" She tried to sit up.

"Roy Jean Toole," said the red raggy wig leaning over her. The Irish setter.

"Stay back, stay back." Eddie was working on crowd control, the shadows like skyscrapers in a blackout. And she could just about make out the nose rings and their manhandlers —

"Oh, say, she don't look good."

"Minds me a Jimmy Sloog fell under his pa's thresher."

"I'm gonna hurl—"

Eddie deputized somebody. "Chopper, go on and get these folks back inside," he flicked the bar towel in their direction.

The shadow she thought was an Astrovan lurched. "You heard Eddie," he gargled at them, "you heard him --"

Chopper was helping out, viewing the wreck. That was reassuring. Chopper, the nose rings, Eddie, Roy Jean Toole—when all Marian needed was Jonelle. This was even lower than dumpster duty behind Sun Won Fa's in Chinatown.

"I'm a paramedic," Ms. Toole rotated her gently to the right, picking off glass.

"Nice uniform."

She could hear him smile. "Off-duty."

Roomy thighs. She winced, "I'm bleeding all over your fishnets."

"Not to worry, Toots," he said cheerfully, "it's just my third best pair."

Sirens came whooping toward them, only half-way through they sounded like the first two bars of the William Tell Overture. "Phone, Eddie," she brushed at his leg, "it's my phone. My phone." He rolled her half up like a couch cushion, felt around for her purse without making a pass, and grabbed the iPhone, letting her flop back in place.

The sirens were getting closer. Where was Khartoukian when she needed him? Where was O'Malley when she needed him? She was in a blaming mood, dagnabbit, and the Mount Hope Community Ed gal back home was damn well going to hear from her about those silly-ass defense moves that were all fine well and good if your attacker was Placido Domingo. If Marian had to, she'd go all the way to the top—the Grange Ladies.

CHAPTER TWELVE

Eddie took the call. "Marian Warner's office, Eddie speaking." She groaned as he listened, then turned to her. "Do you have a sister?" He held it up to her good ear.

"Marian?" came Joan's voice.

She hacked out one more piece of Styrofoam. "Joanie?"

"Who's Eddie?" Joan's clear voice, sweet and unexcitable. Roy Jean was rotating her like a skewered chicken. "What's going on?"

"I was jumped. I'm okay."

She handed the phone back to Eddie, who got to the point. "Why are you calling?"

Marian slapped at Eddie. "Tell her not to come."

"Don't come." Then: "Who?"

"Tell him not to tell Penelope."

"No Penelope. Marian says no Penelope. Lynn Harper? Ellen Harper?"

"She's cutting my grass."

"Not anymore. She hit a stone in your yard, it popped up and hit her over the eye, and now the ER has to file a claim against your homeowner's insurance."

"*What!*"

Into the phone: "She says, *What!*" He listened, then turned to Marian. "Medicare only pays what's left."

She felt tormented. But it was altogether a good thing to hear Eddie Estremera tell her sister how they had been discussing the universe, and he had figured on continuing their conversation—he'd worked up some hard evidence he thought she'd like by way of added persuasion—and he stepped outside. When he saw some kind of struggle at the end of the parking lot—fist fight, attempted rape, hard to tell, it was so damn dark—he yelled, and a guy took off toward the train trestle.

"You're saying because you can't keep it in your pants," she struggled to sit up, "I'm alive?"

"You might put it that way," Eddie said, looking her over. "I really think part of your ear's gone." His voice dropped. "Very elfin."

THE DAMAGES

* * *

Marian flat-out refused to go by squad to the ER. Khartoukian cursed and spat, then drove her over to Quick, where Jim Carney met them. Rotator cuff injury, he diagnosed. Multiple contusions. Multiple lacerations. Part of her ear was indeed gone. Nicked off. "Sweet little triangle right at the top"—Carney scrutinized it—"but you should get some decent scar tissue there to keep it all together."

What was left of her got injected, cleaned out, and stitched. Nineteen times. Her scalp, her ear, her shoulder, her arm. The way Marian figured it, she had enough Telfa pads on her to find work as a gym mat, and her neck felt like an overinflated tire. Carney grabbed a clinic laundry bag and stuffed in her bloody clothes and enough Tylenol #3 samples to float her to the Fourth of July, telling Marian to rest the cuff and see him in the office tomorrow afternoon.

"On the whole," she said, sounding like Joe Cocker on a bad day, "I'm making out better than Beth Prescott"—which was her first complete sentence in maybe two hours.

Jim Carney said nothing.

She left Quick wearing scrubs, staggering from a combination of codeine and exhaustion. Getting into the front of Khartoukian's patrol car was like pulling bamboo through wet cement. "The only place you go alone," he shaped her into an upright position, "is to the john, you understand me?"

"Don't yell. I've got Betadine in my hair."

Barbara Hauser put her to bed with only the light from the hall while Khartoukian and Nan Kemp stood in the doorway discussing whether it was too late to go out for a drink. Marian moaned. *I look like something out of a crewel kit, and they're making a date.* "You want me to call Charlie?" Barbara said softly into her non-elfin ear as her eyes closed.

"Hell, no," she heard herself say, drifting, remembering his crack about always bailing her out. She rolled over, wincing, to face the window. Lightning pulsed, casting the alley in bright shadows. Then came a dull rumble. During the night, her shoulder was throbbing, and Marian could

CHAPTER TWELVE

swear Carney had stitched the left half of her body to the right, but she said to hell with the codeine and pushed the packets across the nightstand. Once she thought she saw Barbara closing the window against the rain battering the glass, and once she thought she saw Jack Girard.

* * *

By 5:35, the codeine had worn off, and her sheets were in a sweaty twist. Outside it was still dark, although Marian could make out the darker shape of the house across the alley, and she heard a meadowlark out there somewhere in the thinning darkness. She kicked off the sheets and grabbed the satin robe she figured was Barbara Hauser's since it was two sizes too big. Everything hurt. And what didn't hurt was probably missing. Hunched over, she padded her way to the hall bathroom. If she saw a tinker or tailor, she'd hurl a doorstop at him.

A nightlight plugged into the outlet over the toilet was all the light Marian could stand, so she used the john in a whopping eight watts. She couldn't go back to bed, where all she had to look forward to was more sweaty half-sleep in medicinal-smelling sheets. It felt about as good as anything possibly could at 5:35 in the morning with nineteen stitches in her, to lean, hungry, and shaky, against the small window. Wrapping the borrowed robe closer, she stared out at the ragged black outline of trees against the night sky.

Someone damn near killed her.

And the only thing that had gotten her out of the Gringos' parking lot alive was Eddie Estremera's libido. It's always nice to know you can count on something. It was strange just how profoundly neutral she felt about the whole thing. Not doped, not scared, not even full of the hysterical reformations she promised the almighty air whenever she scraped by with something. The fact was, Marian had nearly died outside a roadhouse in Carthage, Ohio, unattached and peculiarly employed, with Joan in line for the payout on her measly life insurance policy. Hell, Beth Prescott, dead at twenty-seven down a ravine, had more going for her. A hometown, a family, a lover, two jobs, and a damn ribbon for twirling. And as good a place as any to head back to dust and bone under a cover of wild raspberries, before the ever-loving interference of man.

Marian started out of the bathroom, then slipped back inside when the dim wall sconces in the hall went on and the stairs creaked. Someone was coming up. She couldn't face anybody, not even a Hauser, kind as they were. When the voices stopped down the hall, she peeked out through the narrow opening. It was Nan, in front of the door to her room, still in her silk suit, which looked like it had spent the last six hours balled up under a bed.

With her was Khartoukian, his back turned, in jeans and a red checkered shirt. They both looked loose and exhausted. "Can you get some sleep?" he said.

Nan's hands slid low on his hips. "Sleep's something I can get any time," she told him with a smile. Then they kissed in that woozy way when there's already been a whole lot of it.

"See you around the courthouse, Counselor." He left, and the door to Nan's room closed slowly behind her.

* * *

"Where do you think you're going?" Barbara Hauser blocked her way, like Marian was trying to sneak out without paying her bill.

"To work."

The woman looked menacing with a full carafe of coffee. "You look like hell."

"Thanks. That's better than I feel."

"You should be in bed."

"I should be lots of places, but here's where I am." Marian felt in her pants pocket for her car keys and wallet. Still there. So were her hips. It was going to be a slow inventory.

Barbara wasn't stepping aside. "Call Jack."

"What for?"

"He said he'd be back at eight. He had to check on his father."

There was a left rib that felt pretty sore, but she wasn't about to mention

CHAPTER TWELVE

it to a woman who, at an easy six feet and 175 pounds, could force-march her back upstairs. She had to fall back on wiles. The key was to appear ambulatory just long enough to put that screen door between herself and Barbara Hauser. "Tell him I'm sorry I missed him."

"He sat here all night."

Marian bit her lip, which was too bad because up to that moment, it was just about the only part of her that hadn't been hurting. "Well, tell him thanks from me, okay?" she said, wincing as she started to pull on her navy V-neck sweater.

Barbara set down the coffee. "You tell him," she said, reaching for her. "Here, let me help."

"I can do it."

"You can't lift your arm higher than your waist—"

"Well, I've got to start sometime," said Marian, shoving her arm through the sleeve with a sharp cry.

"Oh, Marian—"

"See you later, Barbara."

"Take a muffin, for God's sake." She thrust one at her. "Cy, get Jack on the phone. *Cy—*"

Marian slipped out, the kitchen screen door slapping behind her. It was only 7:40 and already the air felt bright and gauzy. As she edged her way down the driveway in search of the car, she felt caved in. Pulverized. Like her body tissue had been pulped and processed, then pumped back under her skin any which way. All a shower had managed to do was give her the comfort of routine, because it sure hadn't improved her looks, although the one-handed shampoo to get rid of the dirt and Betadine stains was totally worth it—the hell with the stitches.

Marian found the Volvo on the street, where some kind soul had brought it back from Gringos. Clamping Barbara's carrot muffin with her teeth, she swung the car around and headed slowly into town in the grips of a caffeine imperative. Cycle shop, camera shop, tobacco shop, copy center, bank, bank, bank—don't any of these people drink coffee? Could there possibly be one intersection in all of the United States that Starbucks hadn't found? And then she saw it: the Princess of Wales Tea Shoppe.

She lurched into the same spot as yesterday and lunged inside. The place was empty except for all the Victorian bric-a-brac an owner had spent a lot of time collecting—porcelain teapots, porcelain cherubs, porcelain music boxes. A waitress dressed in a wench costume rustled over with her hands dug in at her waist like she wanted to break out in a naughty song, until she got a good look at her only customer—Marian—and decided she was the poster girl for the Domestic Violence hotline.

Marian stood up taller. "Got any coffee?" When you've seen the Devil, or at any rate, the sleeve of his blue nylon jacket, your social skills take a header. The wench, whose lacy name pin said MAUREEN CALL ME MO, tried to interest her in a seat festooned with beaded bows, scones with lemon curd, and any one of a dozen different black or green teas.

But Marian didn't want to play tea party, so she slouched and asked again if they had any coffee. MAUREEN CALL ME MO suddenly understood that she was dealing with a desperado and backed away, saying, "Yes, yes, I do believe we can fix you right up." What Marian wanted to tell her was that it would take more than Chock Full o' Nuts to fix her right up, but instead, she murmured something that reminded her of the cinematic moment when the blind man was going to ladle some nice soup into the Frankenstein monster's bowl. "Great," she told MO, her eyes narrowing, "make it large, black, and put a lid on it. The coffee, I mean."

It took nearly an hour at the Sheriff's office to file a report on the attack. The deputy they sent her to sported an Adam's apple the size of a golf ball and zero keyboarding skills. Khartoukian was nowhere, which was fine with her. Marian sipped her coffee and wondered if he was home washing his sheets while the deputy at a vintage IBM Selectric next to her was using enough Wite-Out to drive up the stock. Starbucks and Apple, that's what this town needed.

When she walked back out into the June morning, it was 9:27. Enough time to get to St. Lydmila's and collar Flyboy? She'd give it a shot. At the very least, she could check to see if Father Pete remembered to pick up his green pepper. Time well spent. Marian parked across from the proud little church

CHAPTER TWELVE

on Church Street and legged it up the front steps. Inside, she headed straight for the peaceful gloom of the stairwell and halfway down, ran into a figure slumped on the lower steps. Even the statues one flight up couldn't match the motionless Flyboy, dressed in baggy work pants and a long-sleeved blue tee shirt. Today, no red Pizza Shack vest. A wet mop lay puddling on the floor, and the day's newspaper was a sopping mess pulled apart by angry hands, hurled into a sudsy pail. Beth's murder had hit the front page of Charlie's paper.

"Flyboy?" she said quietly, sitting down beside him, noticing his clenched hands and the open door to his rent-free apartment just across the hall.

Slowly, Lucius Barker turned to look at her, trying to place her. "I know you."

His eyes were red. Maybe she should go look for Father Pete. Instead, she nodded. "The other day, at Beth Prescott's. Her brother hired me to look for her."

"Rodie." He sighed, staring straight ahead. Then: "Before."

A beat. "Before they found her. Yes."

All he could do was grunt.

Finally, Marian spoke. "I'm sorry about Beth Prescott."

"Miz Elizabeth." He squinted up at the low ceiling, looking either for light or sense.

"Did—you hike with Miz Elizabeth?"

Suddenly, Flyboy grabbed Marian's sleeve. "She never left me behind. I like to look at things, you know? See things I don't see when I work the Shack. Or here. She was plenty fast, that's for sure, but she mostly stuck with me."

"While you looked around."

"You bet," added Flyboy with some spirit. "And then we made the plans for the big surprise. Her birthday's coming up end of this week." He added solemnly, "She'd be twenty-eight. Us Carthaginians always make the birthdays special. The birthday girl gets to pick the trail, and we all eat deluxe pizzas, courtesy of the Shack and the club treasury, and the gift has to be one-of-a-kind."

"No two alike."

"You got that right." He lowered his voice. "It gets pretty tricky." He leaned closer to me and dropped his voice to a whisper. "Some people are hard to pick out for, if you know what I mean."

"I do."

Suddenly, Flyboy bounded up off the stairs and started to pace. "And now, what do we do? Gina Marie made the card, and I got these pictures for the Shutterfly thing."

"What pictures, Flyboy?"

He waved his hands. "I had this idea about twenty-four hours of Miz Elizabeth." Marian followed him into his apartment. "Samuel Bart was writing the—the—words for each of them, and then we'd order it." He was glad he started a few weeks ago because it proved hard to get a few of the twenty-four. The Carthaginians had to give him permission, at last, to take pictures of her condo at 2, 3, and 4 in the morning, and they would just label it "sleeping."

Marian glanced quickly around Flyboy's apartment. Spotless, two chairs carefully set at a small drop-leaf table, one Sierra Club mug, one dinner plate, one skillet, one saucepan, one electric tea kettle. A twin bed made up with military precision. A multi-colored crocheted throw folded over the back of a gold brocaded loveseat. A few books, from what she could tell, all on hiking. Hiking the Pacific Coast Trail, hiking the Camino de Santiago, hiking the Cotswolds. Framed and mounted on the wall was an Employee of the Month citation from Pizza Shack. A Crucifix, obscured by drooping palms, and an 8x10 photo matted and framed with the etched heading, The Carthaginian Club 2023.

Two rows of hikers on a spring trek in the Wade County hillside. While Flyboy slipped a couple of dozen photos from a vinyl case onto his table, Marian stepped closer to the club photo. There was Flyboy, in the back row with the other tall hikers, his poles raised high over his smiling face. And there was Beth Prescott, in the front and on the far end of the photo, wearing boots and a jaunty beret. Behind them, buds greened up the day, beneath them, what was left of the last snowfall.

CHAPTER TWELVE

She went over to the spread on the table. Flyboy pursed his lips, looking at the only jumble in his small living space. Then, crossing his arms tightly over his chest, he made what seemed like a shameful admission. "I never did get 10 o'clock. In the morning! It was the final one, the only one I still needed, and then Miz Elizabeth was just never around. I didn't see her anywhere. Not anywhere at all."

Suddenly, as he remembered the murder, he was crestfallen.

Marian had a thought as her fingers lightly worked their way through the twenty-three photos. "Did you take any shots, say, even close to ten in the morning? Say, 9:30?"

He was shaking his head in abject refusal. "Wouldn't count."

"Well, you do have all the 'sleeping' photos, when really, you're just guessing."

"What do you mean?"

"Maybe she was actually on a train in California, where it was not even midnight."

He almost smiled. "Or—or—maybe she was inside but binge-watching something."

"And not sleeping at all."

"Well," said Flyboy reasonably, "I did get a couple of 'resting' shots." His long pale fingers pushed through photo after photo until he came to one of Beth Ann Prescott sacked out in the middle of the day in a lounge chair in the Girards' backyard, and one of Beth's Kia Soul parked in a nearly empty lot at dusk, and one of Beth on a bench outside Mercy Hospital, cross-legged, earbuds inserted, her head tilted back, an open and empty personal pan pizza box from Pizza Shack at her side.

"Now, wait just a second, Flyboy." She made herself look skeptical.

He shot her a crafty look.

Marian went on. "This," she tapped the Mercy Hospital shot with the backs of her fingers. "This could just as easily be captioned 'Eating' or 'Listening to Music,' not necessarily 'Resting' at all."

Found out, he laughed with delight and gave her a little push.

"Don't worry about ten in the morning. Maybe her friends happen to have one. You can ask." Or maybe, she thought with a pang, as Father Pete rapped lightly on the open door, maybe Beth Prescott's funeral will get scheduled for ten AM.

The priest stared at her. "What happened to you?"

Suddenly alerted, Flyboy looked her over, and she wasn't sure he noticed anything.

"I was jumped." The abridged version.

Flyboy staggered back and scowled at the ceiling. "Bastard," he shouted, then eyed the priest, working up to what he thought could pass for a look of shame.

Killing a smile, Father Pete agreed. "Bastard indeed," was all he said.

It was the best Marian had felt in a day.

Chapter Thirteen

Letting herself into the Barish trial, Marian found Nan looking refreshed in black silk palazzo pants and an Errol Flynn white blouse. Kelvin O'Malley, standing near the jury box, turned and gave Marian a quick look. She got the idea he wanted to hand her his business card. A TV on a high, metal stand had been rolled to the center of the courtroom, and she had a quick, fizzy hope that everyone had decided just to kick back for a while and watch a little *Queer Eye*, where Jonathan could get across to the pig farmer the importance of moisturizing his outdoor hide, or Tan could suggest to Craig Clemm that white socks are for basketball and absolutely nowhere else on God's green Earth. But it took her all of ten seconds to see that the video described a typical day in the life of Courtney Clemm.

The voice-over was Jeannie's as Craig helped Courtney brush her teeth— "Courtney hates this part, don't you, honey?" the voice said, and a couple of jurors chuckled, O'Malley giving them a comical look that said *that's a four-year-old for you*—and the camera then cut to Courtney easing out of her wheelchair, all smiles in her Paw Patrol pajamas, dragging herself over to her mattress on the floor. The little girl shouldered her way across her *Frozen* sheets and flipped over, grinning, while the voice-over said, "Good goin', honey, do you want to hear a story?"

The video went on to show Courtney riding a school bus to Vanguard School, Courtney being wheeled by Jeannie around their trailer park, and Courtney being pushed up the narrow ramp into their trailer while a Craig voice-over explained how they could really use a regular house. Nan looked neutral. Even Dave Barish looked neutral. But she'd bet every stitch on her head that it was a tough look for him to manage.

Marian slipped out into the lobby to make some phone calls, catching Joan heading into a meeting where—she said airily—she'd be addressing a bunch of museum directors on the latest issues in certifying the gifts by the de Vries estate collection of Russian samovars. "I'm damn sick of Russian samovars, Sis," Joan blurted. "Goddamn it, I wish you were here. From the looks of these folks, I could use you as a bodyguard."

"What about the Poe extortion?"

"A couple of days left before it goes up in smoke. We're not paying." Then: "How the hell are you?"

Marian laughed weakly, told Joan she was getting along okay, Joan said so was she, and they promised to share a Pu Pu Platter for Two when the Prescott case was over. "I'll get there as soon as I can."

Then she called Jim Carney's office on Hospital Way to see if she could change the 3:30 appointment he had made for her to 1:30 instead, but the front office person told Marian that Dr. Carney only has morning office hours at that location on Thursdays; maybe he meant she's supposed to see him at Quick? Marian then called Quick, where the scheduler told her she's totally sorry, but no Marian Warner is down on the schedule, and even if you were, you couldn't come in earlier because Dr. Carney doesn't start seeing patients until three on Thursday afternoons.

"Well, can you have him call me with a time?"

She was hit upside the head. "For an *appointment?*"

"Right." He called Beth. He does those things.

"We have me for that."

"What about the other—"

"They have me for that, too."

Why was it so hard? Marian rubbed her eyes. The man falls through the cracks one day a week while the offended little scheduler went on about how he never makes his own appointments, and he never makes reminder calls. "We have a system," she said, "and he knows better than to go fooling with it,"—making him sound like a third-grader trying to disarm a bomb—

CHAPTER THIRTEEN

"but if you want to come in at 3:30, he'll just have to work you in somehow."

Marian rolled her eyes. 3:30 was the time of the original appointment—the scheduler at Quick was actually saying he was going to have to work her in at the time of her original appointment—and Marian had the feeling she had just fallen down the rabbit hole and was arguing with the Red Queen. By the time she disconnected five seconds later, she didn't know whether she had an appointment at all—or whether she even gave half a damn.

Finally, she called Ernie Diodakis at home to find out if they still wanted to keep her on the case, and Rodie said what Marian thought he would—after first dropping the phone—that yeah, he wanted her to stay with it. "It's too late for Beth, but it's still the right thing." His voice started to trail off. "And I'm sorry for what that fucker did to you."

"How did you—"

"Hang on."

The phone got passed. "Marian?" It was Jack Girard.

She mumbled something.

"Where are you?" He sounded tense and maybe a little bit pissed.

"I'm at work." She looked around the rotunda. "In my office." She'd really have to work on getting back her irony. Last she saw of it, irony was sinking into the the gravel outside Gringos—along with blood, earring, and part of her ear.

"Don't tell me you're fine."

"I won't, I'm not. But I can work."

He exhaled. "I'd like you to go back to Cy and Barbara's."

"Not likely."

"Then I want to see you later."

"Okay."

"When? No more stalling, Marian. Not after last night."

"Whenever. I'll find you."

"After dark," he went on, "until they get this guy, plan on company. Like it or not. Mine or an off-duty cop's. Your choice. Save your solitude for when this is over and you're back home, okay? I'm not going to have you dead on my doorstep." His voice dropped. "Or anywhere else."

It felt good to smile. "It lets me off too easy."

"So does that remark."

He was right. "I'll be careful," she told him. "And I'll find you."

But first, she'd clock the drive from Gringos to Trillium, that Wade County spot for four-star food and five-star trysts. Marian got into the Volvo, lowered all the windows and FM station-hopped until she got the local time and temp, 78 degrees at 10 AM. Heading north on Highway Eight, she hit State Highway 53 and found the entrance to Hopewell Range State Park about fifteen minutes east. Crossing the other side of the highway, she passed a rest area 200 feet from the park entrance and drove into the park. According to the map, if she stayed on Adena Ridge Road, sooner or later, she'd come out at Trillium. And if she could do it in half an hour, she could go back to Barbara Hauser and strut around her kitchen.

Then Marian glanced at her watch. Right—if she's airborne.

Marian was already thirty-five minutes from Gringos, and she wasn't even halfway through the park. She passed the ranger station, the maintenance yard, and a couple of roads pointing off to places called the Buckeye Picnic Grove and the Great Seal Shelter House. The road took her higher, where the air changed, and the fragrance of black locust blossoms drifted in. Finally, the sky took over, the white-blue of humid days when the air wiggles out of reach, and she slowed.

It was the highest point in Hopewell Range State Park, and the road bulged out where cars could pull over. *Scenic Overlook,* the sign pointed into the woods along the ridge. Where Beth Prescott had been dumped, by the looks of the sheriff's two black and whites parked side by side. Not all that scenic, after all. Marian swung the Volvo around but didn't get out. Crime labbers, was her guess, still gleaning for physical evidence.

She squinted down the trail, but it dipped out of sight and Marian couldn't tell a thing about the place where Beth had been lying for the past two weeks, missing work, missing appointments. Beth, the runner-up in twirling. Beth, the runner-up for Tulip Time Queen. The one you use when the good one goes flat. Now appearing in a second-rate death, falling through a final crack. Like Jim Carney on Thursdays.

CHAPTER THIRTEEN

Like Jim.

Slowly, she shifted into Drive and headed back to Carthage.

* * *

Parking a few doors down from The Briars, Marian hobbled far enough up the driveway to see that Barbara's Blazer was gone and Cy was on his haunches in the back garden, weeding and singing "I'm Called Little Buttercup." In the wide-brimmed straw hat and gardening clogs, he looked a lot like his wife. Marian got a whiff of lilac from the bush by the back door, but then got a bigger whiff of the paper mill, and her eyes started to water. She slunk into The Briars through the kitchen door, careful not to let it slam, and pocketed a scone as she eased her way through Barbara's command center.

The parlor was empty.

Marian did a two-footed stump up the stairs, where all she found was a delicious dead quiet. Not a flush, a slam, or a bleat anywhere. In her room at the back of the Briars she dug out Beth Prescott's Rubbermaid bin from the blankets tossed off the bed. The sheer curtains were billowing lightly in the breeze. Settling onto her bed, she grabbed her phone and called in for Beth's new messages. There were three.

The Carthage Public Library announced the new James Patterson Beth had placed on reserve was waiting for her up at the front. Weezie Tiller from the hospital said in a heavy-breathing panic that she sure as shoot thinks Beth's out of a job, but does she want to go in on Narkeytah's birthday present, seeing as they're friends and all, which is a gift card to Olive Garden? Then there was the final message. "This here's Jeannie Clemm, and my number's 774-0406, thanks, bye." Click. *Jeannie Clemm?* What was the connection? Not intimate—Jeannie had left too much information.

Then Marian plugged in the answering machine and listened again to what she'd left Hopewell Range to hear. "Hi, Beth," pause, "this is Dr. Carney calling, to—" he spun it out slowly, choosing carefully, "see how you're doing and remind you of our—" short pause—"appointment for 1:30 tomorrow

153

afternoon." The message was left the Wednesday Beth Prescott disappeared, putting the appointment on a Thursday.

She listened to Jim Carney's message two more times. *Hi, Beth, this is Dr. Carney calling, to see how you're doing and remind you of our appointment for 1:30 tomorrow afternoon.* He was a good-natured kind of a guy, all right, but on Beth Prescott's message machine the good doctor was being funny. He was choosing his words carefully because he was being funny. A quick reminder call to a patient—only that wasn't how his office worked. *We have appointment secretaries for that*, the indignant scheduler had said. *He never makes his own appointments, and he never makes reminder calls.*

Marian pulled out her phone and tapped in the number for Jim Carney's office on Hospital Way. When the front office person answered, she put on her best Wade County accent. "This here's Sandy in the canny sheriff's office investigating the movements of one of your patients. Beth Prescott?"

"Oh, we all just read about it in the *Toiler*. Terrible thing. What can we do?"

"Well, I'll tell you. A friend of the deceased thought Beth Prescott had a doctor's appointment last Thursday or Friday in May. Could you please check?"

"Certainly, be happy to," she said, and I heard fingers tapping away at a keyboard. Silence. More tapping. Then: "Dr. Carney's down for nothing here on Thursday the 26th—but then, he never sees patients Thursday afternoons—and Friday, Friday, let's see. No Beth Prescott down any time at all that day, sorry."

"Must have been another doctor, ma'am, thank you kindly."

Only it wasn't.

She had the right one. It was a reminder call, all right, but Jim Carney wasn't reminding his patient. He was reminding his lover. The operas, the fancy furniture, the name too important to cough up, even to Lila. She felt shaky. Her hand flew to her ear, then eased down over her shoulder. Criminy. Had he really almost killed her last night just to stitch her up half an hour later? *Why?* It didn't make sense. Marian lurched into the hall bathroom, suddenly sick to her stomach, but nothing came. Then she

CHAPTER THIRTEEN

rested her head against the cold porcelain rim of the bowl, remembering Khartoukian when he told her they had found Beth's body: *Carney's having fits. He says he won't autopsy someone he knows.*

That wasn't why he was having fits.

* * *

On her way back to the entrance of Hopewell Range State Park, she called in for her own voicemail messages. There were four. One was from Charlie, who sounded incoherent with anger, and the second was from Lila Ketchum, who just blubbered for a bit, sniffed she'd call back later, then hung up. Eddie Estremera left a five-second message about his phone bill, and the last was from Jack Girard, who said he'd be in and out of the office all afternoon, but it's still the best bet in terms of keeping her promise. Nothing from Jonelle who could do her all sorts of good by just saying there, there, honey, that there lunatic don't stand a fly's chance in my kitchen up against such a fine B-B-Q Beef eater like yourself.

As Marian passed Gringos she felt a high, vast vagueness set in, and she worried it was just a matter of time before she collapsed. There's only so much she could do on four months of bad sleep and a pretty fair assault. Not all the carrots in Barbara Hauser's Vitamix could shore up an energy she no longer had. She dialed The Briars, just to round out the message pick-up, and got Barbara, who sounded like she was stacking cans.

"Briars."

"Barbara, it's Marian."

She groaned. "God, have you got messages. Just a sec." The phone jiggled, slammed against something, and got put back up to her ear. "Okay. Khartoukian called and said you're a damn fool, and if he gets his hands on you, he's going to violate your civil rights."

Marian rubbed her head. "That's love for you."

"He loves you?"

"No, I'm just caught in his afterglow."

"Nan Kemp."

"That's the one."

"What?"

"Is she mad at me, too?"

"Not at all. She'll call back."

Marian scratched her chin. "I'm so tired."

"Come back. You've got a nice back room all to yourself. Flaggie and his cretinous humans are off somewhere—"

"Not just yet." For some reason, it didn't sound good.

"Oh," Barbara added. "One last message. Jim Carney."

Her heart pounded. "What about him?"

"He called you. He wants to see you."

She could hardly move her arm. "What about?"

"The stitches, the bruises."

"Is that what he said?"

"That's what he said. He wants to see how you're doing."

Like hell. She made a decision. "Thanks, Barbara. And don't worry about me."

"I don't like the sound of that."

"I mean it. Don't."

"Marian—"

She clicked off, feeling scared. And then she reached the entrance to Hopewell Range State Park. Something from the morning's drive to the ridge had stuck in her brain: the timing. From Gringos to the highest point of the park was roughly forty minutes, too far to finish the trip all the way to Trillium. But not too far to see where a rendezvous thirty minutes away would put her. And on that score, she finally had an idea. Fifteen minutes north from Gringos, then east on 53, and fifteen minutes to the park entrance—and the rest area 200 feet away.

She pulled into it slowly and checked her watch: thirty-two minutes from Gringos. Close enough. As she drove leisurely through the rest area parking lot, where there were spaces for maybe a couple of dozen cars. Only, right then, it was deserted. Getting from Dayton to Wheeling, West Virginia, didn't seem to be a high priority. Marian studied the lot. Had she been there

CHAPTER THIRTEEN

before? It had a familiar feel to it. But then, one rest area was very much like another.

At the center of the rest area was one of those dark-stained wood buildings that houses public johns and snack machines. Outside were a couple of picnic tables invitingly chained to concrete-studded rings, and a glass enclosed map of Ohio and the State Park System. The landscaping consisted of pink rhodies in full bloom.

Neutral ground.

A dump for rich, discarded lovers.

Some poor asshole was about to get the shove, Roy Jean Toole had said. Carney's hot for their Thursday afternoon toss, but Beth's suddenly off him. *You don't have to look at him every day,* she tells the new quarterback. Then she sets up a kiss-off meeting at the rest area, where they weren't likely to be seen at nightfall, the final nod to his standing in the community. But from his point of view, he and Beth would meet, then go in one car through Hopewell Range State Park and into Trillium for a meal—and, maybe, an overnight.

And then Beth told him. And he snapped.

What was it like for Dr. Jim Carney on Monday when Marian found him in his office at Quick and asked him about Beth Prescott, the courier from the hospital lab, who turned up missing? Jim Carney in his crisp oxford blue shirt, with his kind eyes, telling her about his wife Jen (Christ, *Jen*), fine, still teaching, some things never change. And maybe that was the problem.

About Beth, he hadn't been much help. *Maybe she just—took off,* he suggested. Like it was an answer. Then he went on: *friendly, pretty, stuck in a small town.* On Monday, the words didn't mean much, but today, they were packed, all their edges crammed. What had it cost him to reduce the lover he'd killed to a few flip adjectives?

Man, she felt weary.

But she didn't want to be resting alone at the back of The Briars. It had something to do with leaving a sliver of her ear in Eddie Estremera's parking lot and something to do with not being able to make any sense out of a kind-hearted Jim Carney who'd turned into an adulterous, violent creep making a practice out of doing something with his hands other than surgery.

No, she didn't want to be resting in bed at The Briars and didn't want to be standing alone in a highway rest area. A blue Ram Charger zoomed by, going west, no snacks, no pit stops today. Marian didn't want sleep. She wanted help. She needed help. Khartoukian was right—she was a damn fool.

* * *

Marian hit the water hard, feeling the pain scatter like gravel and glass. It was cold. Girard was right. He had told her so back in January when they stood on the snowy slope of the gravel pit, where Charlie's girlfriend was killed. And ever since then, she had stayed away from Carthage, from Jack Girard, and from the gravel pit. What was stuck in the broken ice four months ago was mourned and—oh, yes—accounted for, she had seen to that.

Only sometimes now in the middle of the night, she'd open her eyes, staring, like they'd never been closed at all, wondering how the hell she could still feel skin—because as far as she could tell, whole slices of her had fallen away. Part of her was left behind in the broken ice, and part of her in the bloody hall, and all the rest of her was still crouched, speechless, somewhere with Jack Girard in the falling snow.

Marian swam down, feeling kind of crippled, pushing the water aside, bubbles rolling back over her cheeks. And she swam down still farther until the pressure hurt her ears. Below her, blots of daylight flickered out of reach; then she kicked up toward the quivering white rim of air. To the place where the blue heat was life, cramped and messy and wonderful. Marian broke the surface, gasping, then swam, sloppy and shaky, across the gravel pit to the place where the rocky slope dropped off into the water. With each stroke, she settled down. As she looked at the steep hillside, at the scrubby firs, what she smelled was mineral, like the sidewalks she and Joan had skated on when they were kids.

Treading water, she looked over at the gravel mountains that shielded the spastic rumble of Girard's earth movers. The workers she had passed on her way into MCG Construction had nodded at her. No one stopped her on the road down through the trees. No one asked what she was doing when she

CHAPTER THIRTEEN

pulled the Volvo over to the silver Airstream trailer. No one shouted when she walked to the crumbling water's edge and slipped off only her shoes. Maybe they all remembered her.

Maybe she had a place there in Girard's crater.

Marian looked up at the tree line. Hundreds of feet overhead, Carthage spun out its history in failed shops and marriages, in a tangle of utility lines and sputtering passions that ended in death of one sort or another. She kept swimming, all the way to the far side of the gravel pit, where she spread her palms out on the warm rockface, then leaned her head against it and closed her eyes.

She felt the daylight change as the clouds collected into thick, low rows. Just a little crescent of sun remained. Marian turned back to the shore, where the trailer glinted, and someone stood at the water's edge, watching her. Jack Girard. Pushing off with both feet, she swam back, taking her time, keeping her stroke long and slow. Even her shoulder worked.

When she reached the shore, he grabbed her forearms and pulled her out. Water streamed from her clothes as she stood with her hands covering her face. Marian felt light, trailing into delicious inconsequence, like the very last thought before you fall asleep. Girard draped something over her, a scratchy wool blanket, for a towel. "It's ninety degrees," she said, which didn't even come close to what she wanted to say.

"It's all I have."

Then she lowered her hands.

Chapter Fourteen

The thunder woke her up.

With her eyes half closed, Marian looked over at the clock radio. Only it wasn't there. Neither was the nightstand. Nothing was where she had left it. Including all the pain. This must be a different lifetime, one without dents and nicks. And her clothes were dry—only, when she tugged the top up to her bleary eyes to get a closer look, she realized she had never seen it before. Some kind of thin, orange, stretchy material (could it be Ban-Lon?), and she never wore orange. Out-There redheads could wear orange. But brunettes in orange looked like old Carnaby Street clichés no matter how distracting the big, white vinyl caps and boots were. Marian might be dragging her feet in the matter of Beth Prescott's killer, but she was certainly making headway on the whereabouts of Ban-Lon.

She rolled over.

Jack Girard was sitting with his back to her at a roll-top desk in the corner. He had brought her home to his house on Providence, where she had gotten through the hall and up the stairs. Beside him, while he was going through a stack of papers, was a long, sash window with the shutters pulled back. Rain was streaming down the windowpane. On the floor next to the bed was Norton, his yellow Lab, in a twitchy dream-whimpering sleep, the smell of his warm paws drifting up to her. Girard stretched and scratched at the back of his short, dark hair. Marian couldn't tell whether his jeans and shirt were going on or coming off, but the place next to her was cold. She figured he was just about as undressed for the night as he was going to get. She cursed the orange Ban-Lon top, then slipped out of bed and went over to

CHAPTER FOURTEEN

him, laying her arm across his shoulder before she had time to weigh all the possibilities.

He circled her hip and pulled her a little closer, entering a final number on a worksheet. Then he pushed back the papers and gave her a long look—one that wasn't quite neutral. The same one he gave her outside the Airstream in the dark last January when Marian flew at him in a fury, and they struggled in the snow until just seconds before she kissed him. Now, with her hair looking like chicken claws, she just stood there next to him, stitched up in five different places.

"You have a funny way of turning up," he said. She noticed he still held her.

"I said I'd find you."

"That you did."

Marian remembered sinking to the rough ground just feet from the edge of the gravel pit, wrapped in Girard's blanket, not giving a damn who was around. She turned on her side, drifting, and felt him loosen the blanket until she was exposed to the heat and whatever the thickening clouds had left of the sun. Girard had touched her hurt shoulder and pulled her hair back over the stitches in her scalp, and finally, his hand had settled on her waist in some kind of terrible defeat. She had wanted to tell him not to be sorrowful, but the words were stuck in her head, and she fell asleep with her fingers in a tuft of green clover sticking up through the cakey soil.

And he had brought her home. "I need help," Marian told him.

"Name it."

"Beth."

"Okay," he said slowly. "But first, tell me why you came back that day."

"Back in January."

"You were already on your way home, Marian. You'd told me what I needed to know about the murder—"

"Only you didn't take it to Khartoukian; you took it home."

"That's where it belonged."

"Christ, Jack, I was scared for you."

"Is that why you came back? Because you were scared?"

She was done for. "No."

"Then why?"

"What do you think?"

His eyes narrowed. "Because you had a job to do."

She touched his cheek. "I thought I had more than that."

The man pulled her in close, wrapping his arms around her hips. "You do." When he tucked his head against her, Marian's knees started to buckle—must have been the attack in the parking lot—and he suddenly let her go. "I called Charlie to tell him you were here asleep, safe and sound."

A pang. "How did that go over?"

Girard inched her back toward the bed. "Not well. He got chilly and asked how the hell did *that* happen." As Marian climbed back into bed, lightning shimmered against the window, and she settled herself against the headboard. Girard shoved the covers against her and sat down, facing her in just the light from the desk lamp. "And I called Barbara Hauser—and Khartoukian, who told me that Sidney Chao, a topnotch medical examiner from Franklin County, was coming down to autopsy Beth Prescott in the morning."

"Which lets Jim Carney off the hook."

"Well, he's sure making himself scarce. I can't find him, and when I called their house, Jen told me he was planning to go to the morgue early, before Quick opened."

She guessed they were crowding Norton because he suddenly scrambled to his feet and stood there uncertainly for a minute. "Tell me about Beth," she said quietly.

"What do you want to know?"

"You hired her. Tell me about her work history."

He scratched his nose. "She had a clerical job at the Bureau of Vital Statistics, where I guess she processed birth and death certificates. Before that, she waitressed at a downtown beef and booze joint that's popular with the business crowd, whose tips came wrapped up in gropes, and neither was very good." Norton had ambled over to the closed door, where he stood whimpering to go out, his big yellow head turned to them over his shoulder

CHAPTER FOURTEEN

with a look of deep criticism. Girard let him out.

"How long was she there?"

Girard sat back down on the bed and took her hand. "Couple of years. Then she walked out."

"What happened?"

"I guess when she took the loaded baked potato from a randy old state senator and dumped it in his lap, she pretty much figured her job there was over."

"And before that?"

"She said she played receptionist for a small Midwest modeling agency until she got tired of looking at anorexics and brats."

"When did she go to medical assisting school?"

"Just before she moved back to Carthage." All of the references checked out—one couldn't remember who she was—but nobody had anything bad to say about Beth Prescott, "although I could tell a couple of them wish they had." She didn't screw up her duties, and she wasn't objectionable, which was just about all he needed to hear. But it was the administrator at the medical assisting school who genuinely liked Beth, telling Girard she had an aptitude for needle sticks and a pleasant way with the frail elderly. " I hired her."

Marian touched the stitches on her elfin ear. No amount of truth or scar tissue could change it. "Jim Carney was sleeping with Beth Prescott."

He met her look, then said the one thing she never expected. "I know."

"You *know*?"

He nodded. "I knew before Beth even came to work for us."

"How?"

"I saw them," he said, "only I didn't put it together until after Beth started coming here."

"Why didn't you tell me before I started the job? For Christ's sake, Jack, I'm on your payroll."

"It doesn't have anything to do with her murder."

"Like there's no possible connection between love in the afternoon and death at night?"

"Not if it's Jim Carney."

"Not my boy. My boy would never do a thing like that."

"Look, Marian, I know it sounds naive—"

She kept shaking her head. "Jack—"

"—but it's what I believe." Over the fall, Girard went on, he and Jim Carney had been playing tennis at the racquet club Thursdays at two. Sometime in December, Jim backed out, saying his schedule was getting complicated. Then around the end of the year, Girard had been poking around the Wade County Landfill with the county engineer as part of a study on solid waste management, and he saw Jim Carney coming out of an apartment at the back of Coconut Palm Estates.

Carney had looked around when he got to his car, which was parked out of sight of the main road, and buttoned his dress overcoat. Then he briefly waved to someone standing at an upstairs window. Girard looked at his watch: 2:45 PM, a Thursday. He decided to take it for a house call and never mentioned it to Jim. Then, in January, when his own home life changed, and he moved back into the family house on Providence, he brought his father home from Sparta Vale, the nursing home, and hired Beth Prescott.

During her second week with them, her car had broken down. He gave her a lift home at seven PM—to Apartment A4, Coconut Palm Estates. Beth thanked him and got out. He watched until she got inside, and after a couple of minutes, a light went on in the same upstairs window where Carney had looked back and waved.

By then, Girard went on; it was colder than he ever remembered, dead black and hateful, and his old Jeep rocked in the wind. Marian had left town without a word to him, and he was dealing with more blood and mess than he ever thought he'd have on his own doorstep. Worst of all, he was left free to examine his own life, and it looked ridiculous to him. During that time, all he had was his father, who liked Beth Prescott, and Girard was mindful of all these things when he asked Beth if she could ever work overtime. But, truly, in the dead January night he just wanted to know once and for all whether something private and pleasurable existed anywhere on the planet. He went on to ask Beth whether she could come to them early some days, as

CHAPTER FOURTEEN

soon as she got off work from the Mercy Hospital lab.

She smiled. *Any day but Thursday,* was what she said.

* * *

"Beth's inside?" Girard asked, nodding at the set of automatic double doors marked Wade County Morgue, Authorized Personnel Only. At 6:50 AM, they had an hour before the staffers came to work upstairs at Quick. Marian looked around at the green, tiled walls and stainless-steel counters, cold in the fluorescent light.

Jim Carney sat without answering at a small metal desk, plunging pencils one by one into an electric pencil sharpener. He was working on his fourth box. There were two rows of blue plastic chairs and a magazine rack, like an ER—only by the time you got to this room, all the emergencies were over. The magazines were two years old, and nobody sitting here, waiting, would really give a good goddamn. You could help yourself to a Styrofoam cup of Mr. Coffee while you marveled how your priorities had never seemed quite this straight. The pungent smell of ammonia told you so.

Girard went on, "Have you seen her?"

"If I could see her," Carney said finally, checking a pencil point, "I could do her. The answer is no." Right about then Marian was wondering why they thought any of this was a good idea without Khartoukian. "Why are you here?"

She took out the CD of *Aida* and placed it on Jim Carney's desk, next to a stack of pencils that looked like pick-up sticks. When he saw what it was, his fingers closed slowly over it. He looked at Girard, who said nothing, and then at her. It was all there in his face. Only Marian couldn't say for sure whether it included trying to blind her, run a major artery over broken glass, or just pop her head like a pimple.

His hand tightened around the CD. "Thank you," he said, closing it in a drawer. "Is that all?"

"You know it's not."

"Then I think you'd better say what's on your mind."

She wanted to ask him if he jumped her two nights ago in the Gringos parking lot, but her knees were shaking, and she didn't want to hear the truth—and she sure as hell didn't want to hear a lie. But most of all, she didn't want to find out that she couldn't tell the difference. "I've been looking for you for days."

"I saw you on Monday."

"I've been looking for Beth Prescott's lover." She couldn't stop shaking her head. "I never thought it would be you."

"Six months ago, neither did I."

"It was so hard to find you, Jim, that it occurred to me, here's a man who has a lot at stake."

For a moment, Jim Carney didn't move, but then his face changed. "You think I killed Beth." He looked quickly at Girard, who crossed his arms and didn't say a thing. "For two weeks now, it's been hell. It was bad enough when Beth missed our Thursday time. No note, no message, nothing. But then the day after turned into the week after, and I couldn't show any more interest in where she was—" he yanked his tie loose, "than if the morning paper hadn't shown up on my desk. Not to my wife, the cops, Beth's family, anybody." His blue eyes slid away from her. "Not anybody."

Carney rested his head in his two hands. "By the time you came to see me, Marian, despair was all I had left—" he narrowed his eyes, "crawling all over me, telling me that Beth Prescott was dead. And there was nothing for me to do but take out the gallbladders I was supposed to, and close up the bleeding ulcers that came in, and try damn hard to impersonate myself."

As close as she came to losing her life at Gringos two nights ago, Carney told them, that's how close he came to spilling it to Marian on Monday when she showed up at his office. He pictured keeping her there in a corner while he uncorked every microscopic detail of his last six months with Beth Prescott. To say that she mattered to someone other than the Prescotts. That maybe the sound of all their collective despair would be enough to unearth her, to rumble her out of hiding and rush her to the safety of Thursdays, where there were no nameless sorrows. No negotiated futures. No compromised desires.

CHAPTER FOURTEEN

"Then Khartoukian called two days ago to say he was sorry, but he had a real nasty one, the remains of a local gal strangled and dumped, and then I knew, I really finally knew—" he said softly, "that insanity's just the sanctuary of a despairing mind." Jim Carney straightened up. "And I don't even have that."

He ran his hand through his white hair. For half a minute, no one spoke. "I'm staying until Sidney Chao gets here," he said. "I figure these are Beth's last few hours—" he blinked at some point on the far wall, "before she wears her liver and lungs on the outside, so I thought I'd keep her company." He pushed himself out of his chair and stood up. "And now—" he glanced quickly at us, "I guess I better hope to hell that when she died, I was at a Reds game where a dozen witnesses could swear I never left my seat, not even to flag down a beer." He ran a hand down his face. "*Shit*, Beth," he said to a woman who could no longer hear him.

Unless Marian got lucky—and she figured she used up about a year's supply of luck when Eddie Estremera decided to pitch her just one more time—she suddenly saw a whole lot more doorbell ringing in the near future. Because what she needed now was more than the name of Beth Prescott's lover. Marian was just no longer sure that what Roy Jean overheard was a dump-in-waiting. It fit. But it only fit because she had nothing else.

If Jim Carney had killed her, then he was caught in a forked stick. Tough out Chao's findings, hope to hell they didn't implicate him, and slip unnoticed back into his pre-Beth life. Or—in an exquisite temptation—fudge his *own* findings. The more she thought about it, it was more than a temptation. It was damn near a necessity. What better position for the killer than to be responsible for determining the time and manner of her death? If Jim Carney had killed Beth Prescott, Sidney Chao wouldn't be coming down from Columbus to do the autopsy, because *Carney couldn't afford not to perform it himself.*

And if he didn't kill her, didn't kill her—outside this room at this moment, here with Girard and Marian, with the sun slanting white through the high windows—Jim Carney couldn't even mourn her. "Jim, listen." And she told him what Roy Jean Toole had overheard.

"You think Beth was talking about me."

"I did," Marian said. "Not anymore."

He looked weary. "Say it again."

It's two weeks away.

I just want it dropped.

You don't have to look at him every day.

Carney folded his arms tight across his chest, troubled. Marian waited. Then he grabbed his reading glasses off his desk and pulled an old copy of *The Toiler* out of his Bengals trash can. "Beth told me the same thing, maybe about a month ago."

"What?"

Picking off a used tea bag, Jim Carney unfolded the newspaper and spread it out on his desk. "'You don't have to look at him every day.'"

"Who?" She moved in closer. "Who was she talking about?"

He smoothed out the paper. Marian had seen it a couple of days ago, the one with O'Malley and the Clemms on the front page, grouped around little Courtney in her wheelchair. Then he opened it to page two, and the backs of his fingers tapped a picture. "Dave Barish," he said.

"Barish?" She looked at Girard, who seemed stumped.

"Beth brought him up about a month ago. She'd heard through the grapevine that he was being sued by the family of some kid he delivered a few years ago." *Too bad,* Carney had told her, meaning it, *because we're all ducks in a shooting gallery, only maybe the obstetricians are bigger and slower than the rest of us because they sure are the ones who get pinged the most.* Still, Beth seemed to have more to say about it. Could Dave Barish go to jail? Could he lose his license? Could his practice fall apart? Could it hurt his family?

All Jim Carney could tell her for sure was that Dave Barish wouldn't go to jail because it was a civil suit, which meant money damages, not jail time. As for the rest, he didn't know. License, practice, family—those things were in the darkest part of the cave none of them wanted to go into, no matter how big the torches. Carney guessed that even if the jury found for the plaintiffs, Barish wouldn't lose his license—hell, if that's how the state Medical Board

CHAPTER FOURTEEN

responded to most lawsuits, women would be driving to Indiana to have their babies—but, yes, his practice might suffer, especially if the jury awarded the plaintiffs something in excess of his malpractice coverage.

I heard the Clemms are asking twelve million, Beth told him.

Well, Dave Barish is probably covered for up to, say, a couple million, Carney said, *which means everybody's premiums go up, mine included—which gets passed on to the patients as rising health care costs.*

Beth stammered, *But how does he come up with the other ten million?*

I don't think he can. He'd have to declare bankruptcy.

Which means?

Which means that the Clemms would get a lot of his assets.

Like what?

*IRAs, savings, cars if they're new, some of the equity in his house—*He ran a finger along her collarbone. *Whatever he's got that can be turned into cash.*

In other words, everything.

Well...

Whether he's responsible for the Clemm kid or not.

But I don't think it'll happen.

I saw the Clemm kid.

Oh?

I went to the Vanguard School and saw her.

He was interested. *Why?*

I know Dr. Barish. I wanted to see the kid.

And?

Twelve million bucks won't get her out of a wheelchair.

Call it seven.

Why seven?

After the Clemms' lawyers take their cut.

All right, then, seven. No one's life is worth seven million.

Not mine?

Beth touched his face. *Not yours.*

He smiled at her. *Not your own?*

She looked him straight in the eye. *Not even my own.*

Barish'll come out okay, Beth, Carney had told her, only he didn't know that for sure, which was why he felt kind of stupid saying it. They were silent, then, the two of them. It was Thursday, and he just wanted to make love, but Beth seemed thoughtful and flat. When he actually told her they still had to have faith in the system, Beth gave him the sort of look he deserved. *Don't worry about Dave Barish, honey,* he said, finally, having run out of anything better. And that's when she said it...

You don't have to look at him every day.

* * *

"Compassion?" Girard pointed a forkful of Texas omelet at Marian.

"Maybe. Only I'm not convinced." After leaving Jim Carney with his head on his desk at the morgue, all they wanted was a ham and eggs interlude at Zack's Stacks half a mile west of town, where two people could down enough grease to slip into the hereafter for something under ten dollars. Zack's Stacks is all red vinyl, grey Formica, and the kind of chrome that puts a '56 Merc to shame. The breakfast crowd, pretty much to a man, looked like Genghis Khan in John Deere caps.

The server, called *Capree* and built enough like Chopper to be his mother, had ringlets the size of empty toilet paper rolls bunched at the top of her head. When she poured, Marian could swear the pot was a foot away from the cup, but she pursed her lips and didn't splash a drop. Then Capree clacked her dentures at them once in a victory lap and disappeared.

Over the rim of the coffee cup, Marian watched Jack Girard—with a tan, open-necked shirt and a close shave—peruse the morning paper, sipping his drink. She found herself wondering whether she could have a serious relationship with someone who drinks tomato juice before 8 AM. That could be a deal breaker. Forking the last of her blueberry pancakes, she pulled over a napkin and made a list of things to do. Find out from Jeannie Clemm why she called Beth. Get Lila to go through Beth's stuff—fresh set of eyes, fresh set of eyelashes, and all that. See if Dave Barish or Bill Rinaldi remembers Beth's ever discussing Dave's case with them. Find out Jack Girard's views

CHAPTER FOURTEEN

on such things as beets and herring.

She put down her pen. "Will you do me a favor?"

Girard was folding Charlie's latest efforts into quarters. "Name it," he said, pushing the paper over to her.

"See if a ticket agent at the Cleveland airport can ID a photo?"

"Right away?"

She nodded. "Forget car rentals. We're looking for a cash purchase here and forget trains because none connect."

"What about a bus?"

"If the airport falls through." She passed him the old issue of the *Toiler* that Jim Carney had pulled out of his trash can. "But I don't think it will."

We looked at each other. "I've got to make some arrangements, then I can hit the road in maybe half an hour. On one condition."

"Namely?"

"That after dark, you're in the company of someone you trust, like Nan Kemp, Barbara Hauser—"

"—Charlie."

Girard slid out of the booth. "Somehow"—he gave her a quick look, peeling off a twenty from a roll of bills for Capree— "I don't think it'll be Charlie." He went on ahead to pay the bill, which was when Marian made the mistake of picking up the paper he had pushed over to her and glanced at the front page.

Well, it was Charlie's bonanza, all right, still crowded with the Barish malpractice trial and now the Wade County strangling of Beth Ann Prescott. An out-of-town strangling would have held some interest on an inside page, but the local aspect of the crime gave it the sort of jittery appeal Charlie had been hoping for. From where he was sitting, he could damn near hear the seagulls.

Then she folded the newspaper back to Charlie's editorial, with the headline, *First, Do No Harm*, and read it, standing next to the booth. He nattered on about "the problem of substandard medical care"—dragging out the classic, tired case of a doctor in Illinois twenty years ago who had amputated the wrong leg—and cited as proof of this substandard care the fact that in 2020, in Ohio alone, 60,000 medical malpractice lawsuits were filed. Tort reform, Charlie went on to say, was "a bad idea" because it may limit citizens' access to The System that can compensate them when they are injured by physician negligence.

Then, the editorial zoomed in on the pending case of Clemm versus Barish. *Had Dr. Barish performed a cesarean section in a timely manner on Mrs. Clemm,* Charlie wrote, *today four-year-old Courtney might very well be able to ride a bike. If his management fell below the standard of care, then Dr. Barish violated the opening imperative of the Hippocratic Oath, 'First, do no harm,' because Courtney Clemm has clearly been harmed. It is only under the present system, free from award caps or so-called peer reviews that injured parties like the Clemms can find proper restitution for what they have suffered.*

Chapter Fifteen

When Jack Girard pulled over to the curb in front of the *Toiler* building, Marian eased herself out of the Jeep and headed for the front doors with the newspaper clutched in her hand like a local crank with the wind up about some grammatical blunder. Since they had agreed that, after a rough night at Gringos, her midnight blue satin and organza wraparound top might really come in handy next time he checks his oil, she decided to hang on to the orange Ban-Lon top for a while—and when he gave her back her pants, washed and dried, she practically wept. But no matter how presentable the outfit, the bruises and stitches still drew some attention as Marian made her way through Charlie's city room, and she realized she couldn't help walking like the expendable character in every 40s noir movie who looked okay until you saw him pitch forward with a knife sticking out of his back.

Charlie's door was open, so she didn't knock, and he didn't notice her, what with his fingers twitching across his keyboard, hammering out the daily libel. She just wanted to take him in, for a minute or two. To see if the guy in the teal shirt and Versace tie, the guy with sleek black hair and drop-dead blue eyes, was the Charlie Levitan she had been through bombings, trashings, and love affairs with. The Charlie who blew the whistle on their high school newspaper advisors for using professional ringers instead of student photographers. The Charlie who told the FIAT urban guerillas who were trashing his college newspaper office that they were full of shit. The Charlie who turned down a cash-obscene job at *Penthouse* because he wanted to be able to tell his hypothetical children what he did for a buck. Now, here he was, running a Gannett white elephant in Carthage, Ohio, and if today's editorial was any indication, he *still* couldn't tell his daughter what he did for a buck.

Charlie looked up and saw her.

"What I want to know is," said Marian, holding up the editorial, "who made you a plaintiff attorney?"

He wheeled back from his computer. "How'd you sleep?"

She ignored him. "For that matter, who made you an obstetrician?"

"You look well rested."

"Fuck you."

"Close the door."

She did, hard. "How I sleep," she said, "and where I sleep is none of your business."

"How about with whom?"

"That, too."

He got up fast, crashing his chair into the wall, and came around the front of the desk. "Do you want to know how I found out about what happened to you? Not from you and not from the Hausers. Not even from Khartoukian. Nobody thought that maybe that little piece of information was something I should have. No, I found out from Kelly," he said, pointing violently toward the city room, where it suddenly got quiet, "a college kid doing a goddamn internship here who wanted to know who was covering the assault on someone named Marian Warner."

"I'm sorry no one called you."

"No one called me," he said, "because you didn't tell someone to call me." His eyes slid over my face like he was trying to identify me. Then he backed off, shaking his head. "Or maybe you told them not to." Marian felt a twinge, remembering Barbara's offer to call him. "Or maybe," he rammed his hands into his pockets and went over to the window, "you just didn't think of it. And that's what it always comes down to, Marian. I only know what's going on in your life when I just happen to turn up."

She saw all over again that night back at Rutgers when he found her at the Sigma Alpha Mu party, she never knew how and snatched her from the

CHAPTER FIFTEEN

consequences of good booze and bad Joplin. *Next time, honey,* he grunted, hoisting Marian over his shoulder, *sing it right and this won't happen. And I won't have to pull your ass out of it.* Even if it was true, it wasn't tender.

And that was why she never came to him.

"I almost died," she said, "and what's pissing you off is that no one *called* you?"

"That's right."

"Not that someone almost killed me—"

"That's not—"

"—but that you weren't in on it."

His eyes flashed. "Let me finish."

"It's always just about the story, isn't it?"

"What are you talking about?"

Marian held up the folded newspaper. "After the job you did on David Barish, who's going to come to him for care?"

"Maybe that's the point. Maybe no one should."

"You destroy a man's life for a 'maybe'?"

"Why not?" he shouted. "You've been doing it for years."

She backed up, shocked. In her whole life, she had never felt this much anger directed at her—even the other night at Gringos, when the object was to kill her. "Charlie," she said softly, "you're dangerous."

He was stunned. "David Barish lands a kid in a wheelchair, and you call me dangerous."

"How do you know he did? Have you heard any testimony? I was there three times this week, and damn it, Charlie, I didn't see you."

"I work for a living."

"No, you don't. Not if this—" she slapped at the paper, "is what you come up with. How do you know what he should have done in Jeannie Clemm's labor? How many labors have you managed? When did you learn to read fetal monitor strips? You're not an obstetrician, Charlie. You're not an attorney—"

"Get out, Marian."

"You're not even a journalist," she cried, flinging the newspaper at him, and walked out.

***

At the corner of Main and Mission Streets, Marian leaned against a utility pole, shaking. Damn him. This was a bad one, and she didn't think they'd recover. Marian wouldn't be going to Savannah anytime soon. For that matter, she wouldn't be going back up to his office anytime soon. She was standing there trying to figure out what her life would look like without Charlie Levitan in it when an old woman with vertical white hair that looked like fiberglass aimed a metal cane at her.

"Are you the crossing guard?"

It must have been the orange Ban-Lon. Finally, a job she could do. "That's right, ma'am." The light changed, Marian grabbed her by the sleeve of her blue blouse with the Peter Pan collar, and they started across Mission Street. The old woman kept clutching at a raffia purse that had NASSAU embroidered on it, with an alarmed look on her face like she thought Marian would try to snatch it, crossing guard wages being what they were. Marian flipped up a menacing hand to motorists a couple of times, and by the time the two of them made it to the other side, they were getting along nicely. As relationships went, it was just about the perfect length. Off the old woman trudged, pulling her raffia bag closer.

Marian hitched herself up the steps of the Wade County Courthouse. No kissers. A few pigeons. In the stony, cool rotunda, she ran into Nan Kemp, who was shouldering her way through a group of sightseeing school kids.

"For Christ's sake, I haven't seen you in two days," Nan grabbed Marian's arm as she walked her down the narrow hall, those dark eyes flickering. "Hank tells me you'll live," said Nan, and it took Marian a few seconds to realize she was referring to Khartoukian. Sex really puts people on a first-name basis. Ahead of them were O'Malley and the Clemms. "Tell me you can do drinks later, Marian, because—" her voice dropped, and she whispered, "unless I miss my guess, this is all going to be over soon. O'Malley rested late yesterday, and I overheard him on the phone to his office, talking about his

CHAPTER FIFTEEN

next case—guy with a throat injury, they're claiming Doritos are inherently dangerous—"

"Are you serious?"

"Twenty million."

"Maybe he could take chewing lessons."

Nan barked out a laugh. "Case starts Monday in Franklin County. O'Malley's just marking time."

"How's Dave?"

"I've got him on the stand next, which, between you and me, has limited value—I've seen taxidermy with more life to it—but that's not something I'd tell him. Besides," she went on, if I'm right about what's coming down, I'm just pedaling with a broken chain." Nan widened her eyes at Marian meaningfully, let her go, and breezed back into the courtroom without waiting for a reply.

Marian looked over at Kelvin O'Malley, brawny in his black pinstripe suit that made him look like a wrestling undertaker. He was finishing off a plastic bottle of Evian while Craig Clemm talked. Craig sounded like every caller on sports radio, going on like an authority about how you can't take a pitcher like Seth Lugo and put him at long relief. "Guy's got fifteen, maybe twenty good pitches in him. You just can't do it."

"Mm," said O'Malley, tapping the last few drops into his mouth, then he did a one-handed crunch of the empty bottle and pitched it into the trash can.

Jeannie Clemm blew a final ripple of smoke and stubbed out a cigarette in an ashtray. She folded her arms across her paisley dress and looked like she was struggling with wanting to light up another one, only she was trying to space out her smokes so she could think she was quitting.

Marian walked over to her. "Jeannie?"

"Uh huh?" She blinked at her, then smiled.

"My name's Marian Warner—"

Jeannie was trying to keep up. "Okay," she said, flipping her hair.

"I'm a private investigator—" *Wow,* Jeannie mouthed, her lips parted. "I understand you called Beth Prescott."

She wrinkled her nose. "Who—?"

"Beth Prescott. Two weeks ago." Doesn't she read?

"Oh." She remembered. "Sure. *Pres*cott. I was just calling her back."

"Well, that's what I—"

O'Malley touched Jeannie's shoulder. "Come on, Jeannie. Time to go back inside." His blue eyes settled on Marian with a look of blank indifference. She didn't figure; she didn't matter—not unless she could tell him the fake butter flavoring in her movie popcorn made her sterile—although he pulled his mouth into a polite frown that was supposed to pass for good manners.

"She called and got my mom," Jeannie went on, "and wanted to tell me something about our Courtney—"

Craig, forced to quit his sports commentary, expanded his chest, making gaps in the front of his broadcloth shirt. "Gotta go, hon," he said, his face suddenly grim, remembering maybe that he was an aggrieved player in the Court of Common Pleas.

Marian reached out to stop Jeannie. "Did Beth Prescott say what—"

O'Malley wrapped a pinstriped arm around his client's bony shoulder and moved her toward the courtroom. Jeannie Clemm looked back. "—something about our Courtney's case, so I—"

"Later, Jeannie," O'Malley said as Craig fell in behind them.

Marian threw up my hands. "When can I talk to you?"

"I'm free after four," she called back. "Leastways, I been all week." Marian heard her say something to Craig about a lady detective, only the information didn't warrant even a glance, and Marian watched the door to Courtroom 2 close behind them.

* * *

The brew of the day at Ketchum Rays was toffee nut. Marian only agreed to half a cup since she preferred to take her candy in chewable form. Lila dumped in some whitener and stirred it with whole-arm rotations. Today, in honor of Beth, she was dressed in a black crepe caftan, and pinned to her breast was a photo of the two of them cheesing it up for the camera, which

CHAPTER FIFTEEN

Lila had trimmed into a circle and glued to a big old campaign button. It was right over her heart.

Holding up her blond hair were black and red chopsticks that really had their job cut out for them since Lila couldn't stop stirring and shaking her head. "Honey, I'm packed tighter than a virgin on her wedding night," she told me, "what with the electrician in Dustin Hoffman and the deputy in Huey Newton. And in fifteen minutes, the pizza guy's going into Bridget Bar*do*."

The pizza guy? *"Flyboy?"*

Lila tucked her head into her shoulders. "Twenty minutes, we have this whole little routine, him and me." Marian picked up Beth Prescott's Rubbermaid bin full of mementos and started to trail down the hall behind Lila, who poked her head around the screen in Huey Newton. "Mm, looking *good*, Deppity Dog," she laughed and winked. She had drawn fine little hairlines on her lower eyelids, giving her a look of permanent surprise at The News About Beth.

"Now, Lila," came the voice on the other side of the screen, and Marian realized it was the bad typist with the Adam's Apple.

"You just take your time getting dressed, honey," she tapped her little fingernails on the door frame, moving her hips to the piped-in mix, this time Aretha the Right Rockin' Franklin singing, "Baby, Baby, Sweet Baby, there's something that I just got to say—" They sailed by Dustin Hoffman—Lila's sonar didn't pick up any sounds from the electrician—at last, someone who actually *tanned* at Ketchum Rays—and Marian got her back to Flyboy.

"What about Flyboy?"

"Oh, just a little thing we do. After he's been in the tanning bed for twenty minutes, I stand there and whack the top and say, 'Lucius, are you going to be good?' and he swears he's going to be good, and I ask it again, and he swears again, and then I let him out." She moved aside the découpaged screen in a doorway on the left of the hall, and Marian ducked by her, finding herself in a room decorated in bordello-red flocked wallpaper—on the wall, the framed blow-up of the album cover for Janis Joplin's *Pearl*. The silver tanning bed stood open like Coffin of the Day at the local funeral home.

Setting down the Rubbermaid bin, she gave Lila the chaise and took the floor for herself.

She started Lila on the shoebox filled with old photos and set aside all the old report cards, twirling ribbon, autograph book, and rock concert programs. Lila kept sighing, with her eyebrows hiked up, as she fingered the photos and came up with nothing. "Jeez, some of these are so old. Even if Beth's in them, I don't recognize her."

"What about the recent ones?"

"Well, there's this one," Lila said, flipping it to her. A dark Polaroid of Beth in a green polo top and black pants, wearing a small apron, presenting a cake with crackling sparklers at a table filled with businessmen. "That's McNifty's, the beef and brew place in Columbus."

"Know any of the men?"

Lila shook her head. "Beth never brought anyone back to Carthage, but she met a lot of suits while she worked there, that I can tell you. A state rep, a banker, a lawyer, a dean, a drug rep. Some were pikers, but some were spenders." Lila pondered the shot. "She got a trip out of one of them, be about two years ago. Just the two of them. Now, where the hell was it?" She sat back. "Beth was already working at Vital Statistics. I remember because she told me the state was tougher to get time away from than the restaurant folks."

Marian handed over the painted coconut, and Lila bounced it gently around in her hands until the name came face up. *St. Thomas, U.S.V.I.* "Yeah," Lila said, "yeah, this was the place. The trip came around the same time as the new furniture. I figured either Beth had saved a whole bunch of tips from McNifty's—or she'd landed someone who was greasing her way in life." Someone who had decided, Marian thought, that sending Beth Prescott to medical assisting school on a sexual blackmail scholarship was a damn good investment.

"When was the trip?"

Lila pursed her lips. "Really," she said finally, "it would have been right around now, two years ago. I remember joking with her that she'd be missing the tractor pull at Tulip Time." Lila held out a hand. "Let's see

CHAPTER FIFTEEN

those forms." Marian passed her the blank passport application, the blank Delta Airlines application, the blank application for The Branch, and the blank birth certificate form.

She watched Lila go through them with a small frown, completely unaware that her chopsticks were sliding on down toward her right ear. It struck her that three of those forms were Beth dreaming—Beth deciding there had to be something beyond waitressing in a town she'd never leave for very long or very far. She could see exotic places, read exotic books, do exotic things like show passengers how to fasten their seat belts. But the birth certificate didn't fit. It wasn't Beth Prescott dreaming, or Beth Prescott hanging on to the aborted plans for all the lives she'd never lead.

According to Girard, Beth had worked at the Bureau of Vital Statistics processing birth and death certificates, and filling requests for photocopies. Maybe the blank form was just Beth bringing home a reminder of what she had looked at forty hours a week for close to two years. In some ways, it was heavier than the coconut. Marian slipped the long blue birth certificate form from the pile next to Lila, who was now looking through Beth's date book and nibbling a fingernail. The top part of the form had spaces for the sort of info on every birth certificate she had ever seen, her own included: child's name, sex, date, time, city and county of birth. Hospital, doctor's signature, parents' names, ages, addresses.

The basics.

What seemed new was the lower two-thirds of the sheet, called *Information For Medical and Health Use Only*, which asked for the kind of info public health officials love to collect. Line items about race, education, occupation, prenatal visits, other births, and what was euphemistically called "other terminations." Marian bit back a whistle. These line items sure seemed like pretty personal info for state clerical workers like Beth Prescott to have at their disposal.

So, for that matter, did the rest.

From there to the end, the form became a record of the woman's labor and delivery, which seemed like a hell of a lot of info the state was asking for just to register the birth of a baby. There were boxes for recording the one- and five-minute Apgar scores, then the attending doctor was told to "check all that apply" under seven separate headings.

Medical Risk Factors For This Pregnancy.
Other Risk Factors For This Pregnancy.
Obstetric Procedures.
Complications of Labor and/or Delivery.
Method of Delivery.
Abnormal Conditions of the Newborn.
Congenital Anomalies of Child.

She counted a total of 88 separate boxes the doctor could mark. Places to check off fetal distress, malpresentation, birth injury, seizures. This time, she whistled, and Lila looked up. Given access, lawyers could graze through this stuff forever.

Given access.

Chapter Sixteen

She swung open the black wrought-iron gate to the courtyard of *Carthage Women's Health,* hoping to waylay Bill Rinaldi between patients and get some answers about the birth certificate form. Two very pregnant women were picking their way at kind of a good clip over slick, white dogwood petals scattered all over the flagstone walk. Their eyes were wide, and they both looked like they had just been told they'd have to reach right in and pull the babies out all by themselves. When Marian opened the front door, she understood why. She could hardly hear Vivaldi's "La Primavera" over all the yelling and crashing coming from somewhere in the back.

The office manager, Mary Jo, barreled right past her, hurrying another patient out the door with bright statements that they'll let her know the results of the glucose tolerance test and have a nice day. The other two pony-tailed assistants were huddled against the wall, torn between wanting to take cover and wanting to hear every last word. Mary Jo had emptied out the waiting room of anyone else who, by God, wasn't about to let a little yelling make *her* have to reschedule that belly check.

Marian went down the hall. Bill Rinaldi, in a dark brown shirt and khakis, was standing just inside the office next to his own, where she was surprised to see Dave Barish pulling down medical textbooks instead of sitting with his trap shut in Courtroom 2. Both men gave her a quick look, but she was pretty sure even if she had been wearing a bandolier and brandishing *pistoles*—naked—Dave Barish wouldn't have given her a second thought. Each book got stacked with a loud thump on his mahogany desk, more like he was trying to crush every hateful thing in the world between two hard covers.

"Dave—"

Barish pulled a heavy hardcover text off the shelf and held it up to Bill Rinaldi—*Obstetrics*—and then flung it at the other stacked books, sweeping a vase of irises and a framed photo off the back of the desk. Something broke.

"Dave, for Christ's *sake*—"

"Go do your work, Bill," was all Barish said, looking quickly at the spine of another book before he hurled it into a trash can.

Rinaldi watched it go. "How do you know the case is settling?"

"Because Nan Kemp told me, Bill, that's how."

"How does she know?"

"Every break, she's on the phone to PQA. They're making noises, is what she said."

"What does she think?"

"How do I know? She gets paid either way. Whether we win—" He grabbed a handful of journals from a lower shelf and hardly looked at them. "Whether we lose." He dumped the journals into the trash. "Whether we settle." He grabbed another handful, gave up trying to figure out what was worth keeping, and sailed them toward the trash. "What does she care? O'Malley's crew gets forty percent, win or settle. I'm the only one who gets screwed."

"Not if you—" Rinaldi stopped short.

"Not if I what? Win? Well, now there's no chance of that, is there? Not when the insurance company makes noises."

"Wait and see." We all knew it was lame, but there was nothing else to say.

"Wait and see." Dave Barish started on the wall, pulling down a framed diploma. "For the last few days, I've listened to a bunch of people O'Malley's paraded—" he swept an arm upward, "in front of the judge and jury say I'm a bad doctor." He pulled down two more framed diplomas and piled all three of them cockeyed on the toppled stack of books. "I've sat there, and the only thing that's kept me sane is knowing that *my* turn would come. A defense, a rebuttal, a chance to bring in our own expert witnesses. Do you know who we had?"

CHAPTER SIXTEEN

"Well, yeah, Daley—"

"Daley, from Cleveland, who heads a top residency program and presents papers from here to kingdom come."

"Okay, I—"

"And Chaikin, from Pittsburgh, who's a pediatric neurologist with a c.v. you need a fucking forklift to put on the bench."

"I know, Dave—"

"These are the ones coming to tell the Avon lady and the pig farmer that I'm not a bad doctor. Only now, of course, they won't." His face looked terrible. "I never got a chance to tell my side of it," he said softly. Bill Rinaldi said nothing. "*Never.* As far as the Avon lady and pig farmer know, I'm a bad doctor—"

"You know you're not—"

"—who's responsible for a brain-damaged kid. That's what they think, and that's what they'll think until they die." He held up a desk clock. "Is this mine?"

Rinaldi flopped his hands at nothing. "I don't remember."

"Every so often," Dave Barish said, setting the clock next to the books, "they'll remember when they sat on the jury for the case against that bad doctor, the one who put that kid in a wheelchair. Let's see, what was his name, Burdish, Barry?"

"The one who ran away."

They looked at each other. "Right," Barish said. "That one." He looked around. "I need a box," he said, heading to the door.

"Look, Dave—"

"Out of my way, Bill." Dave Barish glanced at me. "Marian, if you're here to see me, make it fast." She followed him into the storeroom, where he kicked a few closed cartons and found one that was nearly empty.

She said, "Beth Prescott." Nodding once, but not looking at her, Barish overturned the box, shaking out some sterile-wrapped instruments, where he left them on the floor. "Did she ever talk to you about the case?"

He threw the empty box at the open doorway and looked around for another. "Christ, Marian, how can I remember?"

"It's important."

He looked completely wrung out, with one of his hands clenched in his red hair. Then he straightened his arm at her. "Once. About a month ago, maybe a little longer."

"What did she say?"

His eyes roved the ceiling. "She said—"

Marian waited.

"She said she knew about the lawsuit, and she was sorry."

"What did you say?"

"What the hell was I going to say? I said thanks." He overturned a box of disposable gowns and started stuffing them feverishly on a storage shelf like he was plugging a hole in the ozone layer. "Then she wanted to know if I thought it would turn out all right."

"And—?"

"I told her no, it was already bad. Maybe it'll get dropped, she said. Dropped, I said, yeah, maybe. She wanted to know if that ever happens, and I said I didn't know. Then she said she just wanted me to know she was sorry, and I actually tried to make a joke. Beth, I told her, you don't have to apologize."

"What did she say?"

"Not a damn thing." Grabbing the boxes, Dave Barish pushed by her, and she followed him back to his office.

Bill Rinaldi stood looking down at his shoes, shaking his head. "This doesn't solve anything."

Barish looked up, amazed. "It solves everything," he said and began loading the boxes.

"What about the patients?"

Barish snorted at him. "The patients are why I'm leaving, Bill."

"Not all of them."

"No, not all of them, but which ones? You tell me. Where's the next lawsuit coming from? Do you know? Because it will."

"It's our job to provide care."

Barish went back to work, cramming textbooks and journals into the

CHAPTER SIXTEEN

boxes. "And what do they provide?"

"What do you mean?"

He didn't look up. "The patients, Bill."

"Why do they have to—"

"You say we provide care. What do they provide?"

"A sense of purpose." Almost a question.

Barish looked unimpressed. "What else?"

Rinaldi came up short. "I don't know."

"Trust for the times it gets tough? I don't think so." He loaded another book. "Gratitude for the times it goes right? I don't think so." They gave each other a long look. Barish stuffed his suit jacket in the box on top of the books; then he picked up a leather pen holder. "Are these your pens and pencils and shit?" he wanted to know, rattling them. When Rinaldi didn't answer, he slapped them back on the desk, ran his fingers through his hair, and looked around. Then he wrenched open a desk drawer.

Marian caught Rinaldi looking at the place on the wall where a diploma had been. Then he spoke. "They provide a livelihood."

"A livelihood." Barish loosened his tie. "You know what? I'll go to work in a college health clinic somewhere, handing out birth control pills. That's enough of a livelihood. Or maybe I'll go to work for an insurance company, going over claims. Or, wait, maybe I'll shop myself around as an expert witness." He laughed, pinching the bridge of his nose. Then he pushed his wire rims back into place. "There you go," he held up a hand, enjoying himself, "that's perfect. Barrett Rance pulls in an extra thirty or forty grand a year at it. I'm younger, more energetic, say I can do a hundred. I'll be retired from the practice of obstetrics, so *that* won't get in the way."

He raked at the contents of the desk drawer, which wouldn't open all the way, grabbing fistfuls of coins and personal letters and dumping them over the open boxes. "Wouldn't want anything like an active practice to get in the way of testifying. Wouldn't want anything like reams of new literature in the field to distract me from my pronouncements on some poor sucker's management of a diabetic mom who shows up at 38 weeks with no prenatal care—" he scraped together a pile of wallet-sized pictures of babies he'd delivered and scattered them like chicken feed in the direction of the trash can, "— and blood sugars just about in the coma range, who by the way—" he made a face, "had a couple of stillbirths along the way.

"Or some other poor sucker's management of a pack-a-day smoker with blood pressure off the wall—" he was tugging at the drawer now, slamming it hard from side to side, "who refuses any interventions like non-stress tests or fetal monitoring or *fucking common sense* --" with a final, violent wrench, the drawer came all the way out, spilling staples and paper clips all over the floor, "who says God told her everything's going to be all right. They have the balls to talk to *me* about the standard of care?" he shouted, hurling the drawer across the room, where it hit the wall with a crack. "Look around you, Bill, there isn't any! Where's the standard of care for these people having babies? Where's the standard of care for lawyers? Where's the standard of care for lawmakers? Where's the standard of care for journalists—?"

"—And partners."

Barish said nothing.

"If you don't know, then I'll tell you," Bill Rinaldi said, moving closer to him. "It means that for these last three months I've been covering your ass with the patients when you haven't been able to get out of your chair, you've been so fucking impaired, Dave." Barish faced him, motionless. Rinaldi went on, "And it means that if you go back to court and this case settles at—" he whipped up an arm and checked his watch, "2:30, I expect you back here seeing patients at three o'clock. Use my office," he said, turning to leave, winking at Marian. "Yours looks like hell."

Back in his office, where the sunlight dribbled through his miniblinds, Marian shut the door as he collapsed into his desk chair. He folded both hands over his eyes and sighed so hugely she found herself wondering whether she should just drive him on over to Ketchum Rays, where Lila could slap him naked into a tanning bed and stand over him, crooning, "There, there, honey." She found a mini-fridge that was doubling as a plant stand, pulled out a small bottle of orange juice, and poured some off into the African violets. Then she rummaged in her bag for the hit of airline vodka she kept for just such emergencies, added it to the bottle of juice, which she

CHAPTER SIXTEEN

capped, shook gently, and handed to Bill Rinaldi, who was watching her.

"Instant screwdriver." She wiped her hands on her pants.

"I've got patients."

"Well, no, Dr. Rinaldi, actually," she winced, "you don't." He made a face, pushed his features around with both hands and reached for the bottle. "They all left." It was unnaturally quiet outside Rinaldi's office, and Marian had a sudden feeling if she opened the door she'd step off into a bright and brainless void. Even the muzak had disappeared.

"Have one yourself?"

"Next time."

"Hey, we're having that date."

"The physician at play."

"Yeah," he said, looking out the window at just another Carthage alleyway. "Right." He took another long swallow.

"He'll be back," she said finally.

"Well, you know, the truth of it is—" he shrugged, "we're done. We can't hang on any longer. It's been tough paying the malpractice premiums for the last few years, anyway, and now Dave's will really go into orbit." Bill Rinaldi leaned back in his chair and slung his feet up on his desk. "I have an OB friend at a clinic up in Cleveland. With no cases against her, her premium went up to $300,000."

"A *year?*"

He nodded. "That's more than her annual income. She had to sell her practice to a hospital. Now she's their employee." He finished off his drink. "A few months ago, I did the math. After Dave and I pay our new malpractice premiums, and after I pay the overhead here, I'll be making what my father does, working for the city sewer district in Philly."

"With a high school education."

"Doctors? We're the new blue-collar workers, Marian—only, we don't even have a union."

They looked at each other. "What are you going to do?"

He tossed up both his hands. "Move, sell, quit OB—"

"Then George Patton Briggs hits the jackpot."

He dismissed it. "Only for a while. Briggs'll go under, too."

For a moment, both fell silent. Then, Marian handed him the blank birth certificate form she had taken from Beth's bin. "Bill, can you help me with this? Why does the Bureau of Vital Statistics go after all that information on the bottom?"

He hardly had to look. It was a form he knew well. "Mainly, it's used for medical research," he shrugged. "Where and how often certain diseases occur, whether strides have been made in their treatment, that sort of thing." He sat up, pulling himself in closer to his desk. "As for the downside, well, if certain items are checked, they're red flags."

"Red flags? Like what?"

"Low five-minute Apgars, fetal distress, cord prolapse, birth injury, seizures. These days," Rinaldi shook his head, "any of that stuff would be powerful information in the wrong hands—"

"Like whose?"

"Well, anyone not working for certain government agencies." He set down the spiked juice. "It's also illegal," he said, wiping the back of his hand across his mouth.

She looked skeptical. "Birth certificates are public record."

His eyebrows shot up. "Not that bottom portion." Then he grinned. "But it's also illegal for lab couriers like Beth Prescott to eat their lunch in their cars where blood products are stored in the back—in a refrigerator—" he flung a hand at me, "—in a plastic bag, in *vials*, for Pete's sake, for fear that HIV will somehow—" he waggled his fingers in the air, "make its way through all of that and contaminate employees' Whoppers." Bill Rinaldi slumped back in his chair, stared at the ceiling, and finished off his screwdriver. Then he crossed his arms over his chest and closed his eyes tight. "Christ, what a country," he said softly.

* * *

Marian called Lila Ketchum from the alcove of vending machines just off the lobby of the Carthage Days Inn. Through the glassed-in breezeway, she

CHAPTER SIXTEEN

could see the outdoor pool deck, where a couple of kids in the water battled each other with Styrofoam noodles while their lounging parents hid behind thick library books. The front desk was twenty feet away from where she was standing, just past a couple of lavish potted dracenas. "I'm here at the Days Inn, Lila. Can you get Kelvin O'Malley's room number?"

"Days Inn out on Cold Spring Boulevard?"

"Right."

"Who's at the desk?"

"Hang on." I strolled over to the front desk and smiled at the clerk, a moussed blond guy in his late twenties, whose sideburns must have been waxed off since his hairline cut like a shelf across the top of his ears. His skin was green gold, that color olive-skinned blonds go when they tan. I grabbed a free trifold on Carthage Area Attractions and ducked back around the corner to the pay phones. "His pin says *T. Strunk.*"

"Tuffy Strunk?"

"You know him?" There was a definite advantage to enlisting ops like Lila.

"I've done him lots."

"And—?"

"Give me your number and sit tight." In half a minute, Tuffy Strunk picked up his phone, and Marian watched his eyes flit around the lobby while he figured out if he could let his work face go for a couple of minutes. Finally, he hung up, tightened his tie, and looked pleased with himself.

"Room 212," Lila said. She told Tuffy she had an appointment to give Mr. O'Malley a massage and needed to have some equipment delivered to his room ahead of time. She laid it on thick and promised to show him some of the deep muscle techniques she'd been learning.

"Thanks, Lila." Room 212 was upstairs in the second building. O'Malley's door was closed, but next door, 214 was wide open with a housekeeping cart parked in front of it. Marian meandered by, swiped three rolls of toilet paper, which left the maid only one, then zipped around the corner and tossed them on top of the Coke machine. She slipped back downstairs to the glassed-in breezeway, where she could look straight up to O'Malley's room.

Marian phoned the front desk. In her best uptown voice, she said, "This is

Regina Hall, Mr. O'Malley's personal assistant."

"Oh, *yes*," Tuffy blurted, as if he'd ever heard of her. "How can I help you?"

"Mr. O'Malley was extremely displeased with the way his room was made up yesterday."

"Oh. Gosh. I'm so—"

"It was totally unacceptable. There was dust on the air conditioner, dust on the TV, and dust on the—toilet tank."

T. Strunk's face lost some of its gold. "I will take it up with the housekeeping staff right away, and I can assure you—"

Marian made a high-handed reply and hung up. Tuffy located the housekeeping cart and went into Room 214. Then he reappeared with a woman in jeans, sneakers, and a polo shirt with a springy tiara of black-dyed bangs and a fierce face. She had one of those tight bodies found in weightlifters, whose muscles kind of get in the way when they walk. Marian watched her brush Tuffy Strunk aside with a powerful forearm, open O'Malley's door, and go inside, Tuffy at her heels.

Ten seconds later, Tuffy power-walked it out of there and headed back toward the front desk. Marian timed her call, so he'd have to sprint to make it. When Tuffy picked up, breathless, Regina Hall said, "Mr. O'Malley particularly mentioned that what he needed today is two extra rolls of toilet paper."

"Two extra—" He flailed around for paper.

"He's having a massage." As if there's any connection.

"Yes, of course." Tuffy rolled his eyes, like what the hell.

"If he finds them in his room this afternoon, he may be able to overlook yesterday."

"Thank you, Ms. Hall. I'll make it clear to the staff." Then he nipped back to Room 212, knocked on the door frame, and the maid appeared, a rag pulled tight between her two hands, like a garotte. He gave her the message and loped back down the steps as she steamed over to the housekeeping cart to snag the two rolls of toilet paper. Baffled at finding only one, she started off toward the housekeeping supply room, which was Marian's cue to leg it up to the open and unguarded 212.

CHAPTER SIXTEEN

Since the bodybuilding maid had already made up the room, Marian was betting she would just unload the toilet paper and scram. She stepped into the closet, slid the mirrored door nearly shut, and waited, crowded by O'Malley's suits and a vague combination of sweat and dry-cleaning chemicals. In all fairness, the sweat may have been hers.

Pretty soon she heard feet treading in the direction of the john, a rattling on the toilet tank as the rolls got plunked down, and feet treading back to the door, slammed hard. Marian stole to the window and peeked out through that sliver between the closed drape and the window. The maid was letting herself into 216. Pulling on a pair of thin latex gloves, she looked around the darkened room. Damn. She couldn't risk a light until the cover girl for *Planet Muscle Magazine* was safely out of range. She started in the john, flicking on the light, looking for what, she couldn't say—unless, of course, it was more rolls of toilet paper than anybody this side of dysentery had any use for.

On the vanity outside the john, O'Malley kept his toiletries, which included toothpaste for sensitive teeth, shave cream for sensitive skin, and lens solution for sensitive eyes. That O'Malley was just a bundle of chirping nerve endings, all right. In his dresser drawer, she found Calvin Klein underwear, two unopened packs of Gold Toe socks, a couple of casual tops, and khaki shorts.

The bed closer to the window was O'Malley's catch-all: true crime books, newspapers, and Expand-O-Flex files. Marian fingered through them, no Clemm, just Hanson, Marino, Weinberg, all looking like pending suits. Tossed around were rain gear, an overnight bag, a blue terry bathrobe, a heap of black silk pajamas, a discarded white dress shirt, and an iPad. It must be giving the maid fits to think he chewed her out about dust on the radiator when he sleeps next to the Everest of disorder.

In the nightstand, just the Gideon Bible, but by the phone, a pen and scratch pad, where O'Malley had scrawled *384 Main*. The Briars. No date book anywhere. She went back to the closet and checked out his hanging garment bag—empty—but on the floor were a couple of cross-trainers and wingtips—and a black plastic garbage bag closed with a yellow twist. Marian undid it and reached inside, lifting out a single item. Shaking, she got to her feet and carried the thing into the light of the john. It was a man's dark blue nylon jacket, and she had seen it two nights ago at Gringos. Splattered on the sleeve were dry, dark blotches she'd need a lab to say for sure were bloodstains.

Hers.

She stood staring at it, awash in that kind of clarity that shrieked *Jackass*, remembering how she had shot off her mouth to Khartoukian two days ago in the hallway outside Courtroom 2 after he told her they had found Beth's body. She had made what was just about a public declaration that she'd be going into Beth Prescott's Columbus connections. Maybe Khartoukian didn't make anything of it, but Kelvin O'Malley, pressed into them both as he passed by with the Clemms, did. She felt around in the pockets, pulling out a little blister pack of Di-Gels—attempted murder's really tough on the stomach lining.

Marian couldn't leave the jacket.

But she damn well couldn't take it, either.

O'Malley was decamping and the jacket was definitely at risk for getting pitched where it would never be found. She set it carefully back in the garbage bag, tied it, and put it back where she'd found it. Then she phoned the Sheriff's Department, where a deputy told her Khartoukian was out. In the mirror over O'Malley's sink, Marian noticed a couple of her Steri-Pads were looking like they'd been dragged through a mud puddle. How long had she been oozing? She'd have to swing back to The Briars to change them. "Tell him there's evidence in the Warner assault in the closet of Room 212 at the Days Inn—and that it won't last forever." Then she hung up.

She quickly turned off the bathroom light, gave the room a once-over, and let herself out. The housekeeping cart was three doors down. Putting a locked door between her and the one clear piece of evidence in her assault two nights ago felt about as lousy as anything, but she did it, and then slipped back down into the main building. She gave Tuffy Strunk a smile as she breezed by on her way out to the Volvo. Now Marian had to stay close enough to Kelvin O'Malley to keep him from the jacket—and far enough

CHAPTER SIXTEEN

away to keep him from her throat.

Chapter Seventeen

In the Days Inn parking lot, Marian opened her car windows and grabbed the bottle of Aquafina she had left in her cup holder. Taking a long swig, she pulled out her phone and Googled the law offices of Crenshaw, Pike, and Haberman. The woman who answered on the second ring sounded like she could either put Marian through to an attorney or dish up some pretty fair phone sex. Working up a vague Caribbean lilt, Marian explained that she was the concierge calling from the St. Thomas Marriott and launched into a story about how, during the recent renovation of their guest rooms, they discovered a few personal checks lodged behind a built-in entertainment unit, belonging to a Mr. Kelvin O'Malley and dated two years ago. "Our records provided us with Mr. O'Malley's phone number, and I'm calling to see what he would like us to do with them."

After two minutes on hold, she was put through to another woman. "This is Mr. O'Malley's personal assistant. What is this in reference to?" Marian spun the tale a second time. "Well, Mr. O'Malley is out of the office at present, but I do remember his trip to St. Thomas two years ago, right around this time—" here she started to sound suspicious, "—only I thought he stayed at the Wyndham."

"It used to be the Wyndham," said Marian smoothly, "until we bought it."

The personal assistant grunted. "Since I'm certain Mr. O'Malley must have had the lost checks voided, there's really no point in sending them."

Marian thanked her and hung up, heading back down Cold Spring Boulevard toward the center of town. Idling at a light, she felt jumpy, chalking it up to Lila's toffee nut coffee of the day, as she watched an old

CHAPTER SEVENTEEN

white Honda with a blown muffler tear through the intersection. Flyboy was at the wheel. She thought about him. No 'resting' shots for Flyboy with his grief and his work ethic. And what she suddenly remembered was how familiar that Rest Area felt to her, half an hour into Hopewell Range State Park. But it was Flyboy's photo of Beth's car parked there—not far from another—at dusk. One of three 'resting' shots he had taken for the 9 PM photo the hiking club could include in their gift to Beth.

Pulling off into the Jiffy Lube parking lot, she shifted into Park and called Flyboy's number. His outgoing Voicemail message assured callers the call was important to him, please leave a message, and have a nice day. Marian left her message. "Flyboy, it's Marian Warner. Please call me as soon as possible. It's about the Rest Area digital photo of Beth's car for her Shutterfly gift. I need the place, date, and time of that photo. It's urgent. And—" she took his lead, "you have a nice day, too."

As Marian drove back out into traffic, she considered her hunch. Four years ago, Beth Prescott was working as a clerk at the Bureau of Vital Statistics, processing birth and death certificates. When she died, Beth had no credit card debt, no student loans chained to her neck, nothing, but she did have a roomful of swank leather furniture, a Caribbean vacation in her recent past, and a diploma from a medical assisting school, where she sure as hell hadn't won an academic scholarship. All of Beth Prescott's extravagances had been paid for upfront.

And not on a clerk's salary.

The light changed, and the biker next to Marian gave her a toothless grin—*You want some of this, Mama?* —and gunned it. Say O'Malley was one of the "suits" Beth Prescott met while waiting tables at McNifty's who kept up the friendship and played her along when she went over to the Bureau. *What was the sell?* She could still hear Lila: "I've never seen anyone softer than Beth Ann Prescott." Straight fee-for-service was out because Beth wouldn't play. She would have to have just enough of a relationship with the guy to buy the line, do the job, and, along the way, get what he billed as "relationship perks." The furniture, she needs it, he can afford it, just let him do this little thing for her. The trip, a couple sort of thing. The schooling, a no-interest "loan."

But first, there was the line.

The line.

Part sales pitch, part pillow talk. She could practically hear it: *There are folks out there, Beth, who are suffering and don't even know that the system can help them. Folks, Beth, with brain-damaged babies, struggling to pay their bills—when there's nothing extra to pay them with. Folks who have been so victimized, Beth, they don't even know it unless I'm there to bring them to that understanding. But first, I have to know who they are. Before I can help them, I have to be able to find them.*

Just how much wine and cuddling would it take for Beth to see herself as a full partner in his missionary law work? The way this guy had taken an illegal activity and rezoned it for the moral high ground was masterful. How many lunch hours did Beth Prescott give up, to thumb through bound volumes of birth certificates, looking for likely babies in neighboring counties? Who needs a ham sandwich when what you've got is a noble imperative?

One of the names she came up with was Jeannie Clemm from Carthage, Ohio—and with her, David Barish, M.D. At the time, it meant nothing to Beth Prescott. She had left Carthage, where she didn't know the Clemms, and she didn't know Barish. They drifted, sooner or later, Beth and the "suit" with a mission to bring multimillion-dollar jury awards to the questionably injured. They both moved on to other beds, other requests, and she thought no more about it. But then Beth Prescott moved back to Carthage, took a job as a courier for Mercy Hospital, and met David Barish, first as just a doc on her route and then as a patient.

She may never have known when the lawsuit first landed on his desk, maybe she knew nothing about all the phone calls between Barish and PQA's law firm of Barlow and Kemp, and nothing about the deposition he gave, and the ones he read. But as the time for the trial got closer, she must have watched him bottom out—like Bill Rinaldi said, "when you haven't been able to get out of your chair, you've been so fucking impaired, Dave."

And Beth Prescott found out why.

As Marian started to pull into the driveway at The Briars, she passed LaVerne Simms-Garber loading a garment bag into a white Chevy Malibu

CHAPTER SEVENTEEN

at the curb. Could mater be far behind? The door to the inn was wide open. At the sight of a black BMW parked halfway down the driveway toward the back of the inn, Marian heaved a sigh and backed out. LaVerne, who had nabbed the last available space on the street, gave her a wave and flung a floral carry-on into the backseat.

Marian zipped around the block, parked on a side street, and legged it up the front steps of the inn. In the entrance hall, Cy Hauser and Viola Simms-Garber were getting in their last round of boring one-upmanship, arguing over whether *bunting* refers to a kind of patriotic decoration or just the cloth itself, while Cy danced around with a lightweight lavender jacket. He was trying gamely to pull it over her arms. She brayed, he bawled, and Barbara was nowhere in sight—off somewhere, no doubt, counting down until the Malibu's door closed behind the darling of the D.A.R., and off they went for good.

When Marian had come up with the missing Flaggie, the Hausers sidestepped a gagging payout on their insurance policy for a piece of patriotic kitsch—not to mention a police investigation Viola would have demanded against what she called "that brown person," Esmé Culp. No, Barbara Hauser was hiding in the back somewhere, counting down the minutes, giving the dangerous Simms-Garbers a token of her esteem with the tip of an imaginary steel-toed boot. Bill paid, risk averted, homestead saved.

"Goodbye, everybody, goodbye," Viola warbled as Cy clamped her by the lavender-covered elbow, and LaVerne rolled her eyes at Marian and grabbed the last of the bags. They headed for the door, LaVerne sagging under the weight of the bags, Viola poking at Cy and stumping along in her Hush Puppies: car minus one minute.

Just then Marian heard voices upstairs—one was Barbara's—and started up. "What's available back here?" said a man.

"For one night, or two?"

"One."

Marian froze, suddenly placing the voice, and stepped back hard against the banister. All week long, she had listened to him jollying the jury, romancing the witnesses, carrying the Clemms, and damn near pressing the judge's pants. "I like this one," O'Malley said. She felt winded—twice in two days, this guy had knocked the stuffing out of her, and there he was, standing in her room. What was he doing here? She inched her way down the hall.

"It's taken."

"For how long?"

"Well, she's here on business from out of town," Marian heard Barbara say, "so I don't know."

"I see."

"But I can put you across the hall."

Across the hall?

"Show me."

Marian was slipping back down the stairs, clutching the banister, when all the shouting began, and she couldn't even pin it on Kelvin O'Malley. It sounded like a tornado warning, a one-note wail, and it was coming from outside. She looked. About four feet from that curbside savior called a white Chevy Malibu, Viola Simms-Garber was unbelievably on the ground. Flat on her back. Legs splayed. Arms flailing. No ice, no cracks, no chunks, no moss, no cat, no skate—*how the hell did she manage to do it?* LaVerne dumped the bags and started yelling at her mother, and Cy hopped around gingerly, trying to get a grip on her. Marian smacked her forehead, then looked around, not even sure for what; maybe some bunting she could cram into Viola's mouth just before hurling her into the backseat of the Malibu as LaVerne burned rubber.

"—not *paralyzed*, Mother—"

"—just let me—"

"Blahhh."

"—have to *pay* for an ambulance, you—"

"—just let me—"

"—out of business if *I* have anything to—"

At the sound of a creak at the top of the stairs, Marian looked wildly around for cover. "Unless I miss my guess," O'Malley purred, "someone's hurt."

CHAPTER SEVENTEEN

All Marian could see were Barbara's feet start on down the steps, with O'Malley hot behind her, and by the time she started shouting something that sounded like "*Son* of a ding-dong doo-wop six-toed devil in a blue dress *bitch*," Marian was out the door, around the front, practically tumbling over a hedge, and bolting around the far side of The Briars—just in time to nose a look as Barbara reached the little crew writhing around on the sidewalk, and Kelvin O'Malley made a quick professional assessment of the situation. He turned, sniffing at the air, on Cy. "Were you helping her?"

"Yes, of course, of course I was."

"You were *helping* her." He smelled an angle.

"Well, I had her by the elbow."

"Did she require this assistance?"

Cy looked baffled. "I don't know."

"Did she ask for your help?"

"I'm perfectly capable of walking by myself! I'm not senile!"

O'Malley planted his feet and framed the picture in the air. "But you *grabbed* her elbow—"

LaVerne piped up. "Get up, Mother, goddamn it."

"—thereby rendering her unsteady on her feet." Marian watched him pull out his billfold and extract a business card, which he tried to hand to LaVerne. By this time, Cy, looking a lot like Atlas, had gotten the old lady half-upright, and she snapped up O'Malley's card. "Mr. Hauser," O'Malley pulled out his cell phone and single-handedly pressed buttons. "I have to ask you to release Mrs.—"

"*Simms*-Garber." Viola whimpered as Cy and LaVerne returned her to a sprawl on the pristine sidewalk.

"Mrs. *Simms*-Garber. We need to have her medically evaluated. Hello, 911?...I'm calling from The Briars, where we've got a possible spinal injury."

Very slowly, Barbara Hauser turned with her hands hanging down at her sides and looked at her Victorian inn with the kind of futile fondness you see in a family who stands by and watches their farmhouse go right up in smoke.

THE DAMAGES

* * *

Marian's knees felt wobbly—and not from the damn attack—as she headed down the alley, darting through back yards, past some stone geese and reflecting balls. The smell from the paper mill was making even the garden gnomes wince. When she got to the Volvo, she wrenched open the door and fell inside, grateful to be out of range of Kelvin O'Malley. No, maybe the stench in Carthage wasn't the paper mill, after all—maybe what hung in the air, what circled them all and made them cry, was really brimstone. No sooner did she hear the paramedics go by than O'Malley's BMW tore back up the street toward the courthouse.

When her phone trilled, she fumbled it, then sat back with her eyes closed. "Marian Warner."

"Marian Warner? It's me, Flyboy."

Marian sat up straight. "Thanks for calling me back. Do you have the photo?"

He sounded glum. "You saying it's important?"

"Very. What's the place?"

He sighed. "Well, it's that rest spot off Adena Ridge Road. There in the park. You know."

Her heart was pounding. "I do." Then: "Can you check the date and time stamp?"

"Yes, I can. You hold on." She listened to him sniff a few times while he tapped his phone screen. Finally, "Says here it was Wednesday, May 25, at 9:03 PM. Is that good?"

"Yes, Flyboy," said Marian quietly, "It's very good. Can you send it to me?"

"I would be happy to."

"Take very good care of it, Flyboy. It's evidence now. Do you understand?"

"Yes." He was emphatic.

One final thing. "Flyboy, can you enlarge the photo on your phone and tell me what you can about the cars?"

One was Miz Elizabeth's yellow Kia Soul.

The other was a late-model black BMW. And very carefully he read off

CHAPTER SEVENTEEN

the license plate.

For a full half-hour afterwards, Marian sat with her head on the steering wheel. Maybe there was no point right now in wondering why the hell she had left her revolver at home in Great Aunt Greta's cabin under her bed. After the shooting in January, she had never wanted to handle it again, and all *that* decision meant now was that she was left to her wits, which was a bit like trying to sculpt The Thinker with an emery board.

Marian pulled out her phone and called The Briars.

Cy answered. He sounded ninety years old.

"Cy, did Kelvin O'Malley take a room?"

He started to laugh in a loony way. "Marian, I think he just took all of them." He started to tell her what had just happened, then suddenly his voice started to spiral up, "Well, weren't you there? Did you see her fall?"

"I didn't see her fall."

"Where did you go?"

"I had to leave, Cy. I'll explain later." She shifted into drive and eased the Volvo down to Main Street, where she waved on spiky-haired boys in droopy jeans lumbering home from school, whapping each other with their backpacks. "Did O'Malley take a room?"

"Yes," he said with Olympian boredom, like none of this innkeeper business made a damn bit of sense anymore, "the one across from you. He said for his last night in Carthage he wanted something special."

Right, like a second try at her throat.

Chapter Eighteen

On her way back to the Wade County Courthouse, Marian saw for the first time that the storm had brought out all the beautiful harshness of the colors—paint jobs looked spanking new, leaves looked polished by the rain, clouds looked like they'd been outlined by a fine tool. If she couldn't change out of her crossing-guard top, she could at least slap on some fresh Steri-Strips over that generalized ooze she still called her body. She got a space down the street from the courthouse, right in front of a place called Soskin's Drug Store. Her hands were shaking as she studied the parking meter. Ten minutes of free time, a nickel for twelve minutes, a dime for thirty, and a quarter gets you an hour. When fear starts creeping up from the soles of your feet, the only solace lies in details. Any details.

Considering she still had to get Khartoukian, stall O'Malley, contact Girard, survive the Clemms, and prop up Dave Barish—assuming he hadn't hopped a bus to Albuquerque—Marian plugged a quarter into the meter and headed into Soskin's, which smelled like rubbing alcohol, where she had a strangely difficult time deciding between butterfly-shaped or rectangular, flesh-colored or transparent Steri-Strips. She paid for them, gamely ripped off the old ones and applied clean ones, groping where necessary under her orange Ban-Lon top while the feathery-haired pharmacist looked on. When he wordlessly held out a hand, she gave him the old Steri-Strips and left the shop, heading for the courthouse.

Marian felt like she was walking on stilts. Apparently, changing her bandages wasn't quite the pick-me-up she thought it would be. All she knew was there was just no damn way she was getting into bed that night

CHAPTER EIGHTEEN

at The Briars with Kelvin O'Malley out there drooling for an opportunity that probably held less charm for him than handing Viola Simms-Garber his business card.

But did she have enough to go after him?

Her phone went off just as she got to the massive front doors, which got thirty pounds heavier since the last time she had opened them. "Hello?" Inside the building it was about ten degrees cooler, and the lobby was empty.

"Marian?"

Girard. "God, it's good to hear your voice," she said. "Where are you?" There were voices down at the end of the narrow hall near Courtroom 2.

"Near the United ticket counter at Cleveland Hopkins. I've got an agent who IDed a picture, only it wasn't one of the doctors, Marian. It's O'Malley."

She took a breath. "I know." Then she quickly filled him in, covering Beth's after-hours work at the Bureau of Vital Statistics, the trip for two to St. Thomas, the blue nylon jacket.

"Now we can place him in the vicinity of Beth's Kia, four hours away from Carthage on the night she disappeared."

"We can do better than that." She described the evidence of Flyboy's Rest Area photo.

Girard was quiet while he added it up. "It's looking good, Marian."

"The ticket agent," she pressed him. "Is she solid?"

"She remembered O'Malley from the first commuter flight out that next morning."

"How?"

"Well, he paid cash," Girard said. "And he needed a shave." Holding out, she guessed, for his Gillette Shave Cream for Sensitive Skin. "His clothes had a day-old kind of look to them, and he didn't have a briefcase. At a Brooks Brothers time of day, this guy stood out."

"How can she be sure of the date?"

"She told the guy he should stick around, catch the Guardians when they came in later off a road trip, where they swept a three-game series with Chicago. The guy didn't react. Didn't say a word. It gave her the creeps."

"Then when he hit Columbus—"

"—he took a bus to Carthage to pick up his car."

"We can check that out," she said.

"Of course, but I think we've already got enough."

"I've got to give Khartoukian probable cause."

"I understand."

"He can't arrest O'Malley without probable cause."

"I know." He sounded patient.

Marian turned. "Hang on." The Clemms reached the lobby, Jeannie chattering away, hanging on to Craig's bent arm like they were king and queen of Tulip Time. Behind them was Grandma, her dainty overbite flashing in nonstop smiles, and a couple of older men with comb-overs dressed in Sansabelt pants. They were followed by a dark, frizzy-haired woman Marian recognized was a *Toiler* reporter—Charlie was still just sending in his lieutenants—who was the only one who actually looked like she had some place to go.

Then came a few hot-weather trial groupies—a Marine kind of a guy in a Hawaiian print shirt, folding up a colorful paper fan, the Grateful Dead kissers, who had moved inside from the steps, and a braless, middle-aged gal with greasy dark hair and a knitting bag. The trial was cheaper than the ten-buck admission to Tulip Time—unless, of course, you happened to be David Barish, M.D. Standing near the Clemms, the groupies helped themselves to cigarettes and took on intense expressions, like they might really have something at stake here.

Coming slowly toward her down the hall was Dave Barish, alone, his hands deep in his pockets. No suit jacket—which was probably still in a heap back in a box filled with a desk clock, a broken-glass diploma, books that had nothing to do with medicine, and some paper clips. No O'Malley. No Nan. The rotunda where they were all standing amplified every little sound, collecting shoes, voices, and coughs into a strange kind of tide that rushed and receded.

"Where are you?" Girard wanted to know.

"Courthouse lobby."

"What's going on?"

CHAPTER EIGHTEEN

"I think the Clemm case just settled."

"O'Malley?"

She craned her neck. "I don't see him."

"Get Khartoukian."

"I will."

"There's nothing you can do with it on your own now—"

"I hear you."

"—except get hurt." Marian heard him blow out air. Then: "Do you need me here for anything else?"

"No, I just want you to come home."

"I'll be back at my place around eight o'clock."

"Then so will I."

"I'm on my way."

They disconnected, and Marian ducked through the glass door into the Clerk of Courts' office, where she could keep an eye on the group in the lobby while she called Khartoukian. Patrolling the counter was a thin-lipped, older lady in a green polyester suit, who gave her a look like she was trying to remember just which one of the Top Ten Fugitives Marian was. The Sheriff himself picked up.

"Get over here."

"Marian? Where are you? What's—"

"Next door to you, in the courthouse. Did you get the jacket?"

"What jacket?"

"Your effing deputy has sunstroke, Khartoukian."

"Probably. What jacket?"

"O'Malley's. The night he attacked me. Room 212, the Days Inn."

A beat. "I'll send someone."

"Right now."

"Relax. What else?"

"He killed Beth. Jack Girard got a positive ID from a ticket agent in Cleveland."

Flatly: "Circumstantial."

She raised her voice. "That's not all."

A beat. "Name it."

Marian described Flyboy's nine o'clock photo at dusk in the deserted Rest Area. Her chest hurt with the truth of it. The car two spaces down from Beth's was O'Malley's black BMW. Flyboy's birthday Shutterfly photo of Miz Elizabeth at nine PM on a dusky May evening placed her Kia next to her killer's probably just moments before her murder.

"Marian?" When Khartoukian told her to "sit tight," she realized nothing could possibly sound fast enough, and she blurted "Hurry" before he slipped away, adding, "O'Malley's got unfinished business." Without another word, he was gone. Marian went back out to the lobby, where Dave Barish was staring at a framed, poster-sized photograph of Michael DeWine, governor of Ohio. When she touched his sleeve, Barish turned and raised his eyebrows. "What's up?" she asked, her voice low.

He gave her a small shrug. "It's over. They settled for $800,000."

She looked him in the eye. There was nothing to say. "Where's Nan?"

"She and O'Malley are polling the jury."

"What does that mean?"

He sniffed out a little laugh. "Nan said it's their chance to see what she called 'the scorecard.'"

Marian's eyes slid over to the center of the rotunda, where the Clemm family stood heavily on the Great Seal of the State of Ohio, laid out in mosaic tiles. Craig was at the end of a funny story about a haircut he once got, claiming no one did haircuts as bad as the Army and that's the God's honest truth. Everyone laughed, a full $800,000 worth of laughter. There'd be pot roast and good fellowship that night at the Clemms'.

"Hey, Doc!" Craig called, waving over Dave Barish and Marian. After a stunned second, they went, slowly. The circle widened to let them in, like they were socializing at an employee Christmas party, as though what they'd all been through over the last week was nothing more than some kind of crazy-ass exercise that ended with a whole lot of money for the Clemms—like hitting the Superlotto. And no harm done. Dave Barish had no expression whatsoever when he looked at Craig Clemm, who got very earnest.

CHAPTER EIGHTEEN

"We just want you to know, Doc, we don't hold nothin' against you." He patted Jeannie's back. "Do we, hon?"

"Right," she whispered with a wide-eyed smile. "We just didn't know what else to do."

The Sansabelts were nodding.

Dave Barish didn't say a word.

Craig went on, "We didn't have the money for all the stuff Courtney'd be needing and it turns out the only way we could get it was if me and Jeannie got a divorce, and she went on welfare." He held up a beefy red hand, his thumb and forefinger pressed together. "We come this close to it, but then this call come from Mr. O'Malley in Columbus, says he heard about Courtney and thinks we might have a case."

"How did he hear?" Marian asked.

Craig and Jeannie shook their heads at each other. Then Jeannie squinted. "I think he said he heard around town."

"What town?"

"Carthage."

"Columbus."

All the Clemms laughed. "Leastways," Jeannie finished, "he heard." She took a step closer to Barish, flipping her waist-length hair. "Tell you the truth," she took a quick peek up the narrow hallway, then wrinkled her nose, "Courtney's not as bad off as he made out. She can do a whole lot more'n Mr. O'Malley let on."

"Hell, yeah," Craig said. "And about the twelve million we were asking for—" He put an arm around his wife and faced the man he had sued. "Honest to God, we never heard all that money would have to come out of you," he said. "Out of your assets."

"Never—" Jeannie whispered.

"Cause we wouldn't want that," Craig said, pushing down the air as though it was jumping too close to his nose. "We never heard about the assets part until Mr. O'Malley told us—" he looked at Jeannie, "—when, hon?"

"Just this past week."

Marian had to stop herself from blinking just long enough to ask them,

209

"Where did you think the money was coming from?"

Jeannie and Craig Clemm looked at each other, then back to her. "The insurance company," they said at the same time.

It couldn't be plainer. File a claim, get a payment—the same as a fender bender or a flooded basement. At that moment Marian saw the counsel for Clemm vs. Barish coming down the narrow hallway—Kelvin O'Malley was four feet in front of Nan. The little group in the rotunda was in plain view, but both lawyers were looking past them, their eyes flickering. Both of them. Their smiles were secretive in some effort to stay professional and impersonal. Nan Kemp and Kelvin O'Malley, frontman for The Crenshaw Blight, were savoring the jury poll, leaping ahead to their next piece of litigation, formulating their next opening arguments—true journeymen in some precinct of power Marian never wanted to have anything to do with.

She turned to Dave Barish. He saw it, too.

Where the hell was Khartoukian?

"Mr. O'Malley," Craig announced, squaring his shoulders.

O'Malley raised his eyebrows, shifting his briefcase. His eyes slid first to the door, and then to the very edges of Marian, and she felt like she had rocketed to the top of his To Do list. Then he looked back at Craig Clemm. It must have occurred to him that he had just made three hundred grand off these folks. He could give them another five minutes. With Beth Prescott, he had driven a harder bargain. With Marian, he had tried. But here he had a public face. His mustache rippled. "Yes, Craig?"

Nan came up behind Barish and Marian, nudging him with her shoulder. "You okay?"

He didn't answer.

Craig clapped an arm around Jeannie, who smiled at O'Malley like he had just turned water into wine. Craig's chest expanded. "Jeannie'n me'd be honored if you'd come back to the trailer with us for a cup of coffee."

Jeannie leaned toward him, sweetening the offer. "You could see Courtney again."

"That might be nice," he said with a toothy smile. "We'll have to see." It was an elegant brush-off. Then, the door to the Wade County Courthouse

CHAPTER EIGHTEEN

opened, and Khartoukian came in, followed by a deputy. Nan noticed, and stopped talking, right in the middle of telling Dave Barish that although the jurors felt she "had a leg up" on O'Malley, they were leaning toward the plaintiffs when the case settled.

Khartoukian took them all in, and as he passed behind Marian, he muttered, "I hope you know what you're talking about, lady."

She flashed him a soft look.

Because one of the Sansabelts had O'Malley's attention with a story about how he fell on an icy patch at the Valley Church of God—did he think there was any money in it? —O'Malley was surprised when the Sheriff stopped next to him.

"Kelvin O'Malley?" Khartoukian said, his hands on his hips.

Even Grandma Clemm shut up.

"Yes?"

"I'm placing you under arrest for the murder of Beth Ann Prescott."

Someone gasped.

O'Malley clammed up as the Clemms stepped away. Maybe they were reconsidering the offer of coffee. Khartoukian went on, "We'll have to pat you down." He nodded toward the wall. "Dwight." When the deputy reached for O'Malley's elbow, he twisted his arm free. As he turned toward the wall, he fixed Marian with a look she never wanted to see again. With O'Malley's powerful arms splayed against the wall next to the picture of the governor, Dwight patted near his armpits and worked his way down. "You have the right to remain silent," Khartoukian began. "Anything you say can and will --"

"Don't Mirandize me," O'Malley bellowed, his face hidden by his outstretched arms.

"—can and will be used as evidence against you in a court of law."

"Clean," said Dwight, cuffing him.

Shifting his weight, Khartoukian went on. "You have the right to an attorney to be present prior to and during any questioning. And if you cannot afford an attorney—" Marian watched O'Malley rotate his head at the suggestion, "—one will be appointed for you at public expense." When

Khartoukian motioned toward the door, the Clemms move aside, speechless. "Let's go."

Suddenly, Jeannie Clemm cried, "Does this mean we won't get the money?"

Chapter Nineteen

Marian got as far as the courthouse steps, where she sat, shaky, with Dave Barish. Everyone else scattered like cockroaches when the kitchen light comes on, scampering off to broadcast the story that would have to replace bad Army haircuts in the Clemm family repertoire. The trial groupies followed Khartoukian and his prisoner over to the jail, where the air was cool and the gossip hot. Even Nan had disappeared. As they sat silently on the steps, Barish and Marian watched a nice Culligan Water Systems van go by in one direction and a Sunshine Bakery truck go by in the other. A ponytailed dad in cut-offs pushed a baby stroller and held on to a Newfie on a long leash. At the bottom of the courthouse steps, two pigeons pecked and cooed.

Across the street, three middle-aged women in white gloves and summer hats got out of a silver Toyota Highlander with a bumper sticker that said *Who Died and Made You Elvis?* and went into the Princess of Wales Tea Shoppe. A delivery truck for a local place called Wade County Potato Chips—*Wade Into Flavor!* —double-parked outside the coffee shop at the end of the street and the driver swung himself down to the street. Marian looked down at her feet. The thing about awfulness was this: on any given day, it's really only yours. And there will always be baby strollers and tea drinkers and pecking pigeons who didn't know, didn't care—and that's altogether a good thing.

The sun was behind the courthouse now, and the sidewalk fell into bright shadows. A woman in a flowered muumuu and rubber flip-flops, wheeling a battered shopping cart, paused in front of the courthouse and started picking through the wire trash can.

"That's Nettie," Dave Barish said. "One of our bag ladies."

Marian grunted. "No 800 grand for *her*."

His eyes flickered. "No malpractice premiums, either."

She looked down the block. "I'd say she comes out ahead."

"So would I."

While they watched Nettie choose a plastic Target bag with handles she brushed off and slipped up to her shoulder like a purse, Marian told Dave Barish about O'Malley and Beth Prescott. She kept it short since he didn't seem to have the heart to hear it, and at the end of it, he let out a long breath that she could have sworn he'd been holding since March. Then: "About the Clemms—" she started.

He pressed her hand briefly, then let go. "There's a story my uncle told me," he said, as they watched Nettie, standing a little taller, push her cart up the street, "about a couple of frogs who lived on a farm." One day, for no reason, the farmer was feeling mean and picked them up and flung them into a vat of milk. They swam and swam, first one day, then two, but the vat was only half full, and they couldn't jump out. By the third day, the one frog said to his friend it's no good, they'll never get out, he's tired of swimming, he's giving up. Then, he sank below the surface and drowned. The other frog kept swimming—what else could he do? —for a third day, and a fourth, until finally, on the fifth day, the cream turned into butter, and he jumped out.

"You're one of the frogs," Marian said.

David Barish stood up. "Only I don't know which one." Shoving his hands into his pockets, he started slowly down the steps.

* * *

Marian pulled around to the back of The Briars and went in the kitchen door. Barbara Hauser was sitting alone in the dining room, heaped on a side chair, her hands loose in her lap. She was staring at a spot on the rug. The only sound was the ticking of the grandfather clock in the entrance hall. The look of pinched fear on her face was just the sort of alarming expression

CHAPTER NINETEEN

you don't want to see on a flight attendant during "turbulence." She went quietly back outside, pulled out her phone, and after four calls around town, got through to The Man.

"This here's Jonelle," Marian heard her say over the clattering of big serving spoons excavating B-B-Q Beef. "*Hang on*," Jonelle told her, explaining to a customer, "Honey, we got but one kind of bun—*bagged*." And then Marian arranged for Jonelle to bring a Grange Lady Supreme dinner—brats, beans, kraut, slaw, strawberry rhubarb pie—*whole*—to Cy and Barbara Hauser, served up with an hour's worth of Jonelle herself. Marian would stick a check in the mail to her for $100.

Then Marian went back inside and poured herself a glass of juice. "Mr. O'Malley won't be joining us," she told Barbara, who was still sitting in the dining room.

"That's what I hear," was all she said, without much interest. Her face seemed to shrink behind her oversized blue frames. Marian wanted to hug her, but she couldn't kneel down too well, what with parking lots and hedge tumbles, and Barbara was suffering from full-blown Barish syndrome and couldn't get out of her chair. In the end, they just looked at each other like a hug would have been nice if they weren't so pathetic, and Marian went upstairs.

Nan was packing.

Two leather Coach bags stood open on her bed. She had changed into gray jersey pants and a white top and was folding her Errol Flynn palazzo pants while she talked into her phone, hunched between her cheek and shoulder. She could do that: she wasn't held together with a carton of Steri-Strips. Marian stood in the doorway with her juice.

"Nate, Nate," Nan was saying, "Terhune won't be back; even the *jury* could see that, I'm telling you—" she mouthed *my partner* to me, and Marian nodded, "—and even Rance will think twice. All but one of the jurors felt I had run the two expert witnesses clear out of Carthage." Nate came back with a comment, and Nan laughed. 'You know as well as I do, the 800's great compared to the two million we thought they'd settle for. PQA should send us a goddamn fruit basket," she added, folding her suit and laying it to rest inside pricey leather. She laughed again, then cupped the receiver and said to me, "Nate says every month for the next five years!"

Marian tried a smile, then sipped her juice.

Nothing about O'Malley. Nothing about Barish, although maybe she had missed it. She went down to her own room, set her glass on the nightstand, and went over to the windows. In the alley down below, three boys sped by on their bikes, yelling back and forth to each other something about worms near Cold Spring Creek at three in the morning. Beth Prescott was dead. Carney was imploding with grief. Charlie was estranged. Barish was swimming. But there would always be boys digging up worms at three AM for their own higher purposes.

Nan came in. Her hair the color of old sunsets was looser, softer around her face. "I hear you're depriving me of my worthy opponent."

"O'Malley?"

"What a shit." She raised an eyebrow and crossed her arms. "Pretty fine litigator, though." Nan fixed her with a sharp look. "Good job on the Prescott girl."

"You're clearing out fast."

"I'm back in court in ten days. The fact that this case settled today is a godsend."

"Dave Barish doesn't think so."

She waggled her head. "He'll get over it."

"You act like it was a success."

Her mouth hung open. "It *was*. PQA's thrilled the payout's no bigger than it is. I took out Rance and Terhune, and Dave Barish won't have a judgment against him. If that doesn't mean anything to him right now, in a few weeks, it will."

Suddenly, Marian felt like she was channeling Jonelle. "What about the truth?"

"What truth?"

"About Jeannie Clemm's labor."

"Dave met the standard of care, if that's what you mean."

"I know," she said. "It seems to me that's what all the testimony was about,

CHAPTER NINETEEN

but the truth was nowhere around at the end."

Nan made a face. "You pick your truth, Marian. I've got skills I need to improve. I've got laws I want to change. I've got cases I want to try. Those are my truths." She grabbed both of Marian's arms, then touched her face. "I do what I can," she said softly, "okay?"

"Okay." She felt like she'd used up all her words. They hugged loosely and Nan Kemp started for the door, calling back to her to stay in touch, and then she was gone. Not a word about Khartoukian, but then maybe Nan managed to make a one-night stand the perfect, pearly distillate of the longer relationships everyone else goes batty looking for and working at. Maybe the night with Hank Khartoukian was the emotional equivalent of changing laws, trying cases, and improving skills. Without the truth, though, daughter of Alexander Kemp, it was all just a quick pop.

Marian made up her bed with a kind of military zeal and cleared off the nightstand, carting a dried, bloody bar towel into the bathroom, along with unused gauze pads, Steri-Strips, and Tylenol. She was wringing out the bar towel in the sink when she heard her phone ring and hustled back into her room to answer it.

"Hello?"

"Marian." Only Eddie Estremera could make her name sound like eight different sex crimes.

"Hey."

"Doing?"

"Better. Washing out your bloody bar towel."

"No hurry." She could hear him snap a cigarette lighter. "Bring it in person."

"On second thought," she laughed, "I'll mail it."

"And miss the possibilities?" he *tsk-tsked*. "How's your ear?"

"Still nicked."

"I've got remedies."

"Eddie, of that, I'm certain."

He switched gears. "I thought you'd be calling me."

"Oh?"

"If not for my charms, then for my phone bill."

Marian scratched her face. "I completely forgot." She found a pen and paper in the nightstand, and he gave her the number Beth Prescott had called from Gringos the night she disappeared. She thanked Eddie and hung up. *The new quarterback,* Roy Jean Toole, had thought, but that was before Marian figured out there wasn't one, because Beth was still tight with Jim Carney. Then who? Could it possibly matter? She looked at the number: 614-753-4200. Then she checked her watch—still business hours—and made the call. On the second ring, a woman with a brisk voice answered, identifying the business.

And Marian's phone slipped from her hand.

* * *

Once she left Cold Spring Boulevard behind, Marian pushed the Volvo up to fifty, dodging a semi, an empty school bus painted green for an outfit called Nazarene Tabernacle, and an old Suburban. She passed Mercy Hospital in a tangle of county highways, winkling off through corn and soy fields. When she finally caught sight of the car up ahead on the right, she gripped the wheel and accelerated. In fifteen seconds, she pulled up alongside the toffee-colored Saab and tried to cut it off. The horn blasted her. Marian tried again, edging the other car over to the shoulder.

Both of them slowed, only not enough, and when they hit the rough slope of the shoulder, they were doing about forty. Marian slammed on her brakes and flung herself out of the car, loping back to the car behind her. She wrenched open the door. "Get the fuck out of the car."

"Marian!" Nan Kemp jumped out. "What the hell—"

"Beth called you."

"What are you talking about?"

"Beth called you the night she was killed. You *knew* she was meeting O'Malley." Nan's face went stony, her mouth drawn out thin. Her eyes darted all over Marian: collarbone, chest, and waist. Marian was furious. "I'm not wearing a wire. This is just you and me, Nan."

"It's not that simple."

CHAPTER NINETEEN

"Oh, yes, it is. Beth Prescott called the lawyers for *both* sides—I don't know why I didn't see it—twice, three times over the last few weeks—just to see if she could get the case against Dave Barish dropped. Only you didn't want the case dropped. You put her off, hoping O'Malley would get her to go away. Well, fuck it, Nan," she shouted, inches from Nan's face, "*he did.* What the hell did you think when you heard she'd been killed? When you heard it was that night? You knew he'd done it, Nan, and you didn't do a damn thing. Not a goddamn thing. And why? Because you wanted to try the Clemm case so bad you couldn't see straight. Hand O'Malley over to the cops?" She looked Nan Kemp up and down. "Not on your time."

"You just don't get it."

"Oh, yes, I do. You've got skills to improve. You've got laws to change. Cases to try."

Nan lost it. "Why not? Beth Prescott was already dead."

Marian slapped her hard across the face, sending Nan staggering against the car, her hand flying to her cheek. "O'Malley practically killed me." Marian went on. "You saw me; you saw what he did. And you could have prevented it."

"Damn it," Nan yelled, "there are more important things than *you.*"

Marian took a step toward her, pounding her own chest with her fists. "But I'm where you should have started," she said. She looked hard at the lawyer, collapsed against the fender of the Saab. It was useless. Marian backed away a few steps, then turned quickly and headed for her car.

"Where are you going?"

"Away from you." She kept walking. The semi breezed by her, then the Nazarenes, blowing her hair across her face.

"What are you going to do? Are you calling Khartoukian?" Nan sounded shrill. "Are you calling Khartoukian?" When she didn't get an answer, Nan ran up behind her, grabbing at her sleeve. "Marian, tell me, goddamn it." Without even looking, Marian shoved her violently away. "Answer me!" Scrambling on the gravel, Nan was back, clawing at Marian's Ban-Lon.

That did it.

She whirled around and grabbed Nan at the neck, yanking her top into a tight ball, and pulled her close. The woman looked terrified. "You didn't have an answer for Beth," Marian said, then released her with a push. "See how it feels." She let herself into her car and started the engine.

Nan was pounding on the window, shrieking. "Goddamn you!"

Marian shifted into first and hit the gas, spitting up dust and gravel on Nan Kemp as she swung the Volvo around and headed back to Carthage.

* * *

She watched the sunset from the front porch steps of Jack Girard's house. For a while, she heard Norton, locked inside, whimpering to come out, but Marian didn't have a key, so she told him he's a good boy, a good boy—*soon*. Then she heard him snuffle, and his toenails scraped along the wood floor as he gave up and sank into a nap. Across the narrow, brick street, two ten-year old girls were setting up a lemonade stand with that kind of confidence that didn't give a hang if it was too late in the day.

Chattering away the whole time, the girls carried out a card table, two folding chairs, a pitcher of lemonade, plastic cups, and a shoe box for the take. For a little while, they disagreed about whether they needed a sign, but then they got past it and sat squirming while they waited for business.

"Do you deliver?" Marian yelled over, needing something, maybe not lemonade. They looked at each other, went with this new wrinkle in their business plan, and nodded at her. "I'll take a large." As she watched them pour her a drink—one handled the pitcher, one held the cup—she could hear Jonelle explaining, "Honey, we got but one size—*sweet*." They both brought it over, Marian gave them a dollar, then they sprang back across the street Jack Girard called home, and she and the girls looked at each other and smiled. It was the God's honest perfect transaction.

Marian had walked over from The Briars nearly two hours ago, after she left Hank Khartoukian with all the information she had to give, and after she washed and changed, shedding herself of Nan Kemp and the Ban-Lon relic she had tried to vandalize by the side of the highway. Slowly, Marian put on a clean blue top and pleated rayon skirt, which was all she had left

CHAPTER NINETEEN

that wasn't torn, dirty, or wrinkled, and suddenly, she felt as light as a frog on a floe of sweet cream butter. Taking a brush to her hair, she felt the place where she hoped the skin was pulling together over the sliced-away space.

A few millimeters of damage requires a very great repair.

The blossoms on the gnarled wisteria canes climbing up over Girard's porch were still small and closed, but pretty soon, their scent would drift off the porch, only she wouldn't be there to enjoy it—and maybe neither would Girard. Maybe he'd be in Denver, visiting the ex-wife Marian was generously hoping would have let herself go. Maybe over their favorite local, hazy IPA, she and Joan could strategize their reaction to the extortion problem with the newfound Poe manuscript.

It was all right.

One night the scent of wisteria would float out in the perfect summer darkness for the boys tearing through the alley, with worm buckets hanging from the handlebars of their bikes. Maybe, by then, she'd be back. Maybe for a few days. Maybe for a lifetime. Marian slipped out of her sandals and set them aside. Her finger slid along a ragged break in Jack Girard's stone steps. Sometimes, she thought she'd never understand how a thing could crack and not split open, or how a blossom could dangle and not break off, or how truth could be carved—and not reduced.

Or how a heart could fill and not shatter.

Marian happened to look up and saw Girard's Jeep turn into the alley from Main Street. She didn't even judge the distance as she ran out into the street to meet him halfway.

Chapter Twenty

Late September

A hand pushed open the creaky black wrought iron gate outside the medical offices of William Rinaldi and David Barish. Rodie held open the gate for Ernie Diodakis, who couldn't help arching an eyebrow at him. It was going to be nine months of Galahad, and she didn't know if she was ready. He was on his lunch hour, and excited, him in his oversized pink t-shirt, baggy shorts, and metal-toed leather work boots. Ernie had dug out an old cowgirl skirt she had just that week packed in a giveaway box. It was the only skirt she still had, and it had suede fringe flopping up and down the sides. She put away the belly button ring.

It was all ridiculous, the two of them, this big old sloppy life they were living, and she wondered how many times she'd be mistaken for her own baby's grandma. She remembered the World's Biggest Rubber Band Ball that had drawn a crowd at Tulip Time. Ridiculous anyone would do that, spend two years looping together rubber bands to make a thing nineteen feet around, and wonderful at the same time. It was harder to see the wonderful—it always was, because you had to believe like a kid again—but you could see it if you looked for a while.

When the little EPT strip turned blue that morning, they shrieked and clung to each other, laughing and crying, and then said Rinaldi and Barish. No two ways about it. They might disagree on nursery wallpaper—he favored forget-me-nots, she favored vehicles—but they agreed on that. On

CHAPTER TWENTY

the way over in the Toyota, they started on names.

How about "Beth," he asked, checking for traffic and bouncing all over, and Ernie had said Beth was nice. How about "Jack?" he asked, and Ernie had laughed and said Jack was nice, too. She reached for his hand, feeling shy for some crazy reason, and had to look out the window. The shops on River Street rippled by through some sudden tears. *You know I'll rub any damn thing on your belly you want,* Rodie said so seriously that she had to laugh.

Biting down hard on her lip, Ernie Diodakis opened the office door, with Rodie right behind, swiping his Buckeyes cap from his head. Mary Jo smiled at them from the other side of the counter, and Rodie explained that the little EPT thingamajig turned blue that morning. Ernie added they wanted Dr. Rinaldi or Dr. Barish to deliver their baby, and they were here to make an appointment. Then they saw Mary Jo look regretful, and they knew something was wrong. She explained the doctors were no longer practicing obstetrics. But there's Dr. Briggs, she said, and when Ernie said we don't want Dr. Briggs, Mary Jo spread her hands and told them what others had already heard: then you'll have to go all the way to Columbus. "I'm sorry," she said quietly as Rodie and Ernie stood there, not knowing what to do, then finally turned away.

Acknowledgements

With thanks to Level Best mavens Verena Rose, Shawn Reilly Simmons, and Deb Well. Warm, capable, supportive, and professional—what a joy.

About the Author

Shelley Costa's story, "The Knife Sharpener" (*Alfred Hitchcock's Mystery Magazine,* July 2023), is an Agatha Award nominee for Best Short Story and has been chosen for inclusion in the 2024 edition of *Best Mystery Stories of the Year* (The Mysterious Press). She is also the author of several amateur sleuth novels and many crime stories. When she isn't plotting murder, Shelley enjoys Art History, violin lessons, lap swimming, and time with friends and family.

AUTHOR WEBSITE:
   http://www.shelleycosta.com/

SOCIAL MEDIA HANDLES:
   https://www.facebook.com/shelleycostamysteryauthor

Also by Shelley Costa

"The Knife Sharpener" (*Alfred Hitchcock's Mystery Magazine,* July/August 2023). Chosen for inclusion in Best Mystery Stories of the Year (The Mysterious Press, 2024). Nominated for an Agatha Award for Best Short Story 2024

No Mistaking Death (Level Best Books, 2023)

Evil Under the Tuscan Sun (Penguin Random House, 2022)

Crime of the Ancient Marinara (Penguin Random House, 2021)

Al Dente's Inferno (Penguin Random House, 2020)

A Killer's Guide to Good Works (Henery Press, 2016)

Practical Sins for Cold Climates (Henery Press, 2016)

Basil Instinct (Simon & Schuster, 2014)

You Cannoli Die Once (Simon & Schuster, 2013). Nominated for an Agatha Award for Best First Novel 2014 by Malice Domestic

Alfred Hitchcock Presents: 13 Tales of New American Gothic (digital, 2011): "As the Screw Turns" (reprint)

Alfred Hitchcock's Mystery Magazine (April 2010): "As the Screw Turns" (fiction)

Alfred Hitchcock's Mystery Magazine (November 2011): "The Burning Grounds" (fiction)

Alfred Hitchcock's Mystery Magazine (November 2012): "Strangle Vine" (fiction)

Alfred Hitchcock's Mystery Magazine (June 2014): "The Specific Gravity of Blood in Sunlight" (fiction)

The Everything Guide to Edgar Allan Poe (Adams Media, 2007)

Crimewave (UK), Fall 2006: "Blue Morpho" (fiction)

The Georgia Review, Fall 2004: "From the Personal Record Collection of Beniamino Gigli" (fiction). Special Mention, 2006 Pushcart Prize

The World's Finest Mystery and Crime Stories, Ed Gorman, ed. (Forge, 2004): "Black Heart and Cabin Girl" (reprint)

Blood on Their Hands, Lawrence Block, ed. (Berkley, 2003): "Black Heart and Cabin Girl" (fiction). Nominated for an Edgar® Award for Best Short Story 2004 by Mystery Writers of America

Crimewave (UK), Spring 2002: "The Generator" (fiction)

The Georgia Review, Fall 2001: "Getting the Story" (fiction)

Crimewave (UK), Spring 2001: "Face Value" (fiction)

The Georgia Review, Winter 2000: "The Chief Creatures of God" (fiction)

Crimewave (UK), Fall 2000: "Double Fault" (fiction)

The North American Review, March 1987: "The Passion of Marisol" (fiction)

The North American Review, June 1980: "A Woman of Quality" (fiction)

Cleveland Magazine, December 1978: "The Great Wings Beating Still" (fiction contest winner)